Awakened GIANT, Sleeping SPIRIT

A Metaphor for Life

Kenny G. Down

New Thought Life

Printed in the United States of America
First Printing, 2019
Paperback ISBN: 978-1-79536-067-8

New Thought Life, LLC
Seattle, WA
www.newthougthlife.org

I dedicate this book to those that have helped me find this path and my supporters in pursuing the only way of life for me. There are too many to list, they know who they are, thank you. I owe you my life.

Acknowledgements

I have always received more than I have given; you cannot out give God. It is with deep affection for those that have allowed me to help them along the way that I include them by acknowledgement in this, my first book. To my personal Gary Goldpeople, Albert Bowker, I give special thanks; you plucked me from the darkest abyss.

To those who have helped whip this book into shape by suggestions, edits and commentary I thank you. For early edits Lori Lisi-Fredeking, you gave me hope that I could complete the book. To Laura Bowles for her boundless excitement, support, ideas and feedback in the founding of all the New Thought Life ideals and her edits and commentary in the final edit of the book. Early artistic concepts were offered and accepted by Tara Duffin, you hold a special place in my heart. Thank you to Heather UpChurch for the final layout, design and beautifully artistic abilities, you have made the book look fantastic.

To my children Jessica and Jake, my life would never have been complete without you, I love you more than you will ever know.

Finally, no acknowledgement would be complete for me without a special place set aside, above all, for my wife of over twenty years, Shannon Down. Or as she is more well known, The Beautiful and Wonderful Shan. She brings me back on a regular basis from extremes and lows with her loving touch and supporting words. She is my best friend, my rock and the rock of our family and many others. She is my secret weapon in success and happiness in life.

Introduction

*"The answer can only be found
in the realm of the Spirit."*

This world is in serious trouble. The answer is not technology or self-sufficiency or "might makes right." The answer can only be found in the realm of the Spirit. In the intuition and inspiration of our people. The answer is within each of us. In the inner life. In the living of the mystical life.

I hope this book will begin or enhance a spiritual approach to difficulties in your own life. This book contains a lesson in each chapter. Some chapters are long, and others are short. If you choose, follow directions and fully absorb this small book, then read it and reread it and apply the simple spiritual principles you find in each Chapter into your own way of life. Begin, or deepen your commitment, to live the spiritual life.

While the characters in this book are fictional, the ideas expressed within are very real indeed. Many of the ideas, in fact, are from my own real-life experience.

We all have problems, every human being alive has them. Some are simple, and others are more difficult and follow us well down the spiritual path. The characters in this book have a myriad of problems ranging from serious drug addictions to depression. The good news is, that even if the problems the characters are dealing with are not familiar to you, the answer to our problems are the same as the answers they find. The answers in this book apply not only to the characters in the book but also to the difficulties in our own life, whatever they may be.

Spiritual teachers are among us traveling in the bodies of normal men and women. Yet, they are so often perceived as flawless. One intention of this book is to dispel the idea that our spiritual leaders need to be perfect.

Note that the term God used in the book is an all-inclusive word for higher truth, Great Spirit, Allah, Christ, Buddha, YHWH, Brahman, and any other iteration the word encompasses. For some the word God can carry a heavy and unfavorable meaning. Unfortunately, the English language lacks multiple commonly understood words for the concept of God. So, for the purposes of this book the term God does not refer to any one religion and in fact includes them all and can be whatever you, the reader are most comfortable envisioning.

This book is a "*Metaphor for Life.*" My intention is to create a format, that while extremely entertaining, offers spiritual hope and a glimpse into our own better selves. If we apply spiritual principles as answers to all our problems deep within our inner beings, we will awaken to a new and wonderful life. My hope is that this book is a demonstration of this and keeps you thoroughly entertained with great spiritual characters practicing a new way of thinking.

We begin to think and act like we know we are capable of thinking and acting. We can fulfill our real and deepest heart's desires, because now we have a Power much greater than ourselves on our side. We are tapped into a source that delivers miracles in our life every moment of every day. We can form loving relationships with another. We are free at last! This is what this book has to offer.

I personally have been wrong about many things in my life. Most things perhaps… I've found that open-mindedness has been the greatest ally on the path to spiritual enlightenment. When I discover that I've been wrong about something I was so sure I was right about, and then I see the real spiritual truth, it is incredibly uplifting. I'm always so humbled in the presence of spiritual truth. In this respect, the more wrong I am, the more right I become. I encourage you to set aside your pre-conceived ideas and what you think you know and take a spiritual journey with me of no distance with no destination. Within these pages, we will take an inspiring journey of life. Let's fasten our seat belts and more importantly bring our sense of humor, we'll need it where we're going. Enjoy the ride. A spiritual experience with seating for one, but to be passed onto many.

"Know the truth and the truth will set you free."

We can all do better and greater things. I was inspired to write this book, to teach what I know to be the truth. Inspiration comes from within, I am inspired, not out spired. I am motivated to do this by what I know to be right, know from within. When I am concerned with what others want from me, I'm motivated by what they will think—I am "out spired" instead of being inspired. I write this simple book for one reason: I cannot, not write, what I'm inspired to write. To withhold any-thing, we are inspired to do is to harm ourselves, but more importantly, to harm the world.

I hope I see many of you on the road as I carry the message of peace for us all, through individual spiritual awakening. I welcome your questions and comments and am especially anxious to hear your life-changing stories.

Until we meet, God bless you all. Enjoy this book and your own life to the fullest. Live your dreams and help a few people along the way.

Love as always.
Yours in service,

Kenny G. Down

Chapter One

In Delusion

I always imagined a spiritual teacher to be a wise Buddhist monk, Hindu swami, Indian medicine woman, or at least to look like a wise mystic. Maybe even Christ himself could teach me a thing or two. I had long ago lost all hope that any human being or Higher Being or God could or would do anything for such a pathetically hopeless person as myself. If there were a person who could help in any way, it would have to be someone with incredible power that looked the part. Like everything else in my pitiful life, I was wrong, not just a little wrong, but on an opposite pole from the truth.

The man who would become my greatest spiritual teacher, my mentor, and my best friend, I had not yet met. His name was Gary Goldpeople, and he was a spiritual giant traveling in the body of a fat, funny, quite erratic, disheveled city bus driver. He looked like he had nothing to offer, and yet like everything else, I was wrong about Goldpeople. He had all any of us ever needs, what most people are after and never find. He had life—real honest to God—life. He knew the spiritual truths of the ages, and most of all, he knew the truth about himself.

I had lost all that had ever contained any shred of happiness, stability, and contentment. Everyone I knew and who had loved me had given up hope and suspected I might be a lost cause. None more than myself. My final days were spent alone in hotel room after hotel room; drugs and alcohol were all that were left. I had long ago stopped the lighter stuff and was injecting the drugs intravenously. I had attempted suicide by overdose many times, but none more serious than one attempt at the bitter end. I wanted to die, I was forty pounds underweight, and I'd shoot speedballs for days on end, going weeklong periods with no sleep. Insanity had crept in and now became my constant companion. I hated everyone and everything and blamed the world for my disgusting condition.

I'd cooked up enough heroin to kill a large roomful of non-addicts. The suicidal concoction was so thick that it would barely pass through the cotton into the syringe. I filled the syringe to the very top and shot the entire load into my arm. The next day, I awoke in a pile of vomit, with an overdue hotel bill, no money, and no hope. I knew then that my time to leave this world was not up to me. I was in a body that refused to die with a mind that long ago had lost the ability to think straight. I was trapped. Hopelessness comes in all types, but for me it took the form of a hope-to-die drug addict, stuck for at least one more day, in pain, misery, and depression.

It was a few months after that I'd met Mr. Goldpeople. There was not one day in those last months that were in any way better than the day of the suicide attempt in the old University Motel. My entire life, it seemed at that time, had been one big tragedy. My childhood family had suffered with abuse, alcoholism, divorces, a dramatic mother, foster homes, and institutions. The list goes on and on, and in my mind, I never had a chance. Later I would find out that I was wrong about all that as well.

It was a summer's day that I met Mr. Gary Goldpeople. I'd spent the previous night on a friend's couch and had been asked to leave and not return. I was doing drugs in the kitchen when they had awakened from their night's sleep. I had the gall to yell at them that they didn't care about me, and I was trying to use their love for me against them. I thought they were selfish and unloving. The truth was, as I look back through new eyes, they were selfless and loving. I know now how hard it is to give up on someone you truly love and ask them to leave. I know now I put them in that situation. I thought they had put me in a bad situation by kicking me out. I was wrong. Not a little wrong, not partly wrong—I had it entirely backwards.

I packed the few belongings I'd left in my small backpack and left, deciding to catch a city bus across town where I knew a few drug deals would be going on. I knew that I might catch some old friend with money and remind him of how when I had money, I shared with everyone.

I really didn't care where I ended up, I really didn't care that I'd just burned one of the last remaining friends I had in the world. I only cared about my immediate need for the drugs that brought me the only relief I had known in many years. It had been that way for as long as I could remember. I didn't care—I couldn't—to care was far too painful. I'd lost everything worthwhile in life.

Chapter Two

A Ray of Hope in a World of Darkness

I arrived at University Mall and went to the large lot where the transit buses in the area came and went. It was early, and most had not even begun the trek to work. It was the cool crisp summer morning that was so common to the Pacific Northwest part of the United States for that time of the year. There was one bus waiting at the stop when I arrived—not yet in service. The driver, eating a huge donut and sipping coffee out of a thermos, spotted me walking up to the stop. He opened the door just as I approached. "I'm not in service for another thirty-five minutes, but if you want to come aboard and stay warm, feel free."

Without thinking I climbed aboard the bus and then noticed the driver. Hard to miss, as he was so large he barely fit behind the huge steering wheel of the bus. His stomach protruded around the wheel on both sides so far that it would take a crane to get him out, at least it seemed to me. He sat atop a large driver's seat mounted by a single hydraulic shock absorber that was as big around as the seat was wide. Even the huge shock absorber was bottomed out under the weight of the oversized driver.

I accepted his offer and came aboard and took a seat across from him.

"Gary...Gary Goldpeople's the name." He nodded in a friendly gesture.

Goldpeople? What the hell kind of a name is that I thought. I said nothing in reply and was beginning to feel the effects of the last drugs I had done wearing off. I began to feel uncomfortable and scared of the reality that I, once again was out of money, nearly out of drugs, completely out of friends, and as always, out of hope.

I watched the curious man behind the wheel. He wasn't especially tall. That made him one of the rounder people I'd ever seen. He had long gray-white hair and a medium, long, gray-white beard. Very much the Santa-Claus type. Small wire-rimmed eyeglasses and rosy red cheeks shined above his full beard. A little too disheveled for a Santa on most days—no telling what he might say to the little tikes. Gary always spoke his mind and would not be likely to humor a spoiled child wanting the world or parents who cater to their illusions—out of guilt for never having the time. Gary would have been fired on the first day of any Santa's gig. His looks, kindness, and good humor however did fit the part.

I noticed that the driver had dozens of buttons covering his beret-style hat and navy-blue uniform jacket that identified him as a city bus driver. The buttons had sayings like, "DON'T TAKE LIFE SO SERIOUSLY, NONE OF US ARE GETTING OUT ALIVE," "WEAR MORE PURPLE," and "MAKE LOVE NOT WAR." Then other buttons said seeming contradictions like, "IF YOU DON'T LIKE MY DRIVING, STAY OFF THE CURB" and "GO SEAHAWKS." A little of everything. I watched this oddball for lack of anything else to do. He ate his donut, and then another while slurping away on his thermos of coffee, as if I wasn't even there.

I slipped to the back of the bus and took a seat, looking up front into the driver's rearview mirror to watch the jolly old bus driver. I used the seat in front of me for cover. I could see he was watching me, but he couldn't see what was taking place in my lap. I brought out my spoon, cooked up the last of the drugs I had right there on the seat, drew it up into the syringe, and began the long process of sticking around in my arm to find a long ago disappeared vein.

I was desperate to make this last shot count and couldn't risk missing the vein but then saw the driver begin wiggling out from behind the wheel. He wasn't saying a word, but I knew he was coming to see what was up. After a gymnastic act to remove his body from behind the wheel and get it lifted off the seat, he began coming toward me.

I was stunned. I couldn't pull the syringe from my arm, but couldn't push the plunger down yet either as the vein I was trying for was now gone. I made my mind up to keep trying to find the vein and get the drugs in me, which I did, but not before Mr. Gary Goldpeople was standing over me watching.

I looked up briefly, then back down at the unfinished job and the syringe hanging from my arm. I spoke to my new friend for the first time, "I'm trying to stop." I really didn't know where the words came from, they were the only words I could come up with. They were nowhere near the truth.

Gary stared at me for a brief moment, and then smiled, "I can see that."

I pulled out the syringe and slumped in my seat as the warmth of the heroin rush came over me. I also began to cry, somehow sensing how my life had come to this, shooting drugs in front of a city bus driver and not really even trying to hide it. I no longer cared about anything, anything except the next fix.

I got up to get off the bus, Gary reached out his hand and held it in front of him, indicating to me to be still.

"Gary...Gary Goldpeople's the name," He said slowly and deliberately with such a soft voice that I didn't feel immediately threatened.

I put the syringe and spoon into my pack, trying as best I could to hide them from Gary, even though I knew I had been caught. "Yes, you told me that, I promise I'll leave now, I don't plan on hurting anyone. Please don't call the police." I tried to look up and give Gary the most pitiful look I could, trying my best to play the sympathy card.

"The police?" he responded wide-eyed, "Why would I call the police? What I have here is a garden-variety human being, suffering... I'd say from a spiritual malady— a bad case from the looks of things." He paused, chuckled slightly under his breath, looked at me from over the top of his wire-rimmed glasses worn low on his nose, then added, "Last time I checked, 911 wasn't equipped to handle spiritual maladies." He laughed at himself out loud this time, a very jolly belly laugh that I would come to treasure. He shook his head as if to recognize my plea for pity.

"Very little to laugh about," I cried. I tried to look as directly at him as I could, but ended up looking at his shoes. "As you can see, things aren't exactly going great for me. I've no money, and those drugs I just did were it...my last. That means I'll be sick shortly if I don't figure some way out of this mess. I tried killing myself, and even that won't work." I felt as though I should run but slumped into the seat even further.

The fat man standing over me interrupted—"Yes, most definitely a spiritual malady going on here. My route starts up in five minutes, but I can help you if you like."

"Unless you have some money or drugs you'd like to give me, I doubt you can be of any real help," I replied with all the sarcastic inflection I could muster.

Gary, reached into his pocket and pulled out a large wad of bills, all crumpled up. It seemed like he had placed each bill, wadded up into his pocket, one at a time. Mostly ones, I noticed, but as he began to unravel the mess of bills, a twenty slipped out and he handed it to me. He then smiled. "Anything else I can do for you?"

I didn't know how to respond, I thought about asking for more money, but somehow knew better. I looked up from the spot on his shoes I had been staring at. "No, but thank you very much." I held the twenty in my hand, not sure how to react to the series of events that had just taken place.

He went forward on the bus and went through a most amusing sequence of moves to force himself once again behind the large steering wheel. He turned on the interior lights of the bus and illuminated the exterior sign indicating that the bus was now in service, route number forty-three, University District to Downtown.

Several people had now gathered at the bus stop and waited to come aboard. Several had been watching through the window at the drama unfolding inside the bus—watching our conversation. The door was opened and the first passengers of the day, six or seven in all boarded.

Each of them looked closely at this round bus driver, then again at me, trying to figure out the conversation and the exchange of money they had just witnessed through the bus windows. Twenty minutes later, I arrived at my stop downtown, twenty dollars richer.

"My route starts at 6:30 AM. I'm usually at the first stop, in my bus by 5:00 AM or so." He added, "You look like the type of fellow who stays up all night, so stop by tomorrow."

I heard him laugh out loud as I took the few steps down, off the bus, and into the street. Gary Goldpeople closed the door and pulled away. I had met a spiritual master but I wouldn't realize this until many days had past.

It was a little early for the drug deals to start going down, so I went into a coffee shop and ordered a donut and a tall Americano. This was the most miserable part of each day… the waiting.

I still had seventeen dollars left to try to score later in the day. My mind raced as I sat and drank the hot coffee. I was already thinking of how I could get the best deal. I thought about how I could get the most out of a dealer with the small amount of cash. I thought that maybe I could get someone to give a little extra and take my seventeen dollars now and promise to pay a little more later. I thought that, I should've asked that bus driver for some more money! He might have given me another twenty if I'd asked.

That day, while starting in a very unusual fashion, had quickly turned into a day like most at that time of my life—every moment was a struggle. I was terrified at the prospect that I wouldn't be able to ingest enough alcohol and drugs to keep me emotionally numbed and physically well. I lived in constant misery.

I thought of Gary as I sat and finished the last few sips of my coffee and took a bite of the donut. The donut was the first food I could remember eating in well over a day.

Garden-variety, spiritual-malady! This bus driver who called himself Goldpeople didn't have a clue. What a joke! What the heck was he talking about anyway? But he did give me twenty bucks! Looking back, I see clearly that Gary was using my character defects, which at the time I also knew nothing about, to keep me coming back. In this case, the defects were greed and my addiction to narcotics.

Chapter Three

Walk Towards the Light

I came to three days later, it was around 3:00 AM. I'd hooked up with a girl I'd known and used for several years. Sierra was a part-timer on the drugs. A dancer at one of the local clubs. Every few months, I could talk her into buying some drugs and going on a run with me. She paid. She always had money. The money and her attention, as always, had come to an end. She once again wanted me to leave. She needed to go to sleep, get up, and go to work. Unlike me, she still slept and worked. Sierra's job was to strip her clothes and dance in front of lonely men for money. She didn't trust me there, in her home, by myself. I wasn't trusted by her or anyone else in my life.

I'd known Sierra for five or more years. I'd met her when things were better. She and several of her friends were customers back when I'd still had a little game left and was selling drugs. Sierra was the youngest and the most beautiful of them all. She had a china-doll complexion, as if her face had never seen the sunlight. Beautiful creamy, soft skin and brown, olive-shaped eyes. She always went heavy on the makeup but could've gotten away without wearing any. Her hair was bleached blond and chopped off all the way around, just a few inches below the ears. Squared-off chopped bangs hung just above her eyebrows.

I was now an unwelcomed presence in her life. She put up with me because I would show her attention and I appealed to her incredibly kind nature. Sierra was someone who had been through literal hell in her short life. Many nights we had stayed up and talked all night. I would listen, not make any sexual advances, and hold her when she cried. She would buy the drugs and allow me to spend the night at her home. She had a decent place. A studio apartment in one of the nicer areas of downtown. The view was beautiful, although with the blinds almost constantly pulled, we almost never saw it.

I listened, as always, to her telling me stories of her broken home life. Sexual abuse by her father starting at age nine, by two of her older brothers, who had themselves been terribly abused. She had been sexually abused by several neighbor boys who saw her as an easy target. In high school, it had continued. Several athletes had raped her at a house party, so she'd never returned to school or to home. Shortly afterward, she'd been offered her first job as a dancer. I had listened all these years as she paid for my drugs and drinks, but now she wanted me to go. We always came to this place. Her begging me to leave and me pressing further, for more money, more time.

I was truly offended at being asked to leave and at not being trusted. I spent at least an hour trying to talk Sierra out of kicking me out of her place. I wanted to stay, while she went to work. I continued to try to talk her into getting me more drugs or letting me crash at her place. She refused at each and every pitiful request. Finally, Sierra threatened to call her bouncers from the club and have me thrown out if need be. I left and felt once again that I was misunderstood. Sierra was totally out of line not to trust me. I considered myself to be a good person and believed you should never steal from a friend. A good theory, but one I could never live up to.

The truth was Sierra would've been crazy to let me stay, because I would've continued to take advantage of her. I thought about my friend, the bus driver, for the first time since leaving his bus and going to the coffee shop. I started walking. But as I walked toward that bus stop, all I wanted was oblivion. I was acutely aware of each passing thought. Dark thoughts, hopeless thoughts, accompanied by feelings of doom, desperation, and panic.

I had been in this condition, the place of no hope, for so long that I couldn't even vaguely remember what happiness felt like. The place of sadness and deepest depression seemed like a better space than what I was in. I welcomed a return to plain insanity. I wanted to die. I wanted everything to end. My skin crawled. My stomach ached all hours of the day from hunger, yet every time I ate I got sick. I couldn't take food and had lost every ounce of the weight I had put on in my adolescence. My body was a bruised and battered pincushion, full of infection from the repeated use of unclean needles to inject my poison.

I ignored the pain in my feet from walking. My feet were swollen from repeatedly missed injections into the veins on the top of each foot. I put one red and swollen foot in front of the other. I thought of Gary Goldpeople, the bus driver. I walked on to my destination. I hoped, I prayed, that he would help me—give me money.

The desperation of my condition created a black eerie frightening shadow around my being. It scared me to look at myself in the mirror, and it terrified anyone who looked my way. I couldn't enter a store without being followed; the police couldn't drive by without stopping to see what was up. It was obvious to me, and to everyone around, that I was desperate beyond description. I was a dangerous man. I was capable of anything and everything. I hated myself, scared myself, and despised myself. I was trapped.

As I walked on, I thought of everyone I loved. I thought of everyone who had loved me. I thought of a childhood, lost in oblivion. These days, those who had loved me at one time in my life, would've broken down into tears if they saw me. At first, not at all recognizing me, and then the shock when they realized who I was. I'd been a loving child who would run and hug anyone who needed attention. I had deeply cared for others. I'd been in love, held jobs, married, had children, and laughed out loud any time I was given the least opportunity.

But still, I was being pulled to my destination by the love and kindness of a man who, though I had only met once, had been quick to give me what I too had once given so freely and what I really needed in that moment—forgiveness, no judgment of any kind, and money.

I was being pushed to my destination by a body and mind that wanted it all to end. I would've given my life to feel like a human being for one, brief, moment.

I had changed unwillingly. I'd been swept away in drug addiction, alcoholism, deep depression, and mental illness. I had spiraled out of control and lost all self-respect. Had it been God's will, I would've died long ago as I'd been trying to die more than I'd been trying to live for many years now. God's will was for me to live, even in this misery.

I was constantly tortured by the overwhelming compulsions for more drugs. The feelings of relief and euphoria I'd once received from the drugs were now in the distant past. I used and drank everything and anything I could get my hands on and with only one purpose. Not for the incredible euphoria I'd once received but for the sole purpose of trying to quiet the maddening compulsion for more. Trying to quell the frightening prospective that I may run out and go through the hideous experience of withdrawals.

I thought, as I walked, what torture it would be to go without the only true friends I had left: drugs, alcohol, and inebriation. When I stopped, for even a moment, it seemed the withdrawals would start. I would shake, then sweat, convulse, and throw up. My legs and stomach would cramp, my fingers would curl in pain, every joint ached, every muscle quivered, every bone hurt. But all this was nothing compared to the unbearable insanity that would return. The insanity that would tell me I was worthless, that I should shoot myself, that I didn't deserve to live, that nobody loved me, that nobody ever would love me. Over, and over, and over.

I want out. I want this to end. God please make it stop, please allow me to die. Again and again. I want out. I want this to end. God please make it stop, please allow me to die. This became my daily mantra.

I continued my walk toward the bus stop and the strange bus driver I'd met. One foot in front of the other, it was everything I could do. I was being pulled, being pushed.

Chapter Four

Only Dreaming We Are Awake

I arrived at the bus depot across from the University District and could see Mr. Goldpeople sitting in the dark, in the bus, eating his donut, and drinking out of his thermos. He had a small radio rigged up on his dash and was tinkering with a cassette tape. Navigating his morning coffee and donut while trying to get the tape to play, he appeared from a distance to be a bumbling fool. He was anything but.

He spotted me coming up on the side of the bus and opened the door. "Wow, look at you... I thought you couldn't get much worse than the last time I saw you. Guess I was wrong." He laughed and shook his head, in disbelief. "Have a seat. Thought you'd be back sooner. Twenty bucks usually brings 'em back the same day," he laughed again, this time even louder. "You must've run into an old friend with money...or did you rob a bank?" He continued...chuckling along—not waiting for or wanting a response.

I thought about getting off the bus right then. What was I thinking? This old coot really was nuts. I wondered if he was even safe to be driving a bus. I took a seat and without looking at him, I interrupted his laughter. "How long have you been a bus driver?" I said sarcastically, as I finally looked up.

"Oh, I'm sorry, did I give you the impression I was a bus driver?" He shot back, looking directly at me and jerking his head in surprise. "Heavens no. I do drive a bus here and there, when I've the time." He looked puzzled for a moment, then smiling added "Which seems to be most days for the last twenty or so years, but a bus driver I'm not!"

His smile widened, he was growing happier with himself as the conversation progressed. But I was growing more and more irritated—unsure of why I was there. I'd walked miles, miserable hard miles, and lonely miles, to see this man. Not really knowing why I'd come. Now he wanted to joke around! I still hadn't removed my jacket and had my small backpack in my lap. I clutched tightly to the pack with clenched fists. Looking directly at him and this time in a voice that left no doubt about my growing irritability. "What is it that you are then?"

He didn't answer my question, but instead broke his donut in half and poured a cup of coffee from his thermos into the lid and handed both to me. "You look like you could use a little nutrition this morning." He paused and wrinkled his brow as if in deep thought. He set down his coffee and donut and leaned as far back as his large seat would allow. He closed his eyes and brought his hands up, held together as if in prayer. After a moment, he leaned forward and began speaking, "Now, we must get some nutrition into you and those drugs out of you before we can really get started here." He let out a large breath, and looking at me, pulled up his sleeves as if preparing to do some manual labor.

His offer of coffee and donuts and the moment of quiet had calmed my nerves only slightly. "What? What do you mean 'get started?' "

Gary took a bite of his donut, washing it down with a swig of black coffee. "Oh heavens, forgive me. I didn't answer your first question, did I?"

I had forgotten what my first question was. I was still wondering what he had meant by "really get started".

He continued. "I'm really not a bus driver...I'm a waker-upper."

"A what?" I responded in surprise. I was shaking badly and tried hard not to spill my coffee. Gary had kindly only filled the cup one third full. I looked up only for a moment and then my eyes sunk back to the floor. I felt horrible and wondered if I would be able to hold the donut and coffee down.

He smiled and paused for a moment to get my attention before continuing. "You know, a waker-upper. I show sleeping people how to wake up."

"I know how to wake up, it's the going to sleep for good that I am interested in." I quickly responded, with all sincerity.

This time we both laughed, only I wasn't sure what we were laughing at. I was serious.

Gary stopped laughing, and while maintaining a wide smile, spoke calmly to me, "In case you haven't noticed, and it seems you've not. You, my friend, are traveling in a body with a spirit that's asleep. You're walking around in a body, asleep, dreaming that you're awake. I help awaken the spirit within."

His comment made me nervous, although I'd felt much more at ease than I had just a few moments before. "Oh really?" I said out loud, thinking again to myself that this Gary Goldpeople may be a little unstable to be driving around a city bus.

"Really. So, you see, I'm not really a bus driver any more than any of us are our jobs. None of us are what we do. What's your favorite color?"

"Blue." I responded quickly, wondering where that question had come from and what this had to do with anything.

"Now I know something about you far more important than what you do for a living, and you haven't told me your name yet?"

I looked at Gary. What a sweet old man, I thought. I was sure he was right. I hadn't given him my name. I then felt comfortable enough to give him my real name, something I hadn't done with a stranger in a long time. "Stanley, Stanley Pearson."

21

"Ok Stanley, whose favorite color is blue, that's your lesson for the day. Gary pulled a large wadded up bundle of bills from his pocket and struggled to move his large body behind the steering wheel of the bus. He handed me several smaller bills. "Should be around forty dollars there. While you're thinking about the lesson I just gave you, you may run across something that'll make you want to come back. One thing however, I'm sure of, is that giving forty dollars will assure his return." Gary smiled and gave me a wink.

I quickly grabbed the crumpled bills. He was so happy this guy, what's up with him? I took his money and knew that I would be seeing one of the local street dealers within minutes. I had to buy from the street. None of the dealers in homes and hotel rooms would have any-thing to do with me. I'd ripped them off before, or one of their friends. They always had trouble getting me to leave, even if they did allow me in. Most of all, I drew attention... the wrong kind of attention.

I got off the bus and began visually scanning the street corner for anyone I knew that was selling. I found what I needed—quickly. I did what I had to do and soon my mind was at rest. I almost felt normal. I knew deep in my heart that the feeling wasn't real, and it wouldn't last, but even the temporary illusion of feeling normal was so much better that the alternative of how I felt when I ran out.

It was the illusion for a few moments that that I was okay. In that state I thought of Gary, he must've known what I would do with the money. So why would he have given it to me? He really must want me to come back, but why? What could he want that I have? I had just gone through a brutal walk to see him, needing help—wanting help. He had responded by giving me money for drugs and asking me what my favorite color was?

He had said he was a what? A waker-upper. He'd given me a lesson: *That we are not what we do.* He wasn't a bus driver, but he sure looked like a bus driver to me. There was definitely something about him that made me believe that possibly he was something other than what I thought he was, somehow more than a bus driver. I thought as long and deeply as I could in my condition.

I recalled our conversation. *He'd said that none of us are what we do for a living. That we are not what we do. That knowing someone's favorite color is more important than knowing what they do for a living.*

In my heroin-induced narcosis, my mind had slowed where I could think only one thought at a time. What if I wasn't what I do, what if I was more than a hope-to-die junkie? Then who would I be?

I wanted to return to see Gary. Partly for the money, but now also because of my curiosity about the waker-upper. I really had meant what I had told Gary. I really was more interested in going to sleep for good than I was in waking up. But I knew, from so many failed attempts, that I couldn't go to sleep for good. If that were under my control, I would've succeeded in that job long ago.

I'd tried so hard, for so long, to make it all stop and yet here I was. I was alone with my thoughts—dark and desperate thoughts. Helpless and empty, once again.

The drugs were already wearing off. I put everything I had left into the spoon and ingested what little remained of my forty-dollar purchase.

The narcotics took their effect. My thoughts slowed again. What if Gary wasn't a bus driver? What if I was more than a worthless junkie, a dead-beat Dad, a rip-off, a liar, and a cheat? I had a favorite color. I couldn't remember where that had come from. It was an inner part of who I was, not the outside appearance, but the inside reality. If my favorite color was important, maybe there were other things about me that were important too.

I hadn't thought about any minute part of myself as having the least bit of importance in years. Maybe there were other traits I possessed, inner things, things I was born with. God-given things? Maybe I was dreaming and needed to be awakened?

Chapter Five

Introduction to Prayer

The money brought me back. I was broke, sick, and out of drugs. That was all that was needed to assure my return. I had nowhere else to go; so, broke and sick, I'd turned my thoughts to Gary. I began the trek of despair toward the bus stop. The walk of hopelessness. The early mornings, endless waits for Gary's bus to arrive.

This is how my days ended, or began, I couldn't tell. I rarely slept. There were no more ends and no more beginnings of the days for me. No waking up and going anywhere. No coming home to anything. Just one, unbearable existence. The days turned into weeks, then into months, and now years had come and gone. I really had no idea how things had gotten to this place. I'd come to the point in life where my greatest hope was that a large, slightly insane, city bus driver would have pity on me and give me the money I needed to go another day. I was a charity case.

I arrived at the bus stop, having survived, against my will, another plunge into the world of deception, despair, and self-pity. The early morning dew was still on the benches inside the small bus shelter. I took a seat to rest my weary legs anyway, not taking the time to wipe away the moisture.

It was the middle of June. A few weeks had passed since I'd first sat down at this stop, since I'd met Gary. The bus stop was covered on the top and on two sides with Plexiglas panels that allowed me to view out. The front was open to the street and allowed the cool morning breeze to enter. There was just enough room to lie down on the hard, wooden bench if I tucked in my knees. This stop was to become my own personal Mecca, a place I would be driven to by desperation, but also drawn to by a mystical force beyond my comprehension.

I wished for the arrival of the bus, to see Gary. I got warm, free coffee and donuts when I arrived early. Most of all, I sensed the possibility that I was being taught something that would help. The idea that we are not what we do. That learning someone's favorite color was important. These ideas were simple, too simple I thought, but somehow I had the feeling that there was more to be revealed.

It was the need for money that had brought me back. Each day was the same, and I never had to ask. It was just enough to keep me well, and for Gary, just enough to keep me coming back.

I curled up on the hard, cold, wooden bench and did my best to stay warm. Time passed as I closed my eyes and listened to the traffic passing on the street before me. There were two lanes of traffic in each direction, flowing north and south. Directly before me was an empty sidewalk. I opened my eyes every few moments to see if I could spot the buses arrival. It was too early for anyone else to be at the stop. I liked it that way.

At last I could make out the bus, no mistake it was Gary's, as even from a distance I could spot his hefty physique hulked over the large wheel of the bus. His button-covered beret atop his head and his near shoulder-length white hair tucked into the hat. I stood up and went to the curb.

The door was immediately opened, and a smiling Gary Goldpeople greeted me. He looked as if he was always smiling. Even when he wasn't smiling, his bright-blue eyes were. His worn, slightly wrinkled face showed upturned crow's feet at the corners of both eyes. The wrinkles that framed his mouth were upturned, giving the appearance that he was always smiling. His demeanor, as always, was peaceful and content, bringing an instant calming to me.

"Happy to see you again, Stanley. We have a few minutes until I need to start my route. I'm so very glad you came early. How about some hot coffee?"

"Yes please," I replied as I took my seat aboard the bus, set my pack down, and noticed how warm the bus was compared to the bench outside.

Gary reached around behind him, struggling for a second before retrieving his thermos of hot coffee. He withdrew a previously used Styrofoam cup and poured a cup of black coffee from his thermos into the cup and handed it over to me.

I wasn't sure if I should say anything to him about the used cup, but thought maybe not. I was happy to be aboard the warm bus. I was happy to be drinking hot coffee, but mostly I was happy to look at Gary, to be with him.

"Gary, I'm not okay." The words came out of me, unplanned. I wasn't sure from where. I had thought them, but didn't consciously utter the words, yet there they were.

Gary turned again and reached behind his seat, this time producing a maple bar wrapped in a napkin. He unraveled the donut, broke it in half, and handed the larger portion over to me. He looked deeply into my eyes. I felt he knew exactly what I was talking about without me saying another word. "Have you tried prayer?"

I thought for a moment before answering. "Hadn't even considered it to tell you the truth." I sipped my coffee and took my first bite of the maple-covered pastry. "I really haven't Gary, I believe there is a God, but he wouldn't listen to me. I've done so many shameful things, bad things. Even if God would listen, and I doubt he would, I wouldn't know what to say, where would I begin?" I stared into my coffee and tried hard not to shake, grinding my teeth between sips of coffee and tiny bites off the maple bar.

"It's not the words that are important to God; it's the meaning of the prayers. The spirit that's important." Gary set his coffee down on the large dash in front of him, leaned back in his seat and closed his eyes. I waited for his next words. After a moment, he let out a breath with an "ahhh" and leaned slowly forward in my direction, looking directly into my eyes, "I want you to do me a huge favor, will you?"

I wanted the money he might offer. I wanted to stay on the warm bus, to be with him. I suspected I might be being lured into a trap, but I couldn't resist. "Sure, what is it? I don't have much to offer you know."

Gary's whole face lit up. "Oh what sad news that is, I thought you were a millionaire." He loved to make himself laugh. He let out a real "ho-ho ho" and shook his head from side to side. He took another large bite of his donut, this time polishing it off. He seemed to only chew a few times before taking a large drink of coffee. "God can use those of us with nothing, so that's an attraction to him. Those of us with nothing are more willing to learn. Have you ever heard that the meek will inherit the earth? Blessed are the poor and all that?"

I'd relaxed quite a bit in Gary's presence, but my legs still bounced and twitched in nervousness. I now looked at him when I answered and setting down the coffee, I began to remove my coat, "Yes, somewhere I think I have heard that." I wanted to know what the favor was he had asked about. I brushed off his lecturing to ask. "What is the favor you want me to do?"

Gary put on his wire-rimmed glasses and gave me a serious glance through the round spectacles. His eyes were brilliant violet-blue, even through the glasses. "I want you to write your own prayer of preparation. Take some time today to think about the idea that if you think you know something about God, then you may be limiting the presence of God in your life. You think you know that God will not listen to your prayers. Maybe you need to be rid of that old idea for a new one that works."

He continued after another huge gulp of coffee and a wipe of his chin with the back of his large hand. "You think you don't know how to pray. If you can talk to me, then you can talk to God. That is prayer, my friend. I want you to take the time to write your own prayer about putting aside your old ideas, asking God for something new." Gary paused and opened his thermos again, pouring me a refill then pouring a cup for himself in his thermos lid. He produced a second donut. This time an old-fashioned one. He broke it in half, and after giving the two halves a close eye, he noticed I had barely touched my first. He set one half in his lap and took a large bite out of half number one.

I ate my donut and drank the coffee from the old cup. I wondered what kind of prayer I could possibly come up with. I'd play along with the old guy, I thought. I leaned back in my seat and smiled at Gary for a brief moment.

Gary smiled back at me, "Can you do me that favor and write a prayer for yourself?"

"How is it a favor for you, if I write a prayer?" I asked as I ate the next bite of my donut.

Gary smiled widely, his eyes seemed to tear as he motioned me with a wave to stand and come closer. He pointed to the floor next to his seat, "Come here close while I tell you something."

I stood up, set my coffee on the floor, and was standing directly in front of him expecting some cash to be handed over.

Gary reached out with one hand and touched my left hand gently. "Stanley, my friend, it is a gift to me every time I see you. I smile just thinking about you. It is a favor to me because by you writing a prayer, I get a better friend."

I pulled my hand back gently. I could feel the power in his words, and even more, I could feel his power by his emotion. I knew that standing before me was an honest man. I had only just met him, but I believed with all that I had that he was a man who not only cared, but cared enough to help.

"I need to get driving Stanley. Best thing about this job is that they actually pay me, so I feel some obligation to drive. My first customers are here."

I turned around to take my seat, and through the window, I observed a young couple approaching the bus. I could tell they knew Gary. They both waved, as they got closer. Gary waved back.

Gary opened the door, and before greeting his first riders of the day, turned to me once more, "Stanley, ride as long as you like today, but please do me that favor and write that prayer."

I headed back and took a seat near the back of the bus. I laid back and closed my eyes. I slept until midday, awaking several times to notice folks boarding the bus, sitting as close as possible to Gary and having conversations. They all seemed so happy, so at ease with Gary. They laughed together, and I could hear Gary's "Ha ha ha, Oh ho ho" laugh. Half of all those who came and went told Gary they loved him when they got off. Many touched him. Some even leaned into him for a hug. He kissed one women ever so lightly on the cheek. I had never observed this type of fellowship. I had to just sit and watch, not believing I deserved to be a part of anything so sweet.

I rode that day through the morning rush for those going to work, the afternoon lull, and the evening rush for those returning home. I caught up on my sleep, and each time I awoke, I noticed Gary still talking to people—helping someone. I noticed others listening in on the conversations and being helped as well. No one disturbed me or asked me to move. I knew Gary had an eye on me, so I was able to sleep in peace for the first time in as long as I could remember. I awoke to find a pad of paper with a pen clipped to the notebook. I knew Gary or one of his friends had left this for me. I added it to my backpack.

The bus returned to the University Mall stop once again. I knew it was close to the end of the day for Gary. So I stood, picked up my pack, and headed to the front of the bus to exit and to thank him. I was beginning to feel the frightening warning signs of the beginnings of withdrawals and wondered where my next fix would come from. As I stepped off the bus, I heard Gary's voice from behind me. I turned quickly—hoping. My entire being relaxed as I saw Gary.

"Stanley... I almost forgot" He was holding in his hands two, twenty-dollar bills. "For you my new friend."

I stepped up, took the money, leaned in, and gave Gary a sideways hug. He hugged me back and did not let go for several seconds. He whispered gently into my ear before letting go. "Come back soon, my friend, and write a prayer for yourself. It's the only thing that can help. I can't write the prayer for you, but if you write the prayer I can help."

I watched as the bus pulled away. I took a seat on the bench that was to act as my temporary home, and before making my journey to find the dealers; I was given the strength to write. I pulled out the pad of paper and the pen that had been my gift aboard the bus. From the depths of my desperate soul the words flowed from pen to paper.

God,
I think I know everything, I know nothing.
I think I know what is best for me,
And also what is best for everyone around me.

I think I know how to stop using drugs,
Tonight I am loaded.

Can you help a know-it-all?
If you can accept me,
A know-it-all that really knows nothing,
I will do my best.
I need your help.
Everything I know is killing me.

I am more concerned with being right,
Than I am with being free.
I think I know everything, I know nothing.
Amen.

Chapter Six

Turning Point

The forty dollars was gone. I'd spent the night, or nights, I couldn't really remember, in oblivion. I waited at the bus stop another night, waiting till early morning. I wanted to get on the bus, have a donut, sleep, get some money, and leave. Gary had another plan.

I boarded the bus as soon as Gary arrived—he shared his morning coffee and donuts. I knew that he saw many people each day, but he always treated me like a long lost friend. He never forgot our last conversation, no matter how long I'd been away between visits.

Gary looked cleaner than normal this morning. His white beard was neatly trimmed about four or five inches away from his face all around. His hair looked clean and shiny. He looked great and had showered. Even his uniform of navy blue jacket and black tie with matching navy-blue slacks had been recently laundered.

"Stanley, it's been awhile. I thought you'd write the prayer and be back quickly, what with the forty dollars I gave you." He smiled at me warmly and chuckled, "Hehehe, I guess I should have only given you twenty. He smiled as I dropped my head, knowing what he was about to ask. "Did you do me that favor and write that prayer?" Not waiting for me to answer, he added, "You do have the prayer with you, I hope? Not much I can do without that."

"I do, but really Gary it hasn't been that long." I took a bite of my donut and almost choked at his next statement.

Tipping his head and looking at me sadly, "Stanley, it's been a week."

I knew I'd lost track of days, there were days I couldn't remember. I'd almost gotten used to losing track of large blocks of time. It was still humiliating to me when someone else knew. Now Gary knew. He could tell not only by my comments, but also by the look of terror on my face when he told me it had been a week. I couldn't remember sleeping during that time. I'd thought about Gary many times, but had lost all track of hours and days, seeking relief any way I could. I'd thought a day or two days had passed since I'd written the prayer. Gary told me it had been a week, and I knew this was the truth.

"Let's try prayer, Stanley. Really try it. I did, and look what it's done for me. Ha ha ha," he laughed. I loved that he could laugh even at himself.

I looked at this man. He did indeed look good today, but still not something you would aspire too. Still a disheveled, overweight, broke-looking, unhealthy, bus driver. Not a picture of success to be sure. Unless you knew him. I wanted what he had. His peace, his sense of humor, his relationship with God, and his love of everyone he came in contact with and especially his obvious calm and contentment with who he was, he was at ease, he knew peace.

"I'll try anything." I wasn't sure I meant it, but was willing to go through the motions.

"Let's hear the prayer."

I ruffled through my pack. Unzipped an inner zipper and withdrew the prayer I'd written a week earlier. As just instructed, I read:

"God,
I think I know everything, I know nothing.
I think I know what is best for me,
And also, what is best for everyone around me.

I think I know how to stop using drugs,
Today I am loaded.

Can you help a know-it-all?
If you can accept me,
A know-it-all that really knows nothing,
I will do my best.
I need your help.
Everything I know is killing me.

I am more concerned with being right,
Than I am with being free.
I think I know everything, I know nothing.
Amen."

My first thought as I looked up at Gary was how Gary was going to be so impressed with such a wonderful prayer, how I had such deep insight.

Instead he calmly said as if reading my mind, "If that was meant to impress me, I must admit it didn't!"

He laughed.

I didn't.

"These prayers only work if we are out of answers, if we still have any answers at all, they will find their way into our thinking, our mind, our meditation, and once more it will be ME HELPING ME. I want this to be God helping you because God is all there really is, and your only chance of a real life, the life God intended for you."

I adjusted myself on the seat. I hadn't expected to be critiqued. I suppose when I wrote the prayer, I was thinking more about impressing Gary than I was with expressing the truth about myself to God. I knew he was right. My head hung low, and I stared at my tattered shoes. I felt depressed and impatient. "What next Gary, I read the prayer, now what? I still feel the same as I did before. I'm not sure writing that prayer and reading it here was the answer to much."

"Certainly, it was not the answer. If prayer was enough, what you seek would have come to pass long ago. What you need is action. Action should always follow prayer. Without action on our part, our prayers are dead. Faith without works is dead.

"I want you to do some things. Take some action on the prayer you wrote and just read. Are you willing now to follow some real directions?" Gary looked my way, took a sip from his coffee cup and an over-sized bite from his morning donut, and peering over his wire-rimmed spectacles, awaited my answer.

I looked up long enough to see that Gary was looking deeply into me, almost through me. I could feel the power of the moment. My stomach churned, and my hands trembled. The coffee in my hand was barely contained in its cup as I took a sip. I drank, looking at Gary and then looking back down at the floor before answering, "Gary I'll do what I can. I'm tired, I'm worn out. I can't go on like this. I think I'm ready to follow directions."

Gary wiped his mouth, lowered his head and cleared his throat, and in the most serious tone I'd ever heard him speak with and looking directly into my eyes he said. "Good then, here is what you will do. Not what I want you to do but what you will do! This morning, tomorrow, or next week if ever, really makes no difference to me. Just *don't come back until you do.* Stanley, I love you too much not to tell you the truth, and the truth is that unless you take some action, there is nothing I or anyone else can do for you. There'll be no more money, no more advice, and no more coffee and donuts in the mornings. If you show up here again, I swear to you that I won't open that door." He pointed directly at the front door of the bus with a straight and blunt index finger of his large right hand.

He smiled at me widely, momentarily breaking the levity of the moment. I'd never paid a cent to be on Gary's bus. I knew that when Gary said he loved me that he spoke the truth. I wanted so much to be free of the insanity I'd been living in. Only because of the beating I'd endured, because of the massive daily suffering I'd somehow come to accept as my lot in life, I was willing to listen.

Gary had taken a position of authority with me. He'd taken the time to give me what I needed, what I wanted, just enough to keep me coming back. All leading to this moment in time. The moment when I was willing to allow Gary to take authority over me and to listen and believe in what Gary had to say. He'd won my confidence. Besides now he was all I had in the world.

"I'm going to give you three simple instructions that will be difficult to complete. Simple, but difficult. Your life and the life of many others depend on your following through, or not, with these instructions.

"First, keep the prayer you wrote with you at all times.

"Second, check into the hospital to detox and stay until you are clean and completely withdrawn from everything.

"Third, read the prayer you have with you at least ten times per day, more if needed. Any time you think of trouble of any kind, I want you to read the prayer and consider God instead of thinking of the trouble."

Gary turned away from me and reached into a bag at his feet, he withdrew a donut. He took a large bite, wiped a few crumbs from his mouth and then pulled a newspaper from beside his feet, turned in a few pages, and opened up the paper wide so I could no longer see his face. It was as if I wasn't there.

I spoke, but wasn't sure Gary was listening. "Gary, I will do it, but I have prayed before. I've been to detox dozens of times. I've been to treatment that many times as well. I've checked into the hospital, it's not like I haven't been willing. I've done these things before." The hope-lessness I'd forever felt was back as strong as ever. I'd built up some hope in my few visits with Gary, and now he was only offering everything I'd already knew and tried before.

I was getting angry, now he wasn't even looking at me. I knew his route was about to begin and could see the first few morning folks beginning to make their way to the stop. I felt I was being ignored. "Gary, I'm not sure this is a real answer, I need more help."

Gary dropped the newspaper just far enough to look at me, exposing to me the top part of his head and his eyes. Looking over his small glasses, he replied, "The prayer is the only help you need. I can't help you anymore until you follow through with the instructions I've given you." He opened the door to the bus, illuminated all of the interior lights and turned the "In Service" sign to ON indicating that the bus was now beginning its route for the day.

"We've nothing further to talk about. I love you, Stanley," he said as he began greeting his first few riders and thoroughly ignoring me. As if things were not clear enough, Gary added, "For us to say another word to each other until you follow the instructions is pointless."

I knew that the open door meant I wasn't riding the bus. My invitation today was only to exit from where I'd come with only the prayer in my pocket and the instructions I'd been given. Today there was no cash payoff.

We sat in uncomfortable silence for a moment; I knew deep down he was right. I gathered up my pack, stood up, and walked toward the open door and stepped down onto the street. I felt emotions well up inside me. I turned to Gary with tears in my eyes, in a barely audible voice I said "I love you too Gary. I'll see you later."

I walked away and back into my self-created hell.

Chapter Seven

Follow Simple Spiritual Directions, and ...

It was now July. Summer was heating up. Independence Day had passed, and I had no idea where I'd been or what I'd done. Most days had been this way in the last three or so years. I was as lost as one gets. I remembered what Gary had told me though, the instructions I was to follow. How I was to read the prayer I had written. I had the prayer with me; I'd taken to reading it over and over.

I couldn't recall the Fourth of July or, really, any other holiday in many years. I could vaguely remember the holiday season, but not really where I'd been or with whom. I knew I'd made promises to my family and hadn't shown, that I did know.

I prayed that day in late July that God would deliver me home. I was physically, emotionally, and spiritually sickened. I had so much fear of the physical and emotional pain that I would have to endure if I stopped ingesting drugs for even a short time. I could get used to the physical pain, I thought, but the emotional upheaval that I knew would come I couldn't endure. So, I added this to my prayer:

God,
Please strengthen me and help me find my way.
I am in so much fear.
I cannot imagine living one more day.
Please help me.

I'd been staying with my dancer friend, Sierra at nights and wandering the streets during the days and evenings when she worked. All my waking hours were spent intoxicated with drugs and alcohol. I had to put some in me so I could feel well enough to find more. I did anything necessary to assure that my supply continued.

Once again, Sierra had asked me to leave. She could no longer stand being around me. I was a liar, a cheat, and a thief. Worse off she knew it, and I knew it, and we no longer tried to hide it from each other. I lied to her, cheated her, and stole from her every chance I could. Sierra would let me get away with these things because occasionally I would tell her that I loved her and that she was beautiful. She was beautiful, but I had forgotten completely what love was or how to feel it.

I would hold her and tell her I loved her, but knew in my heart I was incapable of love and that I would have to leave if she stopped buying drugs. We were using each other. We both knew this as well. It was sad to leave her, to be asked to leave. I saw scars that were just starting to heal on both of her wrists, signs of how desperate her life had become. I tried to tell myself I was doing something for her, but the truth was that I was doing something to her and in the process killing us both.

I left her company, this time for good. I thought about Gary and wanted to see him. I knew it wasn't possible now. There were requirements I needed to take care of first.

I began walking and headed into town toward a hospital I knew would at least consider taking me in. They knew me there, although I wasn't among their favorite customers. I walked and walked for over two hours. I could feel the first wave of withdrawals from the heroin hitting my body, but by some miracle I found the inner strength to keep walking. The more I walked, and the closer I got, the sicker I felt. The wave of fear I could feel cresting over me had now began to break.

I pulled the prayer I'd written from my pocket and read. I went on. It was a hot day, and my vision wasn't able to take anything in. I was aware of the people and the traffic, but all was a low hum, a blur. Sweat poured over my face, and my clothes were soaked in the sweat from the heat and the withdrawals. I could smell on myself the all too familiar smell of the heroin leaving my body. God was with me that day; I could've never made it on my own. I was experiencing firsthand the power of a prayer honestly made followed by personal action. I was putting one foot in front of the other, and a power larger than myself was giving me the strength.

I walked the three or four miles needed to arrive at my destination. They were hard miles, very hard miles. Hot miles, drenched and sweat-covered miles. My hands shook uncontrollably. My legs cramped. I placed one foot in front of the other, refusing to stop for fear I would be unable to start again. I thought of Gary's demands, his requests, and his requirements. The thought that Gary might help me if I followed through made the difference and somehow, I didn't give up. I had nothing to give up to. I had no choice. I had to make the Mountain View emergency room, and do everything I could to get admitted.

As I approached the hospital, knowing I had only a few hundred yards to go, I stopped and read out aloud the prayer I was told to repeat. The prayer I had written. I could see folks staring at me as I stood by myself, reading out loud from a crumpled-up paper. I was a spectacle everywhere I went, so it was nothing new to me. I folded the prayer up, placing it back in my pack, and continued the final few yards of my journey.

I stood at the entrance of the emergency room and the automatic doors opened, exposing a familiar scene. I'd been to Mountain View Hospital many times before, for detox, and for observation. This was the bottom of the chain for hospital help in this area. No one here had money. Those affluent-type drug addicts went elsewhere. This was home for the desperate and hopeless type. Most came with police escort, as I had on many occasions in the past. Today, I was here, praying for help and repeating the prayers I'd written and recited to my friend, Gary Goldpeople.

The lobby was full of police checking patients through on their way to jail. I could hear one ambulance after another as the sirens came to a stop and pulled up to unload patients. The smell of an overtaxed hospital wing hung heavily in the air. I waited my turn and approached the nurse sitting behind a piece of glass, a sign that said "ADMITTING," hung over her head. I thought of myself, admitting for the first time that I was nothing. The sign seemed to be apropos.

"Hello Stanley, go ahead and grab a clip board, you know the routine."

I didn't recognize her, but she seemed to have had my acquaintance in the past. I filled out the information asking for detox. The woman now before me had a nametag introducing her as "Shelly."

As I reached for the clipboard hanging in front of the counter, I trembled and shook, I blurted out, "I have no idea what I need. I walked most of the day to be here. I've been riding the bus and praying and now I'm here."

She looked up at me and smiled. "I'm a friend of Mr. Goldpeople. He called ahead and said to be expecting you. He pulls quite a bit of weight around here you know. You must be a very special person, Stanley, Gary sends us a few customers a month I'd say, but this is the first time any of us can remember him calling ahead."

My mind raced. I was starting to feel the leg cramps, and my nose was now running uncontrollably. I felt a wave of emotion, and tears now accompanied my running nose.

"We're going to help you, Stanley, but even for a friend of Gary's we have to follow procedure. A quick trip to the social workers on the third floor and they'll check you into Detox or Psychiatric. Either way, you'll get in. I had my husband sign your admitting documents. There's only one person here that has more say than Gary and that would be my husband. He's Chief of Staff here most days." She smiled a warm, lovely smile, and I was comforted. She winked, indicating that we'd shared in some inside secret. I was completely unaware of what the secret was or even might have been, but her wink and smile warmed me to her presence.

I had no idea what was going on or how they knew me or how Gary knew I'd be coming, but I had no real desire to question things either. I was content to just go along, knowing there was a bed to lie in at the end of the check-in procedure.

After an elevator ride, clipboard in hand, I stepped off at the third floor. I wobbled to the desk and sat in front of a blurry-faced man. I could barely make out his features as sweat now poured from my face and into my eyes, my vision blurred. His voice was high pitched, his face thin, long and pointy.

"How long have you been addicted to drugs? What drugs have you taken lately? How much? When? When did you first start? Why are you here? Where will you go from here?"

The questions seemed endless, and I was getting sicker by the minute. I thought about leaving a few times, but knew I was now too sick to do what it would take to get well. I was here for the duration. I answered what questions I could. The social worker behind the desk told me that my thinking seemed a bit confused. I knew that I was thinking as clearly as I had in a long time. I knew now that I knew nothing. Prior to this day and reading the prayer, I had known nothing. Before this day however, I had known nothing and thought that I had known everything. That was a very hard place to be, a know it all that was wrong about everything. That delusional thinking had led to this day. That idea that I knew everything, when I knew nothing, had led to my self-inflicted misery.

Chapter Eight

Power of the Spoken Prayer

I had a room; there were three other beds. Each one of them was occupied. We never talked with the exception of asking each other for cigarettes, only to discover that we were all out. I could tell by the smell, the red faces, the broken blood vessels in their faces, the wine sores, and the shakes that these fellows were alcoholics. Some say that alcohol is a slower death than drugs, but it will get some, and when it does, it takes you to a place drug addicts never have to go. These three fellows were in that class, the final stages of chronic alcoholism. Repeat customers I'd guessed.

I was able to sleep only brief periods. Fifteen or twenty minutes at a time, the first few days. The familiar acute anxiety that comes with withdrawals overtook my psyche. I was in much physical pain, my legs cramped constantly, cramps so bad that my whole body shook and convulsed uncontrollably. I threw up in a bed pan and made my way, only out of absolute necessity, to the bathroom we all shared and sat on the toilet. I was freezing cold one moment and overheating the next. I sweated even when cold. The cold sweats, the leg cramps, the diarrhea, the running nose, the upset stomach still did not compare with the loneliness, the all aloneness, the worthlessness that I felt.

I'd pull the crumpled prayer from under my pillow and read what I'd written just a short number of days ago. The prayer, and the thought that I could go see Gary when this was all over kept me from going insane. I knew he'd found an answer for himself and that he may have an answer for me. These thoughts battled with suicidal thoughts. I had no idea, which thought would ultimately win out. I only knew I wanted it all to end. The withdrawals and insanity were so severe that I welcomed death. Death was preferable to the sleepless horror I was experiencing.

Unable to sleep, minutes passed like hours. The physical, psychological, and mental torture I experienced condemned me to crave the very substance responsible for my downfall.

Every thought contained equal parts of the drug or suicide. The nurses checked me often and their loving kindness offered some small relief. The physical pain, unbearable at times, was constant. I watched the clock and felt some relief as each hour and then day passed, knowing that I was closer to the end. And I prayed every few hours, remembering the instructions Gary had given me and my instructions to read the prayer I'd written at least ten times each day. By the second day, I'd somehow found the energy to drop from the bed for prayer. I was desperate, and on my knees.

God,
I think I know everything, I know nothing.
I think I know what is best for me,
And also, what is best for everyone around me.

I think I know how to stop using drugs,
Today I want to be loaded.

Can you help a know-it-all?
If you can accept me,

A know-it-all that really knows nothing,
I will do my best.
I need your help.
Everything I know is killing me.

I am more concerned with being right,
Than I am with being free.
I think I know everything, I know nothing.
Amen.

And I added.

God,
Please strengthen me and help me find my way.
I am in so much fear.
I cannot imagine living one more day.
Please help me.

It had been two days since I had ingested anything but water into my system, including drugs or alcohol. I had changed the prayer from being loaded to wanting to be loaded. It seemed fitting.

I began to realize that prayer was the only real power we have to change anything. This prayer began to change me. The hopelessness opened the door for grace and the prayer allowed the grace to flow in. And flow in it did.

Chapter Nine

Spiritual Basis for Life vs. Basis for Life with No Spirit

O n the third day, I had two visitors: Shelly, the nurse, and a man I had assumed to be a doctor by his white overcoat and the stethoscope around his neck. Nurse Shelly introduced my visitor.

"Stanley, this is my husband, Dr. Malik."

"Nice to meet you Stanley, my wife and Gary Goldpeople have both told me about you. Sorry I've been so slow to get into see you, but honestly, most of the time, detox patients with your history don't stay." He smiled with a little sideways grin, exposing pearly white and perfectly straight teeth.

Dr. Malik was in his mid-thirties, on the taller side, and of dark complexion. He spoke with a heavy East Indian accent. Very clear English, but a distinctive high-pitch tone to his voice.

"Thanks for coming, it's nice to meet you. Thank you for all the help here at the hospital." I uttered, as politely as possible, sitting up in my bed. I recalled Nurse Shelly telling me how her husband was the Chief of Staff at the hospital and how he had pull at Mountain View. I had no money, and they knew it. I knew I was here by someone's good grace, most likely his.

The good doctor was the first to share after our brief introductions. He was of average good looks, his dark complexion, black hair, and wide bright smile combined to make he and Shelly quite the good-looking couple.

Continuing to smile, the doctor sat at the edge of my bed. "You seem to have made quite an impression on Mr. Goldpeople. Yes indeed, Gary feels very good about you." He looked up at his wife, and they exchanged winks and a loving glance.

I was having trouble piecing this together, but resigned myself to the not-knowing-everything mode. Somehow, I intuitively knew I wasn't to understand all this.

I sat up slightly in my bed as Nurse Shelly adjusted the bed to allow me to speak sitting up. I was still very weak as the withdrawals had taken their toll on my little remaining strength. I struggled to clear my throat, and wiped my brow with the back of my hand. I still shook uncontrollably and my hands quivered. "I have a question: Why me? Why is Gary helping me? Why are you helping me?"

The doctor stood, once again standing next to Shelly, and Shelly moved closer to answer. She was shorter than the doctor, also a few years younger. Her face showed the wear and tear of a past life of hardships but she still retained much of the beauty of her youth. She was dark with a golden tan and wide, brown, youthful eyes with long lashes, giving her a bit of a mysterious presence.

She was dressed in surgical scrubs with a long, white coat and large, open pockets on both sides of the jacket, filled with papers, pens, and the tools of her trade. "Gary believes, the more hopeless the better!"

They giggled together. An unsettling laugh for me, I didn't see the hopelessness of my condition as a laughing matter, but they knew better. They knew that God comes to many in that moment of deepest despair. In that time when prayer is offered by one who has no other place to turn.

I struggled to sit up further in the bed, swinging my legs around and letting my feet dangle, almost touching the floor. Nurse Shelly touched my hand, turning it over to check my pulse. Her touch was gentle and comforting to me. Still holding my hand, she softly spoke to me. "Just try to sleep if you can. I know how hard all this is, but it is always darkest before the dawn. Gary always told me that."

Her beauty, shining through rugged features of a previously difficult life, impressed me. Her long dyed-blond hair, brown eyes, and slender build along with a spirit that glowed made her attractive. It was so nice to have a pretty woman speaking to me. It was her inner beauty that radiated. I just wanted her to give me a hug, hold me and tell me it was going to be OK.

"How do you know Gary?" I wanted to know. I was confused. I liked what was happening in the moment but was very uneasy with the bigger picture. What did these people want with me?

The doctor answered, "He introduced us. I wouldn't have ever met Shelly if it weren't for Gary. She was one of the first twenty or so patients Gary had brought in and was in worse shape than you when she came in." They smiled at each other with wide, loving, real smiles. "Gary brought her to me in person. It's a long story Stanley, but you are a part of something very big. Gary's helped many, perhaps hundreds since I have known him. If you include those that have been indirectly helped by folks who have had direct contact with Gary, it would number in the thousands. Will reach millions some day. Gary is very particular these days with who he helps, so I'd say you are one lucky junkie."

The good Doctor and Shelly both had the same bright eyes and awakened presence I'd seen in Gary. He was a few years older than she, although they looked very close to the same age. Gary had brought her into the hospital as a kind act for a lost passenger on his bus. Shelly had lain where I was now. Most of the signs of those days were now wiped away from her features. The chewing surface of her teeth were flat across from the years of abuse and the constant grinding of the teeth that goes with the hard life. I could see it, but also, I could see and feel her soft aura, her awakened presence. I knew those days were now gone for her, and she had a new life now. Just looking at her and getting all that from just being in her presence for a few moments gave me a shiver, I felt as though I was in the presence of greatness.

I wondered what they had that I didn't have. How they were seemingly so together, while I was so obviously flawed. They stood so happy, and I laid in self-induced misery. I would come to understand the difference between them. It was that they had a spiritual basis for life and I had a basis of life with no spirit. Relying on myself had failed.

Chapter Ten

Ask and You Will Receive

ay four and five were always the hardest for me in the past. By then I would feel physically better, good enough to have some game back. I'd failed many times, seized by the delusion that I could use one time and get back on the wagon. A little relief, then back to the unbearable. I'd never return to the water wagon until health, mental breakdown, or jail forced me once again to attempt a clean life.

This time was different though. The prayers were different. The nurse and doctor were different. And then there was Gary, he was the biggest difference. Somehow, I knew he cared, but most of all I knew he had a real answer. Not just for me, but an answer to the meaning of life. How to have a real life. Not the dream, the delusion that something outside myself was going to make me happy. Gary had the truth, pure and simple. God is love. Love then, is the answer to any problem. The only problem is a lack of love. This time was different all right. Everything was different, but most of all, I began to feel the presence of God for the first time in my life. It felt like hope.

Everyone had long since given up on me, including myself. Gary was willing to meet and talk. I told myself he was just a crazy bus driver and that I was going on to the bitter end without seeing him again.

But there was a force that was more powerful than my thinking or my willpower that drew me to him.

I like to believe that I came to God sometime during that summer, but the truth is God came to me, long before I came to him. God came to me incarnated in Gary Goldpeople.

I'd resisted the idea of God and could've never heard the message from a preacher or a missionary. Somehow the imperfectness of this funny, somewhat insane man was the thing that made him so attractive and believable. It was that imperfection that gave him a humble attractiveness, it made everyone who met him, like him, and then love him.

I believe that our flaws, not our perfectness, are the things we use to attract people to our message. It was just that, his flaws, his overeating, his weight, and his sometimes-foul language, that made me believe he could understand me. I came to believe that he understood just how hopeless I really felt. I came to believe that he was like me at one time and that he had overcome that. He said God had made that possible, and I believed him.

I believe there are many noble folks, intent on helping others, but afraid to show their own flaws. This fear poisons the spirit necessary to help others. This is a lesson Gary taught me not with his words, but with his actions. Be quick to admit your own flaws and shortcomings, the admission makes us real. Not to do so makes us phonies and hypocrites.

I was thinking about Gary when the doctor and Nurse Shelly came to see me. I was prepared for a long talk and had many questions. They, however, did most of the talking. Each in their turn talked to me about a real recovery. They explained that through an in-depth experience with hopelessness, such as I had experienced, that God's grace was possible. That by applying spiritual principles, the desire to destroy myself with drugs and alcohol would be removed. The doctor, from his experience with dozens of patients, and the nurse, from her own experience, both spoke to me. I listened as one by one the questions I asked were answered.

I felt much better and had showered. My clothes had been laundered and brought to me, allowing me to remove the hospital robe and put on my own clothes. Shelly and Dr. Malik arrived together and pulled two chairs close to the bed. I sat on the bed's edge, facing them.

Shelly took my hand into hers. "What can we do to help you Stanley? We're almost ready to send you back to Gary."

"I guess the real question is, what do I have to do?"

Doctor Malik inched his chair even closer and touched my knee. "Nothing you can do would prepare you for what you need. You are powerless to change your own life. If you could've done anything, you would've done it long ago. This is about praying to have everything you think removed. You only need to follow directions."

"If I can't do anything, it seems I have no say in this?"

Shelly squeezed my hand even tighter. "Let us put it another way. You cannot fix what needs fixing. Your job is to pray for God to do for you what you cannot do for yourself."

"Sounds like I need faith, my prayers can feel so empty."

Dr. Malik smiled, showing his bright and friendly grin. His voice was a faint whisper, and his accent softened each word even further. His speech was comforting, slow paced, and believable. "Faith comes to people in many ways, but for us it is in hearing a message of depth from other people. It is the story of how others found their way out that gives us faith. God made it possible for us to be here today. If you can believe that, you can have faith."

"How long will it take for me to be well? To have what you have, what Gary has?"

My two friends gave each other a knowing glance. Shelly spoke for them both, "A lifetime." This process is about getting a new way of life. You will either put your reliance on a higher power and will continue to awaken to a larger spiritual life, or you will begin going back to sleep. Just to the extent that you rely on God above your reliance on yourself, you'll continue to emerge deeper into the spiritual life."

"When will I leave the hospital?"

Shelly was still holding my hand and smiled as she looked at me and answered, "Tomorrow at noon, Stanley. We want you to go see Gary when you leave."

I felt my stomach drop and knots begin to churn within. I didn't want to go. I wasn't sure I was ready. I had nowhere to go. I pulled my hand back from Shelly's soft grip. "Why am I getting this help, why me?"

Dr. Malik stood and pushed his chair back. His voice was louder now, more authoritative. " 'Why me?' " is the wrong question my friend. It's not about you!"

I still felt so weak and wasn't used to the idea that anything that happened to me wasn't about me. I had to ask. "What is it about then, if it isn't about me?"

Shelly now stood as well and took her place alongside her husband. She looked at him, then at me and answered my question with a wide grin. "It's about love, God's love."

Chapter Eleven

Will To Live

Shelly and Dr. Malik left the room, and I was left alone. My roommates had left the night before to return to the life of drinking, and I was still here. I wondered in my mind why I was spared on this day, then the answer I'd just heard from Shelly came back to me. It wasn't about me. It was a novel idea for me that somehow things happen in my life and they aren't meant for me. Maybe they were meant for me, but certainly not for me alone.

I felt grateful for the help. The help from God. I wondered where I'd go tomorrow at noon. I was afraid at the prospect of leaving. I knew I'd be faced with returning to my old life or accepting spiritual help.

I was feeling better. Mentally and spiritually, I was feeling good. I slept the night through, awoke, showered for almost an hour, shaved slowly, cut my fingernails and toenails, combed my hair, and looked into the mirror. I liked what I saw. Physically, I was feeling better as well. I was OK for the first time in as long as I recalled.

I was dressed this morning in new clothes, given to me by someone at the hospital. I had suspected that the Maliks were the generous gifters. New Levis, white socks and underwear, a white t-shirt, new Chuck

Taylor converse shoes, and a hooded sweatshirt with the hospital name and logo over the heart area.

I began wandering the halls of the ward. I could see Shelly and Dr. Malik going from room to room and doing their work. I saw many patients and realized how easily I could recognize the hopelessness on the faces.

I talked with a few patients and one nurse whom I'd not met. She was working the desk and seemed willing to listen. I told her how I'd felt some hope for the first time in a very long time.

I returned to my room and waited. I knew today was departure day. I was daydreaming about what would be, where I'd go. I was brought out of my inner thoughts by the sound of Shelly's voice. She was standing at the doorway to my room.

"Come on, Stanley, it's time to leave. You need to get up and get packed."

The worry turned quickly to panic. I had no idea where I was going. "Where do you think I should go?"

Shelly had already turned to leave the room. She turned and moved toward me. "Go and be helpful, go and allow God to find you, pray and allow yourself to be led. The resources beyond that are many. Go see Gary, go to church, an AA meeting, a NA meeting. Go to the Salvation Army, God knows you can use some salvation."

We both smiled at each other, and Shelly moved closer and took my hand in hers. I felt shaky and cold, her hand in mine felt so warm and so calm. I knew without her saying anything that this was a time for prayer if there ever was one. In my mind I thought, "God please help and give me the words."

I scooted off of the bed, and Shelly joined me on my knees. We joined both hands and I prayed aloud.

God, I am small.
I, without you, am nothing.
As I leave the comfort of this hospital,
Please let me leave with a spirit of gratitude.
Show me the way to the spiritual life.
As I feel the flow of your love into me,
Allow that love into the lives of others.
Amen.

The words felt powerful. I felt empowered. We stood together. I knew the words had come through me and not of me. Shelly knew it too by the look of pure joy on her face. I could see in her deep brown eyes, a happiness—an inner light. It was burning brighter after our prayer than before. She looked alive and full of life.

I wondered how this simple nurse and recovered addict had come to a place in her life of being so completely devoted to serving others. I knew that she had come from the same source that had just given me such an inspired prayer. I wanted what she had. I cried at the thought that just maybe I would have it.

At noon, sharp, I walked out with my new clothes and a few things in my pack. I'd gained so much in those last five days, but I felt a million tons lighter.

As I retraced the steps, in the opposite direction from my walk of hopelessness of just five days before, I realized I'd been given a new perspective on my chances to live. Where before I'd not cared if I lived or died, I now wanted to live. There was no conscious decision on my part to live, it was just there. There was also no conscious decision on my part to follow directions but I found myself walking toward the bus stop to see Gary.

I feared somehow my thinking would wonder and lead me astray so I kept my head to the pavement and put one foot in front of the other. I walked away from Mountain View Hospital with purpose. The purpose of doing my part, to save my life. I followed the directions I'd been given by Nurse Shelly and Dr. Malik. I walked toward Gary, and I prayed.

God,
Please protect me,
Carry me back to Gary.
Amen.

It was early evening by the time I reached the bus stop. I asked a passerby for the time and ascertained that if was 6:15 PM., I checked the posted schedule only to discover Gary's route 43, University District to Downtown had departed for the last time at 6:05. I'd missed his last round of the day.

I settled into the bus stop shelter, taking a seat on the bench. I stood again and checked the schedule. His route started the following morning at 6:00 AM — I would wait. I feared for my life to do anything else.

Chapter Twelve

Follow Directions

I'd been homeless many times in my life, so it was nothing different for me. I knew how to be homeless better than most. I rarely spent the night outdoors as I was mostly able to scrape together a deal and get a motel room for the night, and when times were good, for a week. Still, it was the first night out of detox, and I really had nowhere to go. I would spend this night at the bus stop and wait for morning, for Gary. I dared not leave for fear I would never find my way back.

I wanted to experience some of what I'd felt in the hospital, and my mind was racing. I had trouble sleeping and many times through the night I was close to giving up, but knew in my heart that something had changed. I wanted to leave and go back to the hospital and see Shelly and Dr. Malik. They had something I wanted. I thought I needed another day or two with them. I thought then of Gary. I had to see him!

Still, I prayed and prayed; I knew I was on shaky ground. I wanted so much to feel normal again, or for the first time? I really didn't know what normal meant, but I did know that I'd need a few things if I were to have even a chance at applying the principles into my life that Gary suggested. I'd decided that I had nothing to lose, so I'd follow directions.

The incredible pounding I'd taken in life up to this point, Gary had convinced me, was the best indicator of my need for a spiritual solution. And a terrible beating it had been indeed. If this was what was needed to affect a spiritual experience, I certainly qualified.

I awakened that morning to the sound of a bus pulling up and the blast of a horn. I hadn't wanted to return to the drug scene at many of the flophouses I knew. I had no desire, being summertime, to go to the shelter or missions. I had been there before. Many times. The smell, being robbed, and men having sex with each other in the night's darkness all made me hate the thought of the shelter. Only under severe cold would I enter such a place, to warm for a few hours, and drift into half-sleep with one eye open.

This night had been a warm summer night. I had felt close to giving up many times, but somehow knowing that Gary would be at the bus stop in the morning brought a feeling of comfort. I could actually feel his presence there. I fell quickly to sleep. I knew I was safe and protected. I'd, after all, prayed before I went to sleep. I'd made it through the first night out of the hospital.

Gary had told me that all thoughts were really prayers and that prayers were the only real power there was. The problem was that my thoughts were obsessed with drug use, ease and comfort, selfishness, and death. This was exactly what was materializing in my life. All of the above. The thinking, my prayers, needed to change, if I were to change. Gary said so, and for some reason, I believed him. So, I prayed that night before I went to sleep.

God, I want to give up so badly.
This fat bus driver told me to pray.
Is there any way you can shut off my mind?
So, I can catch a few hours of sleep
Amen.

I don't remember a thing from that moment until I heard the sound of Gary's bus pulling up and his horn sounding when he saw me. I'd slept! I pulled myself up from the bench and stood up. It was another beautiful morning, and I noticed it. Something was changing. I'd seen many beautiful mornings in the past few years but this one I truly noticed.

I boarded the bus, feeling that I'd slept for a thousand years.

Gary was drinking his coffee and eating his morning donut. He offered a cup and poured it full of steaming coffee from his thermos. "McDonald's coffee. I always stop there, and one of my students that works there fills my thermos first thing every morning. The best coffee there is, you know."

"Your student?" I thought aloud. "Am I your student?"

Gary sipped his coffee, washing down a huge bite of maple bar, grinned, and answered as he did so often with another question. "The question is not if you are one of my students Stanley. The question is whether you feel I'm your teacher?"

I looked at Gary. A sip of coffee had missed his face and dribbled down his chin, dripping onto his city bus driver uniform. He hadn't noticed. The stain on the front of his shirt appeared at the crown of his overly large stomach. He was stuffing the second donut, since I had boarded, into his mouth. This time, it was a jelly-filled one. It squirted out the end, and he barely caught it with the other hand. He looked perplexed for a moment, wondering what to do with the handful of raspberry jelly. He licked it off his hand, and a small amount stayed in his beard. If this was my teacher, I was in big trouble.

As if he knew what I was thinking about, Gary began to smile. The smile grew larger, and he let out a laugh. "When the student is ready, the teacher appears. Or is that the other way around? God knows I'm ready."

I was through trying to decide that I knew what God looked like. At this moment, he looked like a fat city bus driver with jelly in his beard and a large coffee stain on the front of his uniform. His day had just started. To some of us, God must come on our own terms, something we can accept. God brought me Gary Goldpeople. I was his student, and he was my teacher.

I sat on the empty seat across from Gary. I was still warming up from the night chill and my hands shook ever so slightly. I was nervous and hoped Gary didn't notice. I sipped my coffee and then asked the question now on my mind. "I've been praying, and God sent me you?" The words fell from my mouth with an inquisitive tone.

Gary leaned sideways in my direction, smiled and answered quickly. "I like to think it was the other way around. My time here on this planet is limited, Stanley. I've so much to give, and I'm aware that I need to give what I have away, so it was me that prayed for someone. I prayed that day we first met. I prayed to God for help, and God answered my prayer. He sent you."

So, Gary had prayed, and I showed up. I had to ask about this. I took another sip of my coffee, looked up at Gary, and asked the question. "Who in their right mind prays for a junkie and a thief to show? Don't most folks pray that God will keep them protected from folks like me?" I laughed a little at the thought.

Gary was equally amused at my question but not enough to answer directly. "I thought God would send me someone I could tell my life story to, maybe an author or a minister that could take on the work I started. God sent me a junkie with a needle in his arm." He laughed so hard he began to sweat. We both laughed, and cried, at the same time. Gary pulled a hanky from his pocket and dapped at the sweat on his brow and wiped the tears from his eyes. The realization that God had brought us together, through prayer, was just as amusing to Gary as it was to me.

"I need to start my route, Stanley, so I'd like you to write another prayer. Write today about learning, about being willing to learn. Come back tomorrow morning, willing to learn, with the prayer."

The door to the bus opened, and I departed. I watched the bus pull away and Gary driving, beginning his day. The morning was busier now, traffic flowed heavy in both directions and the silence of the early morning was now replaced by the loudness and intensity of the morning commute. The only thing that I really noticed however was the strange feeling of how good it felt to be at the bus stop. I pulled from my pack the tablet of paper and a pen that had been left for me on the bus what seemed like an eternity ago. I sat at the bus stop and with no thought of doing anything else before I was completed I wrote my prayer as instructed.

God,
I have never seemed to learn too much.
Not much of value.
The fat bus driver seems to have something.
Something you want me to learn.
Please allow this know-it-all,
To know nothing.
So new ideas can fill me.
Amen.

Chapter Thirteen

Quality of Our Prayers

I showed up as I was told, on time, and by sheer grace willing to learn. I had the prayer with me. I was a little apprehensive after re-reading my prayer and seeing that I had written "this fat bus driver." I wasn't sure if Gary would like this or if he would think that it was a proper prayer. This thought faded into all the other thoughts I had going. My mind was swimming with ideas, including bagging this whole deal and giving up. Waves of hopelessness continued to overwhelm my emotions. I had only the words of Shelly, Dr. Malik, and Gary to offer hope in what was a seemingly hopeless situation.

I saw the bus pull up, the door open, and as I had done many times in these last few months, I boarded and took my seat across from Gary. He was eating his donuts and drinking his McDonald's coffee. He was dressed as he always was, in his uniform. His signature beret topped his round head. His large body was stuffed into a city bus driver's uniform with a tie and a dark-blue overcoat.

Before a word had been said, I felt myself calming down, feeling at ease. Just being on the bus, in Gary's presence, brought a sense of wellness. To look at his bright-blue, shining eyes and his smiling face was a softening and soothing experience in itself. I settled comfortably into my seat.

Gary wiped his mouth with his handkerchief, washed down what appeared to be close to half a chocolate bar, and asked, "Did you bring the prayer?"

"Yes," I answered nervously, reaching into my backpack on the seat beside me to withdraw the prayer.

"Well then, let's hear the quality of your prayers, Stanley."

I froze for a moment, thinking about the low quality of this prayer and what Gary would have to say about that. I hesitated.

"Well, let's hear what you have, Stanley," and looking directly at me, as if reading my mind, he added, "All of it."

I pulled the notebook from my pack and opened it to the page containing the prayer. Even knowing that we were alone on the bus this morning, I couldn't help myself from looking around to make sure no one was watching. Not so long ago, I was willing to shoot drugs on a public bus and not worry if anyone saw. Now, I was worrying about someone seeing me reading a prayer. Insane thoughts dominate the minds of tortured souls, the insanity of that thought struck me and temporarily removed the fear of reading the prayer to Gary. I read aloud.

God,
I have never seemed to learn too much.
Not much of value.
The fat bus driver seems to have something.
Something you want me to learn.
Please allow this know-it-all,
To know nothing.
So new ideas can fill me.
Amen.

I looked up to see if I could catch Gary's reaction. I was happily amused to see a large smile appearing on his face. I was less amused though at what he said next.

"So that is how you see me, as a fat bus driver that has something God wants you to learn?"

I was unsure how to respond. I tried, "It's just what came out, Gary. I really didn't mean anything by it."

"Prayers should be written with divine thought and recited with purpose. Always remember this."

"I thought, I'd thought about this prayer. I really feel bad about the fat thing."

He smiled wide and gave me a wink. "Who do you think I am, Stanley? I'm a fat bus driver. I do have something God wants you to learn. I know your prayer was divine, I was seeing if you knew it was."

His statement and smiling bright face had put me at ease. "I don't seem to know much, Gary, and I'm beginning to question what I do think I know."

Gary thought for a moment and responded once more. "Know this, Stanley, God is in me. The spirit of God is traveling in my body —a fat, sometimes funny, slightly crazy bus driver. But know this also, Stanley: God is also in you, traveling in the body of a hopelessly addicted, suffering, spiritually empty human being. The difference between me and you is that I know that I am one with God and you do not."

I was pondering this thought as a few passengers had boarded and Gary's route for the day was about to begin. I looked up at Gary as he reached out with a cup of coffee, I could see the shining spirit within him, I sensed the real humility that was his. I took the coffee, smiled and responded after moments more thought.

"Gary, thank you so much for everything you've done for me. I can really see God within you. I feel something's very special about you. I think that traveling in whatever body would be so much sweeter knowing things the way you do."

Gary wiped the remaining crumbs off his white beard from the second donut he had devoured since I had boarded. "The knowledge of God, of our oneness with God is all we need. All other thoughts you have now are irrelevant. I'd love to answer them all for you, and in time I suppose I will. For now, though, pray and remember who you are. You were born with this knowledge, your oneness with your creator, you have simply forgotten." Gary had turned on the interior lights, he opened the door once again and a few more passengers boarded, each taking a moment to nod a good morning to Gary and get a seat up front.

I picked up my pad with the prayer written on it, put it into my pack and headed to the back of the bus. Somehow, I knew that was the end of the conversation for the day. I'd been given much more in these few minutes than I could absorb in a lifetime. Indeed, even today, sometimes I'm far from remembering who I am. I am one with God as the wave is the ocean. I am one with God as the mountain is the earth. I am one with God as you are.

Gary, again as if reading my every thought added as I was walking to the back of the bus "The only thing necessary here is an open mind and an honest desire to change. The power of prayer will provide everything you need. Keep writing prayers and trust in God." I turned around and smiled at Gary.

He smiled back. Gave a wave behind him with the back of his hand and greeted the next few morning passengers.

I had so many questions about the way of life Gary, Dr. Malik and Nurse Shelly were living, but at the forefront of my thoughts were, where would I live, and how would I eat. I thought to myself that maybe the spirit of God was within me, traveling in the body of a homeless and hungry recovering addict. If that was to be, I was OK. It beat the heck out of anything I had ever experienced.

Riding the bus for warmth and safety, sleeping at a bus stop, taking money from Gary to eat. It was still the best life I'd known. The realization of who I was and what I'd become would be even sweeter.

Chapter Fourteen

Am I One?

The next several weeks I wandered in town, panhandled what I could, and slept each night at the bus stop. Waking each morning to the sound of Gary's bus, I'd spend the early morning of each day with my teacher, Gary Goldpeople. Riding the bus each morning, I slowly became a calmer spirit and gained some confidence in my newfound way of life. The obsession with my old way of life was fading. It was now September, and the summer was slipping away. It'd been the best summer of my entire life, although I hadn't realized it at the time.

And I prayed. I followed directions. I became comfortable with writing and reciting each prayer. I began to feel the presence of the Great Spirit. I had a seeming awareness of something new. I knew that this was not new really. In reality, I'd been asleep and was just waking up. It was as simple as that, so Gary said.

Love was the real answer and Spirit knew I needed a real answer. I believe now that the requirements for a happy life are not the same for everyone. This is likely the most important question we face in life. To what extent do I need to follow the spiritual life? Some are called to give all of themselves in service, and I am convinced that for these people, nothing less than giving all would lead to a satisfactory life.

For others, a normal life not aware of a need to nurture the spirit seems satisfactory. For me, I knew I needed an entire spiritual overhauling. Anything less would fail. Love was the only answer. I'd tried everything else.

I knew that cooler weather would be approaching soon. The fall equinox, signaling the end of summer, a change in weather, and a change in me, was just a few days away. I would need a place to stay. I talked to Gary, and his answer was always the same. Trust in God, love others to the best of your ability, and all your needs will be provided.

I thought of Sierra, my dancer friend from all those months ago. I really had a desire to carry this message that I'd found to her. I thought of the scars I had seen on her wrists the last time we had seen each other. I saw her desperation in myself; I now had true compassion for her and wanted to help. I'd found a way out, and thought constantly about sharing what I was finding, with her.

I'd gone to her apartment, and it appeared that she'd moved. Her name wasn't on the list in the lobby of the building. Several different times I'd tried to call, and her phone first had no message, and then came back with a recording that the line had been disconnected. No forwarding number had been left. I panicked and thought of the worse.

I went to the club uptown where she'd worked and there received the horrible news. Sierra had died, she was found dead in her bathtub. She had drowned; having passed out and never awakened.

There was with me now tremendous guilt and a longing to know why she'd died and why I'd been spared. I knew I had so much now even without a place to live, because I had hope. It was something I knew Sierra had lived without for a very long time. I knew her history and knew why she couldn't live on any longer. I felt anger at those who had abused her only to realize in a way I had participated in hurting her myself, instead of helping. When I was ready to help, it was too late.

Sierra was one of the kindest, most lovely women I'd ever known. Now she, along with my old life, was gone. I wanted to know why I'd been spared and why she had had to die. I had the feeling that God had kept me sober for a reason and I wanted to know why.

I would soon come into a way of life that would lead me to answers for this question and many more. I was chosen, not for me, but for the message that would come through me. It would never be about me, never was about me. It would be about those I would help. It would be about my own children's need for a father. It was also about the love of God for Sierra, God knew she had suffered all she could take, and God brought her home to rest, with Him.

I knew that I was one who would need it all. The full-blown spiritual awakening. Nothing less would save me. I needed to follow every direction Gary would give me. I needed to pray for the awareness of the presence of God in my life. I also knew I could never look down my nose at any man. I'd participated in the ruin of Sierra, one of God's children. I could never judge another human being for anything. I had been spared, God had given me grace, another chance at life I didn't deserve. My life belonged to God, and that meant my life belonged to all of God's children as well.

Chapter Fifteen

Safe and Protected

During those first few months of what would become my new life, I struggled to find a safe haven. I talked to Gary about my search for a safe place to spend nights and my fears that spending the night in the wrong place could wind up in disaster. I was struggling with trying out a few of the God concepts Gary had been teaching me and trying to apply these new spiritual tools into my life. The season was changing and spending the nights at the bus stop would prove unbearable. I didn't know it at the time, but that night was to be the last night I would spend outside. That is, the last night I would spend outside when I didn't want to.

I woke up, as most mornings, to the sound of Gary's bus pulling up in the early morning darkness. I hadn't slept well. Tiredness had overwhelmed my thinking as well as weakened my body. I really just wanted to lie there and sleep. I heard the door to the bus open and Gary's voice calling my name. I ignored the calls, hoping he would give up and let me sleep. Surely, we could skip one day. I just didn't have it in me this morning to withstand any deep spiritual message from Gary. What did he know anyhow? I just wanted to get some sleep. I heard the bus horn sound, not once, but twice.

Then, Gary's voice again calling, "Stanley... Stanley, come on. Another day has God made, let us rejoice in it."

I could hear his unmistakable laughter. Damn him, he knew I wasn't feeling well and here he was mocking me. Let us rejoice in it, what a crock. I held my head in my hands, lying on the bench. I struggled to roll over so my back would be to the bus.

The sound of the bus horn sounding was ringing again in my ears, and the sound of Gary's now obnoxious laugh, and my own building anger, awakened me fully. I knew Gary wasn't going to let me sleep. My mind and his laughter were both growing louder. I clenched my teeth in anger and abruptly rolled over. I sat up, facing Gary, and glared at him with fire in my eyes. Through a tight-lipped, teeth-clenched, phony smile, I somehow managed a "Good morning." I gathered my pack, stood up, and took the few steps needed to board. I took my seat across from Gary aboard the bus.

Gary was all too pleased to see me. He was grinning from ear to ear. He spent a moment rocking from side to side trying his best to settle his large body into the seat and behind the steering wheel. He responded to my nasty glare by lifting his thin wire-framed glasses from his nose to above his eyes and matching my zombie-like glare with a friendly smile and an acknowledgement with a nod of his head.

I wasn't at all pleased to see Gary taking some sadistic pleasure in my obvious discomfort and I said so. "Damn glad to see you're so happy about my suffering."

Gary looked at me from under his spectacles, "My happiness today comes from my connection to the infinite and certainly not from your suffering. I am however, very happy to see you overcome your feelings of discomfort and be here with me anyway. This is the day that God has made, let us rejoice in it." He poured me a small cup of coffee and handed it to me.

Hearing his voice and taking the first few sips of the small coffee he'd poured me made me happy enough to begin to awaken to the fact I was grateful to be there.

We drank coffee and shared a few colorfully sprinkled donuts. Gary reached into a bag, on the floor, next to his seat, and ruffled through a few papers before handing me a map.

I looked at the paper he'd handed me and saw directions to an address in the city. It said on the top, "Arrive by 7:00 PM."

"It's my home, Stanley. I've a few days off, and I'd like for you to come stay with me. I have something I want you to learn. Something I can't teach you in a bus ride or even in a few bus rides. Bring an open mind, a sense of humor, and most importantly, patience."

I was somewhat shook. I somehow had never really thought about where Gary lived. Intellectually I knew he had to have a home, but just always thought of him as living on the bus. He had a life outside of driving a bus and giving spiritual lessons to the riders.

He opened the door. "See you tonight." Some lessons were shorter than others, this one was one stop, door open and a "see you tonight."

I wandered the remainder of the day, looking every few minutes at the map and the time. I started walking hours ahead, knowing it would take time to walk across town. The neighborhood I was going into was one I knew well. I'd been there many times to score or sell drugs. I wanted to walk through while there was still daylight. I was somewhat nervous, but had the unfamiliar feeling I would be safe and protected. I knew I was going into the old neighborhood on a much nobler mission.

Chapter Sixteen

Listening, with a Quiet Spirit, to the Sound of Silence

When I arrived at the address, I had trouble imagining what motivated Gary to live in such a place. This was gang central. Drug dealers, many of whom I knew, frequented this area daily. I knew Gary could afford to live in a much better part of town. Why here, I wondered? I was several hours early, so I opened the narrow gate and let myself into the small front yard. It was a decent house, a little run down, in need of paint and gutters, and by the looks of the moss growing, a new roof.

The house was a simple one-story affair with a small front porch and a smaller side porch that led from the driveway alongside to the back entrance. The lawn was mostly weeds, but had been recently cut. I always imagined, from Gary's personal habits, that a clean house wouldn't have been his strong suit, but this was actually very nice coming from where I was. The neighborhood was rough, no doubt about it, but the house was just fine.

I sat on the front porch and waited. It seemed like an eternity. I really had so much going through my mind. It seemed like forever waiting for Gary. I needed to talk to someone! I couldn't wait to see Gary and tell him about all the questions I had for him. I had the realization that he was a man with answers and I had plenty of questions.

After what I thought an unreasonable amount of time to wait for anyone, I heard a car pull up outside the driveway. I stood from the top step I'd been sitting on and could see Gary struggling to get out of the driver's side door of an older model Ford.

He looked up and saw me, but did nothing to acknowledge my presence. Looking down, he left the car door open, slowly approached the chain-link gate to the driveway, and swung open the wide gate. The rusty hinges of the gate squealed as it was swung in to the open position. Gary looked up and waved. He was still in his driving uniform complete with coat and beret. He turned, letting out a long sigh as if he had just completed a major effort, and re-entered the running automobile.

As the old green Ford pulled over the curb and into the driveway, I could hear the undercarriage scrape the cement. The car leaned to the driver's side, and when Gary opened the door and stepped out, raised an additional half-foot.

His car, like his house, was old and run down, but acceptable and ran well enough. An old Ford Galaxy, twenty-five years old or so. A faded green four-door. In good shape for its age, but obviously feeling the strain of hauling such a large man around. The old car sat closer to the ground than it should, and the springs allowed the car to sag toward the driver's side slightly even after Gary had exited.

Gary approached to greet me, but immediately sensed my impatience at having to wait. He smiled and shook his head back and forth slowly, showing once again that he knew what I was thinking. His bright-blue eyes twinkled like stars in the mid-evening dusk.

As I began to utter my first, "Hi Gary," he put his index finger over his lips to signal me to not speak and then placed both hands in front of himself, holding his palms facing out, as to signal me, to slow down.

Then his large swollen and weathered hand went back to his mouth once more with his index finger over the lips. I got the idea and silently followed him into the house. He must have a dog or someone sleeping that we should try to avoid disturbing, I thought.

As we entered through the front door of the home, I was struck by how calm I felt immediately upon entering. I stood in the front room of the home, and Gary motioned for me to take a seat on the only couch in the room. An old vinyl job with a few tears that had been repaired with some type of brown hot gun glue. I sat, and Gary left me alone and went back into the kitchen.

Gary re-emerged from the kitchen with a few glasses of ice water and sat in the chair across from me. His chair was an old, well-worn black and tan plaid recliner, slightly worse in condition than the couch I was in. I could tell the old chair was giving way under the weight of Gary night after night.

The floor was not level, or the chair was leaning slightly to the left, a little of both I decided. I began to speak, "How's it goi—"

I was cut off once again by Gary's motion to be quiet. Gary looked at me as he reclined in his chair. The chair went back much further than it was designed under Gary's weight. The large plaid recliner creaked under his mass as he shifted his weight side to side. He looked sideways, in my direction, as I sat on the couch. He pointed to his own ear. "L-i-s-t-e-n." The one word was drawn out, his speech intentionally slow.

I had no idea what the heck I was supposed to be listening for? I was mystified and beginning to steam with anger. *What the hell was this? I came to talk to Gary, and the first time I get invited to his house and so full of questions, he tells me to listen and then says nothing?* I tried once again to talk. "I need to talk to you Gar—"

Again, I was interrupted. This time with a gentle, "Shhhh." Gary made the sound a mother would make, for a small child who had fallen, to quiet the situation with hugs, a gentle reminder that now everything was OK.

I sat quietly, looking at Gary. He was smiling, looking back at me, and shaking his head in a validating up and down motion. Like the child that had fallen and was beginning to be rocked, I felt myself comforted.

"L-i-s-t-e-n." again, slowly spoken, Gary uttered just the one word; he smiled at me, his grin a bit sideways, exposing his squared-off but straight row of teeth. A slight gap between each tooth made for a friendly and warm smile. He was breathing slowly, large breaths in and then a release... breathing out. His belly and chest, rising and falling with each breath.

I did as requested, and as I felt myself calming, I noticed things. I noticed the sound of Gary's breathing and the sound of the old chair under him creaking as he slowly moved. I could hear a faint hum, the sound of the refrigerator running in the other room. I heard my stomach growl, as I realized, I was hungry. I listened more intently and could hear the traffic going by the house in the street out front. I sat quiet for two or three minutes. The longest I'd just sat, and listened, since I was a small child, first discovering life.

I now got the idea, and each time I even looked at Gary I got a response,

"L-i-s-t-e-n.... ," or "Listen deeper, shhhhh... quiet now... " Gary's soft spoken, calming words, slowly voiced.

I began naturally, and without prompting, to settle into the old and worn, brown couch. I could hear my own breathing and notice it slowing. I was matching Gary's slow breathing, breath for breath. I could hear my own heartbeat and noticed it slowing. I could feel myself quieting, calming. I could hear a bird, then two, outside the house through a small window on the side of the house that had been cracked. I could hear the breeze gently carrying the sound to me through the windows. I then heard three birds, then four, and noticed each bird had a separate song.

Something, very important, was going on in the bird's world, and by listening I was part and parcel to this exchange. In my quietness, was the invitation from the birds, to join them, for a moment, in their world.

I found my eyes had closed, and I was intently listening to the whole world around me. I would recognize each sound and the still quiet voice within would gently remind me what the sound was. "This is a bird, that is another bird. Notice the different songs each sings. That is a child, outside playing, that is another child, outside playing. Notice the different songs each sings. That is a car going by. That is a car going by faster. That person is in more of a hurry that the other person."

I wasn't doing anything, but was learning much. I was no longer in control, but was gently being rocked and comforted. I opened my eyes one last time and received a gentle, silent, reminder from Gary, to remain quiet and listen.

Then, I fell asleep.

Chapter Seventeen

Falling Asleep? Or Awakening to the Spiritual Life?

I awoke inside my dream in a sanctuary. Beauty surrounded me in all directions. Sweet gospel music played gently in the background. "How Great Thou Art" by Elvis Presley was the song. It had been my grandmother's favorite song. As a child, I could remember it being played over and over, until I could stand it no longer. This time, I wished the song would never end. And it didn't.

The sanctuary's interior was round in shape, the inside topped with a large, high-domed ceiling. The domed ceiling's interior had been painted a light sky-blue color with the edges painted even lighter blue to reflect back the lighting from the dome's edges. Puffy-white, low-level, cumulus clouds were painted over the blue, covering just enough of the dome to allow the blue to still dominate the color and warm the room. The light reflecting back from the dome's interior warmed all in the room.

The sanctuary itself felt large and open, although actually was quite small. The room was empty of any furniture or chairs. No pews or an altar. I knew however that I was in a holy place, a sanctuary, a safe place. I could see a light smoke in the air and smell burning incense.

The interior walls were dark wood, the domed roof held up by pillars surrounding the room.

I was standing in the center of the room looking up. Under my feet was soft carpet, almost as dark in color as the wood. I looked down from the dome, and standing around the outside walls looking at me, and I at them, were many people from my past life, the life I had been living. Around the room starting at my left was my mother, my father, and my grandparents on both sides, who had long ago passed away. They all appeared as I had remembered them in their primes, healthy, and happy, and young, and strong. My grandparents, as I had remembered them from my childhood, brought back memories of days when I had mentors in life, examples of right and wrong. I was filled with love and shame at the same time at seeing them.

My parents appeared as they were before sickness, financial setbacks, infidelity, and their own personal struggles had caused separation and then divorce. They'd reconciled prior to my father's death. To see them holding hands, smiling and embracing each other, just as they had done so many years ago made me realize I was truly in a holy space.

My brothers and my sister were there. I hadn't seen any of them in over four years. I had borrowed money from each of them and never paid anyone back. I shifted step by step and faced each of them.

First my sister, Stacy, the oldest, looking so very much like my mother, as pretty as ever. Next my older brother, Steve, my idol as a young boy, and the one I had hurt the most. He'd always been there for me and protected me throughout my youth. I'd repaid him with nothing but contempt for his chosen way of life as a born-again Christian.

I shifted and faced directly toward my younger brother, Sammy. He had been still at home when I had left for good. He looked so much like myself, a younger and healthier version, but as we looked at each other, we saw ourselves. Sammy always saw in me what he might have become, but for the grace of God. I always saw in him what I might have been. He was always content with himself, a quality I had always mistook as naivety. I thought he was a square. In reality, he was at peace with himself and was not driven by what other people think.

I was weeping and smiling at the same time. I held my arms out to my side, palms facing up, showing I was open to all the love in the room. I felt so grateful, in this moment. I was being given another chance. I shifted once more and looked directly at my children, Andrea and Alex, arm in arm with my ex–wife, Olivia. I was now openly crying, tears streamed down my face and onto my shirt. I felt elation and humility. The children looked at me with happiness and contentment. My son, Alex, now nine years old and Andrea two years younger. I hadn't seen either in so long.

Olivia, the mother of my children and the woman who'd done so much to help me, was sandwiched between the children. She smiled at me, and I knew she was here with me with nothing but love and support.

No one said a word.

The temptation to speak or to even ask where I was strangely absent. I had no desire at all to speak or to be spoken to. I was communicating, only in a different language, a silent language. This language was spoken in waves of love in differing intensities and vibrations.

I had no idea where I was or what I was doing there. I thought briefly that I might have died somehow, died at Gary's home. Possibly this was heaven. If this was the heaven the preacher's spoke of, I would take it lock, stock, and barrel. I felt at peace.

Around the room I continued to turn, pausing briefly at each person. Waves of love and forgiveness coming and going between us as we each smiled widely, at each other, in deep and loving respect. I saw many of my past teachers. Many childhood friends, as well as enemies. People I'd stolen from. People I'd crossed, after they had trusted me and attempted to assist in my struggles.

As I moved around the room, I came to Gary. He was standing to my right. He was smiling, his head tilted to the side. The beret atop his head was shifted slightly to his right. He was surrounded by a light glow of soft, white light. He smiled his crooked smile at me.

I smiled back, at the same time fighting off the sobbing and the urge to drop to my knees with joy. Dr. Malik, and his wife, Shelly, stood with Gary. They both embraced Gary, then each other. They turned directly to me and both held their hands together in front of their bodies in a prayerful motion to me. They both looked up into the domed cathedral ceiling, then back at me.

Gary, without speaking, communicated to me to continue to listen by just smiling and shaking his head gently up and down. His hand went to his mouth with his index finger pointing up. He held the finger tight to his lips, closed his eyes, and paused for a moment in prayer.

I did as instructed and remained silent. I could hear myself in a prayer of forgiveness. I looked at Gary and he smiled back, knowingly. Although I wasn't moving my lips, I could hear the words clearly. The prayer came through a power greater than myself, and into my heart, from my heart to all in the sanctuary.

God is present in every way with us here and always.
I forgive each of you for any transgressions you may have caused me.
I know you were all doing your best with what you had.
As was I.
Here today in the presence of all.
As witness to God's grace and forgiving spirit.
I ask your forgiveness for all the pain I have caused in your lives.
We all need to be free. It is the only answer we have.
Love and forgiveness.
I stand ready to receive each of you separately.
To listen to how my selfishness and self-centeredness affected you.

To find out in each instance what I need to do to make it right.
In God's presence here, I promise to see each of you in the physical world or
the spiritual realm to listen to you, to do whatever is asked.
God loves us all so much he has brought us here today to be together.
I am so grateful for you all.
Amen.

As I finished the prayer, I could feel the receipt of the love from each of the other people in the room, and one by one, I noticed their faces happy, some with tears of joy, all with smiles. It was my first real experience with the love of God flowing through me. I knew in my heart this was a beginning. I would now need to see and be with each of these people in the physical world.

I turned to Gary. His arms were outstretched. I was sobbing heavily, remembering to the extent I'd harmed many of these people. The extent that I had fallen into the selfish life and away from God. I'd harmed the people who loved me the most. I'd harmed them the deepest. I turned and moved toward Gary and fell into his outstretched arms. I was surrounded by his love and comforted by his mammoth hug.

Shelly spoke to me. Again, in the world of the spirit. I could clearly hear her words, but her lips did not move. In the vision world, in this spiritual dream state, I saw this as it should be and was not the least bit surprised that I was hearing a voice come from someone whose lips were still. In that moment, I'd accepted the supernatural.

Shelly moved to my side and placed her right hand on my left shoulder. I looked directly into her eyes, and she communicated not only with me, but also with everyone present. "I came here with Gary in the beginning as well, Stanley. I come here now, when invited, to help welcome the new person out of a life of delusion and into a life of service and truth."

I already knew the answer to my first question, but I asked anyway. I was communicating without words. "Have I been in delusion?"

"Thoroughly deluded." Those words came from my right, from Gary. We all laughed. Inside, we all felt the same thing, joy. Bliss at having had an experience with the truth.

I turned one last time around the room and met each person's acknowledgement with a nod of the body forward and a shallow bow, showing my humility and gratitude for their presence. I turned to Gary, looked up into his eyes, and asked my last question. Again, my question came through my heart, but not the words from my lips. I was communicating as naturally as if we were sitting on the bus, across from each other. In fact, I was communicating more comfortably and more naturally than I had ever before.

"Where am I?"

Gary looked at me and smiled but didn't respond. Still I knew the answer.

I was home.

Chapter Eighteen

Mindfulness

I could smell food cooking, the smells in the air made me realize how hungry I was. The sanctuary had faded, and I was acutely aware that I was no longer dreaming and was now back on the old brown vinyl couch at Gary's.

I sat up and looked at Gary sitting forward in his chair. In front of each of us was a bowl of steaming-hot, tomato soup. A large grilled-cheese sandwich made with thick yellow bread and lots of cheese. A glass of milk and a cup of hot coffee.

Had Gary been cooking or was he with me in the sanctuary? I was pretty sure I had been dreaming or had I been in another realm? I knew something dramatic had just happened and cared not to try and intellectualize it.

I knew better than to talk. I felt a complete peace with the surroundings and myself. I looked at Gary and paused in silent prayer for a moment and then we both began to eat. I took in each bite and slowly allowed the food to dissolve in my mouth. I ate slower and with more intention that I had ever before. I noticed how each bite tasted, and I could see that Gary was enjoying eating, just eating.

This was the first time I'd ever thought about the concept of enjoying one thing at a time. I was always doing one thing, while working on another or at least planning on what I would do next. This was Gary's first lesson to me in doing one thing at a time. I always ate and watched television. Ate and listened to music. Ate and talked with whomever I was with. Ate and allowed my mind to wander into problems. Ate and wondered how I would conduct myself, to appear in control of everything, even though life was out of control.

This evening at Gary's I ate. I ate my soup, savoring each spoonful. Allowing each spoonful to melt away, before ingesting the next. I ate my sandwich, enjoying each bite. I concentrated on only the sandwich, about what it took to bring the sandwich to my table. I could taste the bread, and the cheese, and imagined the farmer working the soil. I imagined the farmer's family. The machinery and all the people that built the machinery. The machinery builder's family. The seed of the wheat, the sunlight necessary to feed the new sprout, the watering and care. The harvest. The driver to take the wheat to market. I was mindful as I ate!

I knew intellectually about mindfulness, but now I was practicing it. I'd found a deep connection with the hundreds, perhaps thousands of people who'd contributed to the bread on the sandwich in which I ate. I felt love and gratitude that they'd given of themselves and devoted a piece of their precious life so I could eat and be nourished. I felt a part of a much bigger whole. I looked at Gary, and he smiled wide and took another large bite of his sandwich. I knew that he somehow knew what I was thinking.

Gary did know, in his practice of loving kindness, he was able to put himself in others' shoes, this time in my place. Having gone deep into the spiritual life tonight, I was grateful. His look told me to continue with the mindful eating and to remain silent. I did just this. I now knew what *he* was thinking. I also knew my place. He was the teacher and I, the student. I was to do as told. I was the *Sleeping Spirit*, and he was the *Awakened Giant*.

As I ate my soup, I tried to experience to the greatest extent possible, what was really in each bite. I saw in the soup, the soil and the sunlight. The farmer and the family, the tomato and the migrant farm worker, and the farm worker's family. The daily struggle to make ends meet for them all.

I wondered if they had imagined where the fruits of their labors would end up? Had there been a mindful picker? Had there been a picker mindful enough of his work to see the bigger picture? That he, like I, was a part of a larger whole. Had the worker seen the possibility in the tomato, of a person eating soup and contemplating mindfulness?

I could see I was ingesting a gift from each one of them and in that moment, I felt the gratitude and understood for the first time in my life why people pray before they eat. Again, I felt grateful.

I took another bite of my sandwich and tasted the cheese. I pictured the farmer and the animal. The milk heating and then aging to make the cheese. I thought of the animal and wondered if I was participating in something the animal was against? I had a strange feeling that I would need to come to terms with this if I would continue to eat this type of product. Mindful eating will do that to you. It was the best (most mindful) meal I had ever eaten. The first in a very long time I had really enjoyed.

We finished up our food, and I got up without being prompted and gathered the dishes. Not saying a word, I took the dishes into the kitchen and slowly, with no time schedule began to clean each dish.

My experience continued with the water. I seemed fascinated by the water, like a small child playing in water for the first time. How soft the water felt on my skin. How refreshing the cold and how soothing the hot. I knew the water also was a part of this life I was living and the new life I was awakening to. I prayed at the sink full of dishes.

God, giver of all life.
Fill me with your gratitude for all that you have given us.
I see now the precious resource.
I have been given a gift.
I am, and you are, this water.
Thank you God.

I continued to wash, and as if time stood still, losing consciousness of all else. I found myself immersed in my given chore. Immersed in joy.

The sound of the water. The feeling of the clean dish. The thought that these were Gary's dishes. I thought deeply about the cycle of the water. From the snow in the mountains, through the river, into the reservoir and now here to Gary's home. I thought about how I took the water for granted. I thought about those who came before me who carried the water, sometimes great distances into their homes. I thought of those whose daily lives were consumed with the search for and the keeping of clean, drinkable water.

I felt serious gratitude and leveling pride as I thought about how many years had passed since I'd given any thought to this great and wonderful gift. I'd lived a life that typified this type of self-centered thought. That the water should flow when I turned on the tap and never a thought about the gift. Never a feeling of gratitude at having nearly unlimited access to clean water. I shut the water off and conserved every drop I could as I finished up the remaining dishes.

I dried the remaining dishes and found a home for them all. I wiped off the counter tops and the stove. It looked as if Gary had other priorities than housekeeping. The place was far from a mess, but looked the part of Gary's personality—a bit disheveled. I shut out the kitchen lights and the room filled with darkness.

I entered the living room to find Gary fast asleep. He'd fallen asleep, as I was in my deep thought in the kitchen. I noticed as he slept that there was a noticeable grin, a look of complete contentment on his face. He looked happy. His body labored with each breath, to keep this *Awakened Giant* with us. His massive chest rose with each breath. Exhaling through his nose and breathing in again through his mouth, it was hard work for his overgrown body. His body shivered slightly between breaths as his heart pounded out each beat. Even so he looked deeply at peace. He didn't struggle. He was free.

I took a seat on the couch, sinking into the old worn cushions. I watched Gary sleep with my full attention. The man who saved my life was teaching me even as he slept. I knew, as he had been sleeping, he'd still had a part in my kitchen experience just a few short moments ago. My doing his dishes was a lesson. One he had planned, I suspected?

I stood and moved towards Gary, took a small, well-worn, old quilt that was over the back of his chair. I pulled ever so lightly to remove the blanket from behind Gary's head.

He flinched just for a moment, and then proceeded in his labored breathing, now beginning to snore. He continued to grin ever so slightly, contented, joyful and free, even as he slept.

I placed the blanket as best I could, to cover his upper torso and lap. I pushed back on the chair to assure he was in the fully reclined position. Removed his glasses, placing them on the table. I saw his grin as he slept. He truly was one who had found peace.

I walked slowly and silently, to the back of the house, finding a tiny bathroom, light on, in the short hallway. Lying next to the door was a clean, folded towel, a washrag and a new toothbrush. Gary had left them for me. Gary didn't just talk about helping others. He thought about others full-time and showed this, by his own actions, how to truly care for another human being. I mindfully cleaned up and prepared for the evening.

I entered through an open door and into what I assumed to be Gary's bedroom. The bed was perfectly made, not a single wrinkle. I had the thought that Gary rarely made it to this room to sleep. The recliner in the front room must've been where he spent most nights. I saw his wardrobe, hanging in the open closet and consisting entirely of his bus driver attire. The city uniform of the Metro bus driver was all I could see. Several, but all the same. I recalled never once seeing him wear anything else.

I pulled a blanket off the end of the big bed and headed back to the living room. I laid down across from my mentor, pulled the blanket over me, and in a few minutes, was fast asleep.

I awoke having not stirred all night. As I focused on my surroundings, and my experience of the previous twenty-four hours came back to me I sat up. Gary was gone. I had slept well into the morning, and the clock on the wall let me know that Gary was on board his bus and well into his route for the day.

I sat there, trying my best to absorb the spiritual movement that had taken place in me the last twenty-four hours, but also in the last five months since I had met Gary. There was a note on the coffee table in front of me. I sat up, rubbed my eyes and stretched gently and read.

Stanley,
Get a job!
Love,
Gary

P.S.
Try the New Thought Church on Highway 99 and 22nd West.
Ask for Pastor Anthony.

Posted to the note was a twenty-dollar bill. A church? I was supposed to go to a church looking for work. I imagined a job center or a shelter. I wasn't too excited about the proposition, but had learned to follow directions. The address wasn't far away. I took the money and got dressed. I locked the front door on my way out and headed for the bus to take me to my destination out on Highway 99.

I had my next set of instructions: Go to the New Thought Church and ask a pastor about work. I had twenty dollars for food and bus fare for the day. Once more, another day, being provided for.

Chapter Nineteen

Happiness in Simplicity

After breakfast at a small coffee shop and a short bus ride, I arrived at my given destination. The New Thought Church was exactly where Gary had said. I'd been by this place dozens, perhaps hundreds, of times in the past few years, but had never noticed the small building. The building had once been a small business complex and sat on an oversized lot. A small white sign in the front parking lot let me know that I was at the correct place. A large, lighted sign, affixed to the building roof, allowed drivers on the highway to see the church, from both directions of traffic. Yet, I'd never noticed.

I entered the lobby through a set of double glass doors. I could see a very large room behind the lobby, with two sets of open double doors. One set each to the left and the right of the entrance, entering into the church sanctuary. I stood in the outer entrance of the sanctuary. To my right was a set of stairs going down and a sign pointing down that read, "Office." I proceeded down the stairs and thought about my experience at Gary's the previous night. I thought about being in that sanctuary and now at this church.

My preconceived ideas, as well as my years of antireligious sentiment had brought me to a place of serious suspicion of all churches and religions. But last night I had gone to a church during the spiritual experience I had while dreaming, and today I'd come on my own free will to see a pastor! Desperation and a failed way of life had caused me to reconsider everything. Where I had previously seen spirituality and religion as a crutch, as a weakness, I now saw it as my only hope. I was weak and broken. It was no attribute that I had to reconsider my prejudices. My old way of thinking had failed, that was all.

I approached the office door, but before I could knock, a woman opened it. I stood face to face with a red-haired, fair-skinned, green-eyed beauty. Nervously wringing my hands, I managed to spit out a few words. "I'm looking for Pastor Anthony, my name is Stanley, um... ah...Stanley Pearson."

"Nice to meet you, Stanley. I'm Pastor Anthony."

I was expecting a man, but did my best to suppress my surprise. "Sabrina Anthony," she added.

I'd guessed that she picked up on my surprise by the tone of her voice, especially since she'd clarified her name for me.

"My friends call me Tony, please come in," She motioned me into a small office. "What can I do for you?" she said with her hand outstretched.

I shook her hand and had a seat in the chair that sat in front of her desk. The desk was scattered with stacks of books and papers. As I surveyed the desk and room she motioned me to sit and continued around to the backside of her desk.

"Please have a seat, Stanley."

There was a classic beauty to her features and a warm glow about her presence. She wasn't the Hollywood-beauty type, but there was something gorgeous about her. I found it impossible to take my eyes off her. She was a few years my senior, mid-forties, I imagined. Her voice was deep and a bit gravelly. I also detected a slight Southern drawl that added to her welcoming features.

Tony's long, straight, red hair and dark, olive-shaped green eyes gave her a professional, intelligent, wise look. Her thin nose and large smiling mouth all added to her rugged beauty. She was the type of woman who men and women alike take a second glance at in passing.

She spoke again, catching me staring. I looked away quickly, then looked at the floor. "Stanley, thanks for coming, what can I do for you?" She picked up a pair of tortoise-shell glasses from her desk, placing them on her face, and looked up for my answer. She sat in her chair and began shuffling a few papers, awaiting my reply.

I continued to look down nervously, fearing I might lose my thoughts if I looked up. "I'm looking for work and was sent by Gary Goldpeople to ask for you."

Tony smiled, and her smile was as soft and beautiful as the rest of her. Her lavender lipstick, matched her lavender blouse. She had one eyetooth slightly crooked and out of place. In her imperfect smile was a friendly attraction, imperfection only added to her attractiveness.

"Awe, Gary you say," she said, as she smiled even wider. Her striking features, her apparently soft skin, and her loving smile combined to keep me deeply attentive to her every word. "I'm one of Gary's students. Love to ride the bus!" She laughed, in her deep voice, and I nervously giggled with her. "Looking for work, are you?"

"Yeah, I guess I am. Just trying to follow instructions. Can you help point me in the right direction?" I was nervous and held my hands together tightly. I wasn't sure why I was there exactly, I knew I needed work but wasn't sure I was doing the right thing. I was following directions.

"Not sure if I will need to point you very far," she pointed out the door and signaled to her right with a wave of her hand. "You can start down here in the assembly hall and kitchen. You'll find mops, brooms, and most everything you need to clean up in the closet next to the kitchen. If you need any help, come find me." Sitting behind the large oak desk she slid her glasses up further onto her face and picked up a pen and started writing. She didn't look back up.

That, was it? I was somewhat stunned, but left the office and started cleaning up downstairs in the hall and kitchen that were outside the offices. They really were in need of a good cleaning up, and God knew I was in need of honest work. I had the feeling I was just where I was supposed to be. I swept, mopped, and practiced staying mindful, as I went. I found I really enjoyed the work so long as I just cleaned.

As soon as I noticed my mind wandering, I began to suffer from thoughts of worthlessness. My mind would go to... "I should've amounted to more than cleaning basements... What the heck am I doing hanging out in a church... How much am I being paid to do this lousy work anyway? I'm ugly... I'll never amount to anything... No one loves me... I'm worthless..." As soon as I recognized the old thinking slipping in, as quickly as possible I would think only of the cleaning, of mindfulness. My thinking would return to gratitude and God.

I would continue practicing the mindfulness and clean. When I finished each area, I returned to the office for the next task. I'd worked nearly all day and was hungry and tired. Pastor Anthony had left her office and in the kitchen made some sandwiches and pulled out a few glasses of iced tea and served us both some late lunch. I noticed as we sat and ate that there was a white glow around her being, a soft aura about her. This added to her attractiveness and poise. Her spiritual light was illuminated, even as spiritually asleep as I was then this fact was impossible to miss.

We ate, as I'd eaten with Gary only one night before, in silence. Once again, I experienced deep gratitude for my food. We finished, and I cleaned up as I also had done at Gary's the previous night. When I'd finished cleaning, I returned to Pastor Tony's office for more instructions.

She was once again busy at her desk, writing and working on what looked like a large project of some kind; She looked up and stopped work for a moment. "Behind the sanctuary is a small stairway. At the top, you'll find a small room. It'll be your room. It needs a little cleaning, and you'll find sheets and towels in the room to make up the bed and set up the bathroom."

I was tired and the instructions by Tony were such a welcome invitation. I hadn't had a real room since my stay at the hospital with Nurse Shelly and Dr. Malik. The truly inspirational spirit of Tony reminded me, in many ways of Nurse Shelly and the good Doctor. I had one more question. I cleared my throat to prompt her to look up in my direction, "Uhm. How do you know Gary?"

She set down her pen and removed her glasses, after a long pause and a look directly into my eyes, she began "I met Gary almost fifteen years ago, and he brought me into this way of life, the spiritual life. I was like you, started with nothing, and now am trying to give back some of what Gary has given to me." She grinned slightly and nodded her head gently in sincerity.

"What did Gary give to you?" I asked.

"Everything you see and more," she quietly answered. She stood up from behind her desk and turned out a small desk lamp with a snap of her fingers. "Now, this will be good night, you've done a good job here, and so long as you are in need, you are the maintenance and clean-up man by day and the night watchman by night. I'll be going home soon and will lock up on my way out."

I had no idea how to express my good fortune and gratitude. I felt undeserving on one hand and overwhelmed with hope and gratitude on the other. "I'm not sure what to say. Thank you so much. I promise I won't let you down." Tearfully and filled with gratitude, I turned and headed back out of her office and upstairs to the sanctuary.

I had never been so grateful for a job before. I'd never recalled being grateful for much, but especially work. I'd always imagined it was a burden pushed on me by society, or I would go the other route and feel I was doing the employer a favor by showing up. I knew then who was helping whom and was grateful for the opportunity. I was grateful for the chance to work. I was grateful for the health that allowed me to complete the jobs.

I was grateful for Gary trusting me enough to send me to the church. I wondered how the pastor came to trust me so quickly. She was leaving me alone in her church for the night. Why?

I wandered through the sanctuary and found the staircase leading to the room upstairs Pastor Anthony had described. As I looked around an eerie realization grabbed my attention. I stopped in the middle of my tracks when I realized how similar this place was to the sanctuary from my spiritual experience I had in my dream the night before, with Gary. I remembered seeing all my loved ones. I recalled, just then, seeing one person I hadn't recognized at the time. It was Pastor Anthony! She'd also been there!

I fell to my knees, in the sanctuary, overwhelmed by the presence of God. I'd always wanted answers to all my questions about God. Was God real? Did God know who I was? Did God love me? I knew in that moment the answer to all my questions. God knew me and cared for me for I was one with God. I'd been brought to this place by the power of love, God's love.

Looking around the room I knew I had been transformed somehow. I felt shivers run up my spine and felt strongly I was home. I never once in my life knew what folks were talking about when they said they "felt at home" in a particular place or why people felt such a strong need to go back to the place of their childhood home. I knew now, alone and feeling for possibly the first time my oneness with my creator, what it meant to feel at home. I was there. It was the sanctuary of my dream the night before and now was my resting place for the night and beyond.

I rose back to my feet, after several minutes of gratitude and thankful prayer, found the staircase, climbed to the top, and entered the room above the sanctuary. A quaint and simple place, with two windows. One window faced south, toward the city. It looked out on the city, and all the city lights appeared, sparkling and dancing. Beyond the city, in daylight, the water was visible.

The other window faced the east, onto the highway. From there I could look out onto the traffic below. I could see the cars going by and I noticed a few folks walking. Not a good neighborhood for a nightly stroll, I knew these were street people passing time, until the next piece of action came along.

The bedroom was simple. A single bed, with one mattress atop a wooden frame. Next to the bed was a nightstand with a large candle for light and a box of matches. I instinctively lit the candle. There was a small simple wooden dresser. I unpacked my few belongings from my backpack and put them into the dresser. It was the first time, in as long as I could remember, that I'd had a place to put my clothes that wasn't a cheap hotel.

In the back of the room was a door that opened to a very small bathroom. A single small rust-stained sink hung from the wall, with a tiny, oval, mirror hanging over. An old claw-foot tub had been adapted with a pull-around curtain for a shower. I washed up, made the bed, and fell fast asleep.

I slept with a peace I hadn't known in years. I had been sleeping in a half-awake state for as long as I could remember. I could never allow myself to fully sleep, for my own safety at times and at other times due to the withdrawals that tortured even my sleeping moments.

I was warm, safe, and I knew even protected somehow. It was the barest of accommodations but to me it was a palace. That night I didn't need or want the home of the rich and famous. I had everything I wanted and everything I needed. I slept contented. I slept peaceful. I slept deep and long.

Chapter Twenty

Spiritual Potential

The sun rising awakened me, as its brilliant streams penetrated through the closed blinds. The smell of freshly washed sheets and the warmth of a bed made with a clean, heavy, thick comforter were heavenly, for I had endured many nights on the hard-wooden bench waiting for Gary's early morning arrival. I'd spent the last two nights in a row indoors; my body, mind, and spirit felt the relief.

I'd been given the gift of showering before bed. I'd eaten before retiring for the evening. This was a stark and welcome change from the self-inflicted misery of sleeping outside on an empty stomach. I laid in the soft bed as long as I could stand, soaking in the long ago forgotten luxuries.

This morning began, what would become a daily ritual that I dearly loved. On this beautiful morning, I pulled back the covers and swung my feet to the side of the bed. I showered again, taking advantage of having hot, soothing, running water and sweet-smelling soap. Refreshed and ready to face my day, I dressed, and then I prayed.

God,
I give this day to you.
I am here to serve you, God,

and your children.
Show me God,
not what I can get from this day,
but what I can bring to the twenty-four hours ahead.
Amen

I headed back down the stairs, through the beautiful chapel and down the second flight of stairs to the offices, looking for Pastor Anthony. I found her in the kitchen, serving tea. She looked every bit as if she had been expecting me. As I walked in, she was just setting a tea service for two, down on the table. She was wearing light-brown sandals with a long lavender skirt and a white blouse. A purple rope belt snuggled up tightly at her thin waste, pulled the outfit together. Her red, shiny hair fell lightly on her shoulders. A small golden cross fell lightly against her blouse and hung from a delicate chain around her neck.

I wanted to just stand there in the doorway and stare at her. I nervously cleared my throat, as so as not to startle her, then spoke softly. "Good morning, Pastor."

"A good, God's morning to you, Stanley. I was just setting up some tea for us to start the day. Please, sit," She motioned with her hand, inviting me to sit. She grinned with her warm and friendly smile. She sat herself, sitting cross-legged and slightly sideways on the chair.

I took my seat across from her at the small round table, I'd had something on my mind all morning so voiced my question. "How did you know I could be trusted when you left me in the church?"

She removed her tortoise-shell glasses from her nose, and placed them to rest, gently, on top of her head, holding her hair back and exposing her brilliant green eyes at the same time. She looked directly at me when she spoke, then grinned slightly. "You, Stanley, can't be trusted."

It hurt and embarrassed me to hear this, but I somehow knew she was telling the truth so I didn't argue.

She continued, "I trusted in the spirit, in God. That Gary had sent you, that I practice every day seeing the spiritual potential in each person I meet. I trusted in God and these ideas, in Gary, but not in you, sorry to say.

"I saw in you, not the man who can't be trusted, but the spiritual potential of the man you will become. I saw in you only the spirit, not the man. Stanley Pearson, the man will let me down. Stanley Pearson, the embodiment of God, created in the image and likeness of God, this is the Stanley I saw."

"I somehow felt you trusted me?" I inquired. As I spoke, Pastor Anthony poured a cup of tea. I picked up my tea, remembering to be mindful and savored my first sip as I listened to her answer.

"That's the real miracle then, isn't it? That's how this works. I see the Spirit in you, Stanley, and you become empowered. That is the power of God working through me to heal you. We become healers. Like Gary. He taught this to me, and now I teach this to you, and you have another assignment."

She noticed the puzzled look on my face and added, "The assignment is to practice seeing the spiritual potential in others. Notice the difference when you look at the human frailties of folks and when you see deep into the spirit. This is all I did with you, and I had no problem leaving you in charge of the church."

She gave a deep, gravely, but sweet and genuine, laugh before continuing. "Besides, the worst that can happen is for you to take something and go...rob us. As I see it, if there is anything I have that you want, go ahead." Her warm smile and glowing eyes melted me.

I wanted what the spiritual confidence she had, and to a certain extent, I knew I'd acquired some of what she was. I was she, and she was I. At least, I was whom she saw. The spiritual potential to become great women and to become great men, to do God's intended work for us, exists in each and every one of us, to the extent we can see it in others. We are all created in the likeness and image of our creator and when I see that I see truth. When I see separation, and feel bitterness then I see delusion.

Each morning when I awoke I would come downstairs and find that Pastor Anthony had prepared tea and was waiting for me. I dearly loved the mornings with Sabrina. Each morning, waking, and drinking tea and being spiritually taught by another of Gary's students was a gift from God, one I never tired of.

I could hear in her, Gary's message of hope and recovery. I could see in her the same light that was in his eyes. I could feel from her the same radiant presence of God that I had felt from Gary. Each morning in her presence I was awed by her kindness and her peacefulness.

Chapter Twenty-One

Delusion and Right-Thinking

I'd been living in the church now, for several weeks. It was late October and Halloween was soon approaching. I loved my mornings with Pastor Anthony. She taught me to see the good in all people. She taught me that this was about being a teacher, not a preacher. In all our morning talks, I'd never once felt that I was being preached to. I always felt I was allowed to take the lead and ask questions. She never insisted that I do anything. She never insisted I believe anything. She'd never insisted I be anything but myself. I'd had many experiences being preached to; this time, I was having an experience being taught. A real leader leads by example; Pastor Anthony was a real leader.

She was here, at church, each and every day, seven days a week from early morning until late at night working tirelessly. Paying bills, answering the phone in her office that seemed to never stop ringing. She had people stopping by all day and many of them she counseled behind the closed door of her office. I never once had her ask me or saw her with any of the other dozens of folks she helped ask for one thing in return.

On this day, I settled into another morning. Pastor Sabrina Anthony had cooked a small breakfast for the past several mornings and I was looking forward to something to eat. My stomach rumbled in hunger and I was looking forward to a wonderful breakfast.

I went to the kitchen for our morning breakfast and tea but didn't smell anything cooking. The tea was on the table, so I helped myself. I sat at our table and wondered where our breakfast was.

Sabrina emerged from the kitchen with two small wooden bowls. She said nothing, and only nodded in my direction and smiled. She had a serious look on her face. Not knowing how to take this, I nodded back and remained silent. Sabrina set one bowl in front of me and took a seat herself. Sabrina bowed her head in prayer, and holding her hands together, made a silent prayer intended for only God and herself. With her head bowed, her red hair fell forward, covering the sides of her face.

I paused momentarily myself. I felt comfortable enough to open my eyes and look at the bowl of food in front of me. I knew I wouldn't be seen, as Pastor Anthony had her face partially covered and her head bowed, with eyes closed. My small, wooden bowl was filled only about halfway with hot cooked oats. No milk, no sugar, not even brown sugar, like she knew I loved?

I began feeling irritated that there were no condiments for the hot cereal. I felt that she should be serving something with the oats. What the hell anyway… If I were cooking, I would've had more than this tiny bowl of hot cereal with nothing added!

Sabrina finished her prayer, smiled in my direction, and began eating her plain, hot oats. She rocked her head back slowly, in ecstasy at each bite and exaggerated her enjoyment, for my benefit, I thought.

I felt the anger well up inside of me. I knew better than to say something lest I sound angry. After all, I was supposed to be learning to live the spiritual life… right? I paused and asked in prayer for relief. I bowed my head again, this time in earnest prayer:

God,
I am in delusion.
I am angry.
Please help me to see the truth.
Please return my thinking,
To who you would have me be.
Amen

I came out of my prayer with a moment of silence, trying to recognize the presence of God. I sat up, opened my eyes, and observed Sabrina, brimming with joy. She looked much less serious, more beautiful and happy than I had imagined her just a few moments before.

I came to rely on this simple prayer as a way of returning my self-centered thinking to the spiritual life. I became, as time went on, quicker at asking God for help. I was now, easily able to receive spiritual help, and increasingly aware of being prepared for something larger.

I looked again at the simple breakfast before me. Looking now through the spiritual eye, I saw something quite different. I imagined myself as the hungry beggar with the outstretched bowl. I saw the beggar that would gladly accept any offering of food. I pictured the beggar's children and family waiting to be fed. I thought about all those going hungry in the world.

Pastor Anthony's eyes shined brightly, her smile illuminated the room. She knew a shift had taken place, and she knew, she had just witnessed the power of prayer firsthand in our lives. First, she had said a prayer, in silence, for me. Then, I in turn had said a prayer that had affected us both. Her breath was audible, as she slowly took her next bite and enjoyed her meal. There was that bright, white aura around her presence that I could now see. She was beautiful, powerful, and obviously connected to the world of the Spirit. To God's world. The only real world.

My feelings of anger had subsided quickly, and I was returned to a state of gratitude for what was in front of me. The fact was, I ate too much. I had gained some badly needed weight, but certainly wasn't hurt by eating less.

I ate my oatmeal in silence with Pastor Anthony. She smiled, and I sensed that she was aware of the transformation that had taken place within me in the last few minutes. I have since seen many situations where there was a transformation in an individual or within entire groups. Times when one or more were clearly off their mark. Sometimes a whole group out of sync. I witnessed a transformation and realized someone had said a prayer.

The pastor sat sideways, legs crossed in her chair with her small bowl in one hand and a spoon in the other. She was freshly showered, and her hair still a bit damp from the washing. She was wearing her normal attire with a large, lavender blouse and a flowing print skirt. She was the first to break the silence and talk. She finished her last bite, set the bowl and spoon down on the table and swung her body around to directly face me. "It's better to live one day in awareness of the presence of God, than to live a hundred years in ignorance."

Enough had been said. I'd understood even before she'd said the words. In my ignorance, I suffered. It was everyone else's fault. I was owed a living. Nothing anyone did was ever enough. I thought about how grateful I was for the New Thought Church, Pastor Anthony, Nurse and Doctor Malik and especially Gary. I knew God had brought these people, and the church to me, and I instinctively knew these were all tools of God. I found much comfort in being grateful to and for them.

Chapter Twenty-Two

Faith without Works Is Dead

I t had been only a few days ago that I'd sat in front of the simple bowl of oats with Pastor Anthony—since I felt incredible gratitude and love for all that had transpired. Now, a short few days later, my self-centered thinking had returned, and I needed God's help. One minute I would be blinded by the sunlight of the Spirit, feeling all the awe of the presence of God. Then I'd fade from the life-giving sunlight of the Spirit and once again find myself angry with many of the people in my life. I was even mad at Pastor Tony for not paying enough attention to me! I needed to ride the bus. I needed help.

I had waves of anger at my former wife and my children. I had, several times, in the last few weeks, made contact with them and was rebuked. Why couldn't they see I was changing? I knew from the outside I was a man living in a small room above a church, but what they couldn't see was the huge change taking place within. Many old friends, skeptical of any real change, I was sure, were waiting for the day I would return to my old way of life. I questioned myself if they maybe weren't right. I deeply yearned for the spiritual life and just as I'd feel its presence I was led astray by my own internal fears and doubts.

I awoke early that morning, knowing I needed to venture back to the bus stop. In the wee morning hour before tea and breakfast, I slipped downstairs and left a note for Pastor Anthony, and headed for Gary's stop. When I arrived, the bus was already in place, and Gary was drinking his coffee. We exchanged exuberant waves as I approached from the front of the bus. Gary opened the door and when I boarded, I stepped right up, hanging my head a bit and grinding my teeth. I managed a grin.

I took my seat, and before Gary could even say hello, I started in. "Gary, I'm angry with most everyone in my life... or out of my life, as the case is with most everyone." I was bitter, and my choppy speech and tight-lipped frown showed it. "My wife won't call, she won't bring the kids by the church to see me. None of my friends will listen to anything I say about this new way of life that I've found. I can hear people holding back the laughter, as if this is some kind of a damn joke!

"My life is better for sure, but I'm still a broke adult man living in a church. I still can't support my family. My mother didn't do the best job raising me, you know! My wife kicked me out, that's why I was homeless. Gary, I'm angry with most everyone in my life... or out of my life, as the case is with so many—" I snapped my head up quickly in angry surprise, rather shocked that I had been cut off.

"Anger toward others and blaming will kill you sure as heck," he said so matter-of-factly it pissed me off. Gary straightened up his beret, looked in the rearview mirror, and didn't even glance in my direction before adding, sarcastically, "Yep, the blame game. Stanley, certain death if you keep it up."

"Blame game?" I said angrily. "What does any of this have to do with blaming?" I'm not blaming anyone, Gary; I'm just stating the facts!

"Facts, are they? Well. let's just see about that." Goldpeople went on, finally looking directly at me. "Your only hope is a contact with this power we call God, right?"

"I honestly can't think of any other way," I responded, calming slightly. I dropped my head in defeat. This sweet, loving old man had suddenly grown a bit too serious for my comfort zone. I shifted in my seat, uncomfortably, unable to sit still. My stomach churned.

"Wouldn't it be great if all we had to do was ask God into our lives or ask Jesus into our hearts and then everything was better?" Gary smiled.

"I've tried that Gary, over and over again."

"So, you see that it doesn't work, and the reason it doesn't work is that there are many things blocking you from the one thing that can and will save your life. That one thing is God, Stanley. You are blocked from God by your own fears, anger, blaming others for your failure and things in your past that you have never made right. To mention a few."

"Imagine this." Gary said, removing his glasses and squinting his eyes.

I could see a light shining from his slotted eyes, as if there was a little man with a flashlight…one behind each eye, the light shining out and warming my soul. I felt as if this old bearded man was the voice of God speaking to me. In fact, I now know that it was just that and nothing less. The same soft white aura surrounded Gary that I had seen in him many times and also in Sabrina, Shelly and Dr. Malik and several of Gary's passengers over these last several months.

"Imagine that God is the sunlight, the sunlight of the Spirit, now hold your hand in front of your eyes."

I took my left hand and tightly held it to my face, covering my eyes.

"Notice how things get dark?"

Yes, of course, I thought. I said nothing, and for the moment, sat in silence.

"Now pull the hand away and notice that you can now see."

I pulled my hand down and looked directly at Gary. His eyes beamed and I felt a relaxation come over me as I calmed. The light from him and from all around me was evident.

"The sunlight of the Spirit is the same way. It's there, Stanley, but you're blocked from it. This is why I say your spirit is asleep and why I can tell you my spirit is awake. I can see the sunlight of the Spirit, and you cannot, or if you can, it is hazy and distant. I want you to know, the sunlight of the Spirit shines in my life every single day." He paused and I could feel the gratitude welling up inside Gary and being passed to me.

"This will be our plan, you write down all of those people who wronged you in any way, those with whom you are angry. Write down all the people and situations that make you, have made you, or are making you, angry, upset. Don't leave anyone, or any situation, off the list. Bring this list to me, and you and I, in God's presence, will review them, and ask God to show us the real facts. Seek the knowledge of the truth and the truth will set you free. So long as you live in the delusion that forces outside yourself are to blame for your failures, you are unable to see the truth in any area of your life. For you to live a delusional life any longer will be certain death."

Gary paused, wiping his glasses on his shirt and bending his wire rims slightly to form to his chubby face. He winked, put his glasses back on just the tip of his nose, and looking over the top of the small spectacles, added, "No worry my friend, it's only a matter of life and death." He laughed out loud as if this was funny, and then he continued:

"We will do the same with all your fears, as these too are blocking you the same way that your hand blocks the light from entering your eyes." He stopped laughing, paused for a moment, closed his eyes, and clutched his hands together.

He emerged a moment later from his deep thought with a question? "So, what do you suppose will happen to you when all the things that block you from God are removed?"

I followed Gary's lead and paused. I closed my eyes and concentrated as deeply as I could on the question… If everything that is blocking me from God is removed, then I will know the truth, I will know the sunlight of the Spirit. I will know God! I let out a loud and exuberant, "Wow!" I looked at Gary, in open-jawed astonishment, with the realization that in the search for truth, I would come to know God.

Gary began laughing at the look on my face, so hard I thought this time he would wet himself, "OK, then I'll see you tomorrow, or if you need a few days that's fine." He managed to say between snickers.

This was always Gary's deal. He would throw something in like a little bean into an empty jar, and these thoughts would bounce around in my head but he would never give me more than a few thoughts a day. I was changing, I could once again feel within me the hope that this God thing was real, and that it was going to work even for as hopeless an individual as myself.

I stood at the next stop, gathered my pack and hugged Gary on my way back onto the street. I knew I needed God or else. I also knew now that something more than faith would be needed to remove those things in my life that blocked me from Spirit. More than ever I would need to follow instructions.

Chapter Twenty-Three

You Don't Need Much, To Have Much To Live for

I was back the following day, to write as instructed and ride the bus. I was most comfortable when I was with Gary. Even after the bus had started its route, I would stay just to be in his presence and around his gentle aura. I loved watching the people board the bus like me and sit and talk to Gary. Day by day it seemed the crowds grew. A seat anywhere towards the front of the bus where one could hear Gary answering questions to life's most difficult problems were at a premium. I always came at least an hour early.

I again was early and so was Gary, parking his bus at the stop and awaiting what God would bring him for the day. The door opened as I approached and I boarded the bus. I started to feel like those early mornings when Gary opened the door to the bus it was like opening the door to a new day. It occurred to me that the simple act of stepping through the door of the bus was symbolic—each morning I open a door to a new day so long as God is in the driver's seat. Thy will not mine be done.

Gary and I exchanged in our usual, friendly conversation. He shared his coffee and morning donuts. The bus began its morning rounds, and the front was full by the third stop, passengers boarded at each stop, heading to work... downtown.

"This is your stop," Gary announced, catching me totally by surprise. I had only been aboard a few minutes and had never gotten off at this stop. He brought the bus to a stop and opened the door. I was more than a little embarrassed by the abrupt comment in front of everyone on the bus.

This wasn't my stop, and Gary knew it. "What's up, I'm planning to ride and write today!" I pleaded. The door remained open, and I knew better now than to argue because it never helped. One thing I'd come to know about Gary was that it was going to be his way, and moreover, everything he had said so far was right. All of it. I'd tried to argue, I'd tried to prove he was wrong about me. He was always right! What was the deal with that? I put my pad and paper in my pack, stood up, and turned to face Gary, "I love you Gary. See you later." Still, I wondered why Gary was putting me off the bus here.

"I love you too Stanley, just remember, 'You don't have to have much, to have much to lose, my friend.' Gary closed the door behind me, and the bus, along with the happiest man alive, and filled with his students pulled away leaving me behind.

I hadn't paid much attention to what Gary had said as I walked off the bus, being somewhat perturbed with him for announcing my departure so sharply. I waved, and the bus horn sounded to reply in the early morning chill.

I walked south along the sidewalk, in the same direction I'd been traveling in on a warm bus. Instead of riding in the comfortable bus with my mentor to ask questions of, and to listen to Gary teach about living the spiritual life, Gary had dropped me off here to walk back to the church and to ponder the questions for myself. I felt overwhelmed with gratitude for everything that had happened in the last few weeks. A special gratitude came over me for being brought to Gary

Goldpeople. He was the teacher, and I was the student—this much was clear. Something else was very, very clear. I LOVED HIM! I stopped and thanked God for bringing Gary to me.

The self-pity and anger I had been feeling subsided, not completely, but enough to feel love for another human being. Again, love was the answer. I stopped walking for a moment and went into prayer:

God,
Lord of the happy, joyous and free
Thank you for love.
The love of others for me.
And my love for others,
Thank you especially for Gary,
My mentor,
My teacher.
Thank you great Spirit,
For speaking to me,
Through him,
Amen.

As I looked up from my prayer, I noticed something on the ground, a small bag— a type I recognized all too well. It was a tiny plastic bag, and I hoped that it was not what I thought it was. I reached over and picked it up. As I did, I noticed a drug deal going on across the corner. Two young men, both with the sunken-in faces and recessed eyes of an experienced addict, I knew I was one of them, separated only by the grace of God. I now had the bag in my hand and began to tremble.

I opened the small Ziploc bag and inside were small pieces of black tar heroin, each wrapped in a tiny bag of their own. I looked around, and my heart raced. I also noticed several bars in the neighborhood, one just a step away from where I was standing, the other I would only need to cross the street. I knew about the money in my wallet. I didn't know exactly how I had received the gift of the life I now had. I knew then however, without a doubt, how I could have my old life back.

I forced myself back into prayer as my entire thinking was shifting. I couldn't let go of the small bag. The only thing I now noticed about this street was the drug addicts and the bars. Late at night, I knew where the hookers would be hanging out. They were always my good friends because they had a way to get money when I didn't. Most were generous with their money, desperately wanting someone to love them. My old world had come to visit.

I began to run now instead of walk. Without thinking I was racing towards the New Thought Church, towards sanctuary! My heart was jumping out of my chest, all I could think of was the warm feeling the drugs would give me when entering my body. I continually returned to my prayer, as I entered the door of the church and headed up to my small room atop the sanctuary.

I burst through the door, still holding tightly to the bag of drugs I had found on the street. I shivered for a moment about the timing of the whole thing. Was this why Gary let me off the bus early? Did he know these drugs were there on the street? Did he put them there? No, I was sure not. Hopefully not. I never knew what Gary was up to. I also couldn't help but think of the irony of the situation.

There had been many days when I would wander the street praying for a find like this. The drugs would have lasted a day or two, maybe more. It would've been the winning of the junkie lottery. Now, it was the worst thing I could think of. It threatened all the good that was now in my life. By most people's standards I didn't have much, but compared to where I'd come from, I had much to lose. I fell to my knees, knowing I was on shaky ground. I said one simple prayer of desperation.

God,
I recognize you as the only presence
The only power
I claim here and now
The truth forever
That these drugs have no power over me.
Grant me the power,
To destroy the insanities of my life,
Before they destroy me.
Amen.

Shaking and now covered in sweat, I went into my small bathroom and was given the power to flush the drugs down the toilet.

I took my first real breath since I'd picked up the bag from the sidewalk. I could hear the voice of Gary come over me. I understood now what he had said just as I walked off the bus. I could hear his voice in my head as if he were in the room with me. *"You do not have to have much, to have much to lose."* These were the words he'd said to me just an hour ago. I knew now exactly what he meant. His timing was always perfect; he intuitively knew what to say. A real connection with God is like that. The voice of God had spoken to me through Gary many times. I indeed did have much to lose, not in the material world, but in the spiritual.

I awoke the following morning feeling rested and at peace with the direction my life had taken. After my morning routine of a shower, tea and oats with Pastor Anthony, and fifteen minutes of prayer in the chapel, I went forward with Gary's instructions. I sat down with a pen and paper and began to make the lists of grudges I held, and fears I had. There were many. I prayed continuously over the next few days, as I wrote every chance I had.

Chapter Twenty-Four

Reasonable Options

Halloween had come and gone, and November had brought with it a cold winter chill, strong winds, and rain. I bundled up after some early morning prayer and headed out to the bus stop. Gary, as always, was early. He saw me and opened the door. I boarded and smiled, notebook in hand.

"Hello Gary" I said as I boarded.

"You are following instructions, and this is a good thing," Gary said with a smile.

"I have a choice?" I responded, half-jokingly, as I took my seat.

Gary paused… dropped his head and looked over the top of his glasses at me with his signature crooked grin. "A choice is one or more reasonable options, my friend, and if that is correct, I would have to say you're right—you have no choice." He laughed with such a lust for life that it was infectious, and I too began laughing.

"I have no choice but to turn my life over to a bus driver?"

"Remember I told you before, I'm not a bus driver."

I smiled at Gary's comment; it warmed my heart to hear him say it again. "That's right Gary you're a waker-upper."

This truly struck both our funny bones. Gary continued to laugh as he poured himself some coffee from his thermos and sipped for a minute or two as I waited for his next words. He set his coffee down and began our lesson for the day. Our lesson had actually started at "Hello."

"Anger is the strongest force of darkness I know. To live the spiritual life, you will have to find freedom from the blaming. Blaming others, finding faults in others, is just anger turned outward. It is self-hatred projected outward onto others. God would have you be free of anger. He makes that possible my friend. You can have freedom from those grudges you've written down. The list you carry is the door to a better life, the door to God. Find freedom from those and you'll find God." He shook his head slowly up and down. He said everything in such matter of fact terms. With such confidence.

I wanted to interrupt him and tell him of the freedom I'd already received through my experience with discarding the drugs I'd found. Instead I listened, as I knew that freedom would be short-lived if I didn't move forward on the spiritual path that Gary was laying before me.

"You're so busy with this over-concentration on yourself that each person's actions are interpreted by you, to have direct consequences on you. When things don't go according to your grand little plan, you resent what you interpret to be the cause of your suffering, your discomfort.

"The truth for you is that all this discomfort and suffering is self-fabricated. You are suffering because you want to and because you are blocked from the truth. This list you have made is truly then, the key. The key to the gate of a real, happy, playful, useful life. Know the truth and the truth will set you free.

"Look at the list of people and situations with which you are angry and pause for each name and consider the reason or reasons why you are angry. When that is completed, go back to each name and look at what you may have done to these people, as well as how you may have played a part in the situations that angered you.

"Don't stop with what you have done to those on your list. Write a list of what you have done to others, all of those things in your life that you know are wrong, those things you were never going to tell anyone. Get it all out onto paper. Leave nothing out, absolutely nothing! He leaned back and took a long sip from his coffee and closed his eyes for a moment, enjoying the coffee and contemplating his next words.

"It is so very easy for us to see the wrongs others have done to us. It's so easy to see what is wrong with the world. It's so easy to write about what others have done to us, but what about what you have done to others? He had left the door open and was getting ready to begin his route. A dozen or so had boarded and were also sitting close hanging on every word.

Another sip of coffee and a warm smile and inviting nods as people continued to board and he continued. "We're angry at that in them, which mirrors what we despise in ourselves. We see what we don't like about ourselves in others and use that as a reason to pick them apart.

"We're so self-centered that we never see our part. Well, Mr. Stanley Pearson, that is all about to change." Gary took a long sip of his coffee, then tipped the cup upside-down finishing that last few drops.

He had my attention. I was making notes as fast as I could, as he hammered out one instruction after the other, on writing out what bothered me about others and what I perceived as wrongs others had perpetrated against me. This part of the instruction was easy for me. I had been doing this for years. Listing to my own sick mind what was wrong with the world and keeping track of all the wrongs that were ever committed against me.

Now, this part about my side, what I had done, where had I been wrong. My ego had kept me from looking at this, but now I began to see that this was where the real freedom lay. I shifted positions and set down the pen for a moment. "Gary, I think I may have done much worse to others, than anything on my list that was done to me." The truth weighed heavily on me as I prepared to turn the pen on myself and continue to write.

"You can feel like you're right, and continue to try and prove you're right, or you can be free and look at what needs to be changed in you rather than always looking at what needs to be changed in this world. What's it going to be, Stanley? Do you want to be right or do you want to be free?" Everyone around me shook their head contemplating this question not for me but for themselves. He had our attention.

A lone tear ran down my face. "I want to be free, Gary."

Gary smiled wide. "Once again, no choice, the only reasonable option, my friend." Gary laughed, pointed his round finger, and shook his large hand in my direction. "Continue writing, but now about yourself, the real problem. Ride the bus today, tomorrow, and the next if needed until you are complete with the instructions."

I pulled my pad of paper and pen up from the seat, then stood up and headed to the back of the bus for writing time. The route was about to begin, and my seat was needed. I took my seat on the back of the bus and started writing; after all, I had no choice. There were no other reasonable options. There was no friendly direction other than a lone seat on the back of the bus.

Chapter Twenty-Five

Darkness Before Light

This November was especially dark and cold. A low cloud cover had hung over the city for days. For the next eleven days, I rode the bus. I wrote, asked a few questions of Gary, and received my next instructions, and then I would write some more. As I wrote, I watched the daily routine aboard the bus.

I saw many people board and disembark the bus, some in the morning and some in the evening. A dozen or more each day, that had obviously received, or were in process of receiving, the same teachings as me. Each and every one of them had something I wanted. They had clear eyes and warm welcoming smiles. They were truly happy and had that attractiveness that's irresistible in truly spiritual people.

I found myself drawn to all of the students and would listen in on the conversations they would have with Gary. I was totally blown away at the exchanges. I'd look up from my writing each time I heard Gary and his infectious laugh to see he had just struck a chord with another one of his students. My love and attraction to Gary grew, as I watched him help others. He was a man on a mission to be sure. He was a spiritual warrior. He preferred to say, "I'm just one of God's kids doing what my father asks."

I wasn't the only one watching and listening. Besides the obvious students many men and women, busloads each day would board the bus and jockey for positions close to Gary. They were there not to ride the bus, but to listen into the words of a spiritual master. Even after the morning rush hour, Gary's bus was still full, while other buses sat idle, awaiting the evening commuters Gary's bus was full from the first stop to the last, throughout the day they came. I would watch many ride for an hour or two and then get off at the same stop they had boarded at. They were there for Gary and his teachings. Word was getting out and I had a front row seat.

The riders were young and old, some taking time off of work to ride. Mothers hurried to ride the bus while the children were in school. The lunch hour each day was packed as businessmen and women rode, listened, and ate their lunch.

As I continued to write and look at each resentment, it became clear to me that these resentments were ruling my life and that the desire to look good at all costs had caused much of my anger. Any time I was wronged, it was about me not getting what I wanted and what would other people think. I would become full of fear (what is everyone going to think?), and then the anger would come. If I didn't get my way, I would become angry at whoever was the easiest to blame—the likely target. I would never look at how I had entered into the situation. How I'd caused the problem. How I'd shared the blame. I blamed others and became angry. All out of fear. Fear of what others would think.

I saw that when my wife had taken the children and left me, I was angry; nobody should leave me. What are my friends and family going to think? Nobody should leave me. I'm such a nice guy. Everyone is going to think I'm a jerk. How dare she leave me and put me in this situation. How will I survive and pay the child support? I want to have a happy marriage. She should love me no matter what.

I was having an experience, that this type of thinking, of blaming everyone else, dominated my being. I began to see that this type of thinking, that this blame game, affected every area of my life.

I looked at my roommate, John, who had left me hanging with the rent when he'd moved out. I was angry. No one should do this to me. My friends and family should see that I have my act together. No one should interfere with the things I need. I should have a nice place to live; no one should interfere with that. I should always have rent. No friend should do this to me. Never remembering that I had stiffed the landlord when I moved out in the cover of darkness. Later a requirement of finding freedom was that I would have to set this matter straight.

These hidden perceptions about myself, that I should be seen by all as having my act together, that my family should see that I am successful in life, that I should have a stable job and be well liked and admired on the job site, that I should have a stable marriage. The hidden belief in all of this was that people should see me this way even when it wasn't true! I needed everyone to see me as a loving and successful father and husband. I needed them to see me as a success in life. I needed them to see me as happy and willing to help anyone, at anytime. I needed others to see me this way *in order for me to be OK*. I needed others to see these attributes in me, even when they had never really existed. *I blamed for my failure anyone who interfered with my delusion.*

I looked at my former boss. He'd fired me. No one should fire me. I'm a great worker (false belief). Everyone should see that I could have and keep a good job. (I'd never kept a job for long.) Without a job, I can't survive, nothing should threaten my survival. No one should get in the way of my wanting to have a good job. I need a good source of income. My boss should like and care about me.

I wrote on all of those I'd blamed in this manner, looking closely at each one. Why was I angry? What areas of my life are being affected? What beliefs, feelings do I have that cause these areas to be affected? I wrote on over one-hundred people (ex–wife, boss, etc.) places (jail, my old public schools, etc.) and belief-systems, prejudices (racism, right-wingers, etc.) and on. I then brought it all to Gary.

I arranged to meet with Gary one hour early and I read some of what I had to him. He stopped me after a few minutes of listening to my delusions and interjected. Waving his large hand in disgust, he cut me off, "Stanley, you have now done something in writing that you do in your mind constantly and have for many years. You figure out whom you are angry at, apply blame in the way of why you are angry, and make it their fault that things are not going well in different areas of your life. How much time have you spent thinking about what your wife did to you? How that affected your life?"

After a moment of silence, I realized I had been asked a question. "I don't know... I guess a lot of time." I replied.

"Almost constantly," Gary answered for me. "Your days and hours have been spent thinking about someone else to blame or what you could get for yourself. What a useless life!" He shook his head from side to side in pity, and then continued, "It is now time to quit pretending and set that all aside. Set it aside entirely. Look at what your part is in this. Look at where you did wrong, what were you trying to get out of it. What were you after? Try to see where you were responsible."

"I'm not sure I know how to do that." I inquired.

Gary laughed at my comment, "Not only don't you know how to do that, but even if you did, you would be unable to do so. Continue to pray until the knowledge and power come."

I nodded, letting him know I understood, stood up, paper and pen in hand, and went to my spot in the back of the bus.

I took my seat and realized I was now writing my life story in the same seat where I had once injected drugs. I was, in fact, on the same bus. God had seen to it that I would see the truth in the same seat where I had sat in compete and total delusion. The same seat, the same bus, the same driver where I had felt like I was in hell. I now sat in that same seat and felt like I was in heaven. Nothing on the outside had changed. I thought about God and his possible plan for me. I began writing, first the following prayer:

Lord of the happy joyous and free,
Thank you for helping me see the truth.
I have always blamed others.
I can never clearly see my part.
Remove the ego that has protected me all these years.
The time has come where ego now creates more harm in my life
than good.
Allow me to worry less about other's wrongs.
Allow me to see the truth about my own.
Amen.

I wrote, looking at each person, place, and thing I'd been angry with. I saw the truth for perhaps the first time in my life. It was a massive blow to my ego and pride. In other words, exactly what I needed. Where my ex-wife, Olivia, was concerned, it hit me especially hard. I was a drunken, drug addict. The children were better off without me. That was the truth. I'd given her many more reasons to leave than to stay. I'd scarred her, intimidated and manipulated the whole family. I'd financially bankrupted all of us. I was a terrible husband and a worse father.

I wrote it all down. The ink flowed from my pen, and it was a devastating blow—I could no longer live in the delusion that Olivia should have or could have stayed with me. I was dealing in truth for the first time.

I looked at my old roommate, John. I was a drug-addict—he was not. He'd tried to help, and I'd lied to him about being clean. I'd conducted illegal activities in the apartment and told myself it wasn't hurting him. The truth was that he was in danger of being associated with my lawlessness. I took his rent and used it for drugs, then lied to him about how far behind in the rent we were. I'd made dozens of unkept promises to get clean and pay up the rent. My fear of what others would think and of becoming homeless was used as a basis for attacking John—for not paying the rent. I blamed him when I did get kicked out of the apartment.

I'd ruined a relationship with someone who had shown genuine love for me and compassion for my situation. I realized that I'd hurt those who tried the hardest to love me. I treated my enemies better than my friends. At least with the enemies they knew where they stood and could get out of harm's way. Not so with those who loved me.

I looked at my old boss, McGregor. I'd stolen from him without ever thinking it was wrong... perks of the job, I thought. The truth was I was a thief. I'd never thanked him for all he'd done for me. Besides providing very good employment, he'd tried in every way to help, putting me through treatment, twice, on insurance he'd paid for me. He didn't let me go until I showed up drunk, one day out of my second treatment, asking for a draw on my next paycheck. I stole from him in the way of calling in sick when I was really withdrawing from drugs or too loaded to show up.

I realized for the first time this was stealing and lying. I lied about my drug use. I never thought about what I could offer on the job, of what I could bring to the table. I always looked at it as in what he owed me. I never thought about how I could be of service. How he needed good employees. I was ungrateful.

I wrote in this manner that day and the next and the next. I felt depressed and yet enlightened. I knew that I couldn't go on another day like I was. It was the dark night before the dawn.

I'd been writing for eleven days, on and off. When I found myself blocked, I returned to thinking about God and my prayer:

Lord of the happy, joyous and free.
Thank you for helping me see the truth.
I have always blamed others.
I can never clearly see my part.
Remove the ego that has protected me all these years.
The time has come where ego now creates more harm in my life
than good.
Allow me to worry less about other's wrongs.
Allow me to see the truth about my own.
Amen.

This process allowed a flow of power the likes I'd never known, and I saw things as if I'd been reborn into a new person. Each time I paused, I thought about God and his hand in all this, I knew that there was a new power in my life as I continued to write. I finished all the instructions Gary had given on this subject. It was, all of it, down on paper.

Chapter Twenty-Six

The Path to God

The day came, after riding the bus and writing for days that I was to read what I'd written to Gary. I had a notebook—full.

Things with the New Thought Church had been going well and Pastor Tony had been helping me with my writing. Any time I felt blocked she would seem to know and would ask how the writing was going. She was truly an angel. The soft aura surrounding her always put me at ease immediately, no matter what my current emotional state. She outlined the maintenance and cleaning I was to do around the church each night after I arrived home from riding the bus.

Cleaning, painting, and preparing for services were the chores of the day. I liked being trusted and given new responsibilities. Pastor Tony always reminded me that I was being provided for, not by her or by the church, but by Spirit. I was being given this work to provide for myself, so I could do the real work of riding the bus and writing.

The small cash I was given at the church was enough, just enough to get me through each day with the necessities. I truly was being provided for, and this time in my life was a gift, a constant reminder that I need not want, for anything. God would provide what I needed, just to the extent that I sought each day to do God's will.

I was late leaving the church after a terrific morning with Pastor Anthony. Gary's route for the day had already begun. I went to the nearest bus stop to the church and waited. Within a few minutes of my arrival, Gary's bus pulled up to the stop. One older gentleman got off; he smiled at me and waved as if we were longtime friends. I returned the greeting and boarded the bus with notebook in hand. I was prepared to talk. The bus was full of students and passengers, only a few seats remained open. The seat directly across from Gary was one of them.

Gary spoke first, "Good morning Stanley, I can see you are ready for a talk."

It was a statement of fact. I was impressed rather than startled. I'd seen this too often, Gary's ability to know what was in my mind even sometimes before I did. I wanted that. The ability to be aware, awake enough, to sense the needs of another human being. It takes the reduction and ultimate goal of elimination of ego to begin the process of having what Gary had. Gary had the ability to feel another's needs and then place those needs ahead of his own. It was beautiful. That's the ability to live the spiritual life. Its beauty is overwhelming.

I took the empty seat across from Gary. That seat was always open when it needed to be. My seat, but not really my seat. This experience was for me, but not for me only. I began to read. I started with my ex-wife and mother of my children, Olivia. I read, and Gary listened. Not only did he listen, but he also rubbed my nose in what I was seeing. I saw that I was in each instance at least partly to blame. In most instances, it was I, and not the other person, who was to blame. I saw I was trying to get something for myself and had placed myself in a position to be hurt.

As I read and we talked, I became completely unaware that we were surrounded by people. Some came and went, others were there for the same reason I was, to be in the presence of Gary. They sat and listened in support of my awakening and to take home some of the lessons that spilled over from our conversations.

With Olivia, I'd left her with no choice, in a position where the only choice left was to leave. For the good of herself, the children, and even me, she left. I had held this against the children and gone over and over in my mind how my downfall was her fault. I had the story so well-rehearsed that I could easily find strangers willing to go along with the idea that I'd been taken advantage of and irreparably harmed by a jealous, money-grubbing, controlling witch. I had even attempted to swing our mutual friends to my way of thinking. Even her family was barraged by a constant flow of rhetoric from me.

The bus came to a stop several times, then it would merge back into traffic and continue its journey. All the while I read, and Gary taught school, using each of my resentments as examples. The driving of the bus, the stopping and returning to traffic, the picking up and dropping off of passengers was secondary to Gary. He was teaching class and I was the example for this day. I didn't mind. I wanted to be in his presence and more I wanted to be free. This was the cost of the ticket.

Gary let me know, in no uncertain terms, the only way to make this right was to visit all of those I'd harmed and make restitution to those I had harmed.

"Are you willing to go to each of these people, Stanley, to visit them and tell them you were wrong?"

The questions flew from Gary faster than I could answer. I wasn't meant to answer I thought.

Was I willing to do this? To go to each and every one of them and admit I was wrong? To find out what it was that I could do to make it right, and then do it? Was I willing to go to Olivia and the children? To each of the former friends I had talked to and apologize for putting them in a position to choose sides? To ask them for their forgiveness, and most of all to admit to each and every one of them why Olivia had left me? To tell them the truth?

To talk to my family, and hers, and tell them the truth as I now saw it? Then, and only then, would I earn the right—the gift to be able to approach Olivia and make an amends to her. I would need to ask her those same questions and do whatever I was asked to do to make it right. Even if this meant living amends, for the remainder of my life. To be a decent father and ex-husband on a daily basis.

"Gary, this seems like quite a bit to do. I know how wrong I've been, but to go back and look for these folks, some of them I haven't seen in years. I'm not sure I'm willing to go that far. It seems a bit much. I haven't used drugs or alcohol in months. I have a place to live and a job. I'm trying to live the spiritual life. It seems that this is enough. Do I really have to dig up the past?"

The two passengers closest to me let out an "oooh" they knew the answer.

Gary didn't answer, but took a moment of quiet time. I thought he was concentrating, for a moment, on his driving. He pulled the bus over at the corner stop. The bus slowed, the brakes squealed slightly, and we shook gently to a stop.

I saw no one getting up to leave, and no one was waiting, so I wondered why Gary had chosen to stop.

"This stop is for you, Stanley," he said, very matter of fact.

"For me?" I responded. "What's going on?" I asked surprised.

"I can't help you any more, Stanley, I only have time for the willing. And you are not willing. My time here is short, and I have no time to screw around."

I was devastated, and at a loss, as to what to do. I'd seen Gary angry with me in the past, but not like this. I had actually witnessed this a few times in the past with other passengers. Gary just pulling over and telling folks they just weren't willing or were not ready when they didn't want to follow suggestions. It was never mean spirited or egotistical. Gary was what he said. A busy man who did not have time to screw around with the unwilling who really wanted to suck up some of his spiritual energy without doing the work he had done to get it.

The door to the bus was open, but I couldn't bring myself to stand up, gather my papers, and walk off. I knew he was right. There would be no room for a lack of willingness; I needed to be willing to go to any lengths. If I didn't, I knew I would lose everything. I had to go forward. My inability to walk off the bus was evidence that I really didn't have any choice. Once again there was not friendly direction outside of my seat with Gary. My thinking that my opinion on this process counted for anything was another of my long list of delusions.

I slowly began to cry and heard myself say the following words, "Gary I'll do anything, please help." I heard the bus door close, and we continued. The bus pulled away and back into traffic and the same people who had gasped when Gary had gotten quiet, now clapped. I felt like I had passed through another barrier, I had passed beyond another obstacle that blocked me from the sunlight of the Spirit. The bus started and stopped as Gary continued to drive, somehow able to concentrate on the bus and his driving, greeting each new passenger with a friendly nod and a smile and bidding farewell to those getting off. All the while I read… many listened… Gary would comment… and I would read some more.

The conversation went on through the day and into the evening. I stayed on the bus for the entire route, and we returned to the bus depot, all along I read. Gary continued to press anytime I had trouble seeing the truth or retreating into delusional thinking.

Gary's day had ended, so he parked the bus in its stall among the hundreds of city buses and gathered up his paperwork. We both got off the now silent and dark bus.

"Wait here for me, Stanley. I need to take care of my end-of-shift papers."

I waited for Gary, feeling exhausted at what had already been a very long day. A few moments later, I saw the large silhouette of Gary heading my way. We proceeded together, through a gate, into a parking lot and to Gary's car.

I recognized the old, green Ford Galaxy as we approached. I got in on the passenger side, and Gary struggled to fit behind the old car's steering wheel. I could feel the car sink under his weight. He managed to get the old Ford to start after pumping the gas pedal with his right foot a few times.

"We'll have to let the old girl warm up a few minutes. She really likes to sit and take her time getting going. We have that in common."

We both laughed. It was a welcome break from our day's work looking at one very selfish, self-centered, deluded, immoral, self-righteous, ego-centered life.

After a trip through the Burger King drive-in, we sat and ate in silence. Gary bought and ate two Whoppers, a large fry, a large chocolate shake, a baked pie, and a large coffee. I ate a hamburger and drank a Coke. Gary loved to eat. I think it gave him as much pleasure as anything apart from talking about God. He loved that even more.

Gary's style of talking about God could only be described as extremely unorthodox. It was a style that had an impact of great depth on many lives. Gary was never afraid to tell you the truth, the real truth. Gary had no desire to provide motivation for you to seek God; he knew that that motivation had to come from a personal life that was becoming overwhelmingly unbearable. Mine had done that. I needed no motivation to seek to know and do God's will. My motivation came from extreme failure in life. I saw just how completely I'd failed as I read to Gary. I had failed utterly in being a son, a father, a friend, a coworker, a productive member of society, a husband, a caring person, and most of all; I'd failed at self-sufficiency. Gary knew where this knowledge of the truth would lead me. It would lead me to God.

Chapter Twenty-Seven

Willingness

We drove to the church and parked, then Gary instructed me to continue. We'd looked at everything I had held against others. A hundred or so items in all. Many began to blend together, and when I looked at the pages, all I saw was delusion. In places where I'd thought I'd seen so much truth, I now saw only a deeper level of delusion, the delusion that I was going to do anything about these on my own. I needed God's help and I knew it at an entirely new level. No amount of therapy, pills, women, money, well-intentioned friends and relatives, prestige, or my own ego could help. I was in deep. Over-my-head deep.

We finished by going over the list of fears I had made. Looking at each one, Gary pointed out that these were preludes to resentment. I was in fear and wasn't getting what I wanted, so I resented. I saw that these fears were the result of my own attempt to live life on my own terms. When I failed to live up to what I thought I should be, I was left in fear. The more I tried, the more I failed, and the worse my fears became.

But there was a better way: to get about the business of leading a God-centered life. My fears were a lack of trust. From fear came anger and blame. I couldn't stand to admit I was wrong, about anything. I lived in fear that, any day, I would be discovered as a fraud. I was afraid of everything. I was afraid to be successful, because I would leave friends behind and what would other people think? I was afraid not to be successful and everyone would see what a failure I really was. I was afraid to live without drugs and alcohol, and I was afraid to go back to my old life. The level of my fear stood exposed. Exposed to God, to Gary, and to the only one who didn't know—me.

Gary reached across the car seat and took my hand in his. His large warm hand gripped mine tight. We bowed our head together, and Gary asked me to repeat after him:

Lord of the happy, joyous and free
I am so afraid.
I fear most of all failure.
And I have failed.
On my own will, I will die alone and afraid.
In your arms, I will survive.
Connected to all.
Knowing nothing but love,
I ask here, in this moment,
To know your love, rather than my fear.
Amen.

Gary had led us in the prayer, but somehow the words were mine. They came from his mouth, and I simultaneously said the words with him, although I'd never heard the prayer. I knew then that God was speaking through both of us, the student and the teacher.

Gary lifted his head from prayer, pulled a handkerchief from his coat pocket, and removed his hat, wiped sweat that had accumulated from his brow. "Stanley, I'll give you three simple instructions that will take a lifetime to complete."

Gary had written the following list on a three by five-inch card and handed it to me.

1.) Seek to know and do God's will.
2.) Give what you have found to others.
3.) Any time you think of trouble, think of God instead.

"You can't live up to even those three simple instructions on your own, can you?"

I sat, looking at the list he had handed me, and knew if I could've lived up to that I would've a long time ago. I breathed out heavily and then answered, "No, no I sure cannot."

"You'll need God's help, Stanley. God helps those who help themselves. There are some things God has already given you the power to do. Do those things, and God will provide you the strength, each day, to do one more day's worth of the right living. You say you are willing, so we will see about that, won't we?"

He didn't wait for me to answer, but laughed. We both laughed. I'd cried many times throughout the day, both sweet and bitter tears. Sweet tears as I was coming to know God, and bitter tears as I saw how terribly I'd harmed so many. I'd promised to see each of these people in time and make a complete amends to them. For now, I was to live a life that would earn me the right to see these people in person.

"See you at the church on Thanksgiving."

I knew this was the end of the evening so I opened the car door and stepped out.

"I love you Gary" I said as I shoved the door closed.

"I love you too Stanley."

The old car started up and pulled away.

Chapter Twenty-Eight

For Those Who Receive
Much—Much Is Asked

Pastor Tony was heading up to what would be the New Thought Church's High Holy Day. Thanksgiving. It was the one day of the year the church went all out. This year, I was a part of the planning and would be a part of the celebration as well. I felt deep pride in the church and was very proud of to be a part of it.

The church felt that Thanksgiving should be a holiday that people of all backgrounds and religions should come and feel a part of. There was no particular religious connotation to the holiday. It was about gratitude, and everyone could share in that. It was a service designed to allow all people, regardless of religion or lack of religion, to experience the spiritual uplift of fellowship and praise. It was a day the New Thought Church showed their gratitude by opening the doors and putting on a feast complete with music, dancing, and a church service on Thanksgiving and Gratitude. I'd heard Pastor Tony and many others sharing these types of feelings for days and was very excited to see what the entire hubbub was all about.

Much had changed in the few days since my reading to Gary. I'd contacted Olivia and the children and told them of my newfound experience, and of the New Thought Church. They were skeptical, of course. Gary had told me not to have any reasonable expectation about them sharing the spiritual experience I was having. In their own time, they would see, that I was a different person. That day would be up to God. For now, I was to show up and be a good father and a supportive ex-husband to Olivia.

Each week I would receive $200.00 from Pastor Anthony for my work at the church. I was, under Gary's direction, sending $150.00 per week to Olivia, for her and the children. I had argued at separate times with Pastor Anthony and with Gary on this issue. I'd made the argument that I should be able to keep half. I'd lost on both accounts. They won, I was one of a family of four and I would be allowed to keep only 25%. Since I'd not paid for so many years they were quick to point out I was lucky they allowed me to keep a dime, fifty dollars a week is not much to live on, but it really was, all I needed. I was being provided for, my rent was paid. My food came mostly from meals at the church. I needed $27 for a bus pass a few cheap grocery items. I truly had all I needed. I was being provided for.

I invited Olivia and the children to come to the church for Thanksgiving dinner, but they declined. They had plans to go to my former in-laws. There was a time when I would've gone with them. I was saddened to be separated from them. I'd loved them in so many ways, but without God, what I had shown them wasn't love in any way. I knew why I wasn't with them on this Thanksgiving. I was grateful to know why. I'd always thought the reason was Olivia, but it wasn't. I knew the truth. It didn't feel like freedom, but indeed it was.

The plan was to open up the church for a day of feasting and joyful prayer and music. Pastor Tony had blessed me with being in charge of publicity, so I made signs and posters, then spent my days plastering the city neighborhoods where I used to practice my addiction, putting up flyers for the New Thought Church. I saw many of the people I had been associated with, and rather than avoid them as I had done in the past when trying to steer clear of temptation, I was now drawn to them. I would cross the street to give them a flyer and tell them of my experience with Gary and the New Thought Church. Most thought I'd finally cracked, but I could see that they were all curious as to what could've made such a huge impact on me. I could see the darkness in their eyes and the hopelessness on their faces. They, in turn, could see the light in my eyes and the hopeful spirit of my being.

The day before Thanksgiving, Pastor Tony came to me as I was preparing to head out with yet another stack of flyers. I'd handed out and posted over 500. Some in the church were worried that too many would show and that there would be a shortage of food. Pastor Tony brought us together each night for a prayer that each person who showed up would be provided for. Her faith was amazing. She knew, absolutely knew, that God was the provider of all things and God wouldn't let us down so long as we gave all credit to the Great Spirit who provides for us all.

Pastor Anthony appeared as I was about to leave for another day of promotion, putting up flyers and extending an invitation, a smile, and a handshake to those who were all alone in this world. She was in a light grey sweat-suit, her hair pulled back, and wearing no make-up. I could see she had gotten up and not showered—going right to work. She had been working like this for days, morning till night. Working tirelessly, she was the director, giving orders, cooking, and making certain every detail was attended to.

"Stanley, hold up there," Pastor Tony barked, as I was about to leave. "Tomorrow will be a work day, do you understand that?"

I had one hand on the front door and a stack of flyers in the other. "Yes, I think so." I answered.

"You are here to serve others?"

I could tell that this was somehow a question, so I answered. "I'm here to serve others, of course."

She said only one word and it was again obvious that this was a question. "And?"

It seems like I've been here to receive, but I understand that it's my job to ask, "What can I do to be of service today?" I answered my hand still on the door but now I relaxed my hand and looked directly at Pastor Anthony and gave her my full attention.

"Good, then you will do as you are asked?"

Again, I could tell this was a question, "Yes, I will do what is asked," I responded. I was getting nervous and was sure I was going to be asked to leave for something I had done or be asked to stay in the kitchen and out of sight tomorrow. My mind raced. The old fear that I was not good enough raced back into my being. I still held tightly to the door in one hand, wanting to push my way out before I received any bad news. I stayed frozen to the inside of the church's door. I gripped tightly to the flyers in the other hand.

"The format for tomorrow is prayer, just with the staff for forty-five minutes in the morning starting at 5:00 AM in the chapel. Then, we'll begin cooking. Music will be playing, and we will serve meals from 11:00 AM till 6:00 PM. At 6:00 PM, we will have our annual Thanksgiving service in the chapel. It will be fairly short, a few guest musicians and a guest speaker who will talk for ten or fifteen minutes on the topic of Thanksgiving." She smiled, put her arm around me, and continued, "I would like it very much if you would be our guest speaker tomorrow."

I was stunned, nervous immediately, and wasn't sure at all I'd heard her right. My hand fell from the door, and I turned and faced her directly. "Why me? What should I say? I...I... just don't know. What about Gary? Gary could do such a great job."

She looked deeply into my eyes to explain, dropping her arm from around my shoulder and lightly holding my empty hand. "Gary doesn't speak in public, just not for him. But you, you will be our speaker. You see in the spiritual world sometimes it is the one with the newest experience that can impact those seeking a better life. Your experience is new and fresh and will have an impact on someone, maybe even a few of those who new b you in your former life. Now head on out and get those flyers delivered. I just picked the pockets of a few more of our wealthy friends and bought twelve more turkeys with all the fixings, so round up some customers. I don't want any food left over that could have gone to feed our friends."

The rest of the day was almost unbearable. I was very grateful and knew I had something to say. I knew Pastor Tony was right. I would be a speaker. I found no particular pride in that knowledge. In fact, it scared me to the point of almost being sick. I posted the flyers and returned to the church and helped with the preparation for the following day's blessings.

Chapter Twenty-Nine

Give and You Shall Receive

5:00 AM came early, or late, as I barely slept. Pastor Anthony, Gary, Shelly, Dr. Malik, and a dozen or more volunteers had already gathered for prayer when I entered the chapel. We prayed and did meditation together. Shelly was asked to close our circle with a prayer and offered the following:

God, as we work this day of Thanksgiving.
Guide our thoughts to service.
Allow us to resist the temptation to preach.
Rather allow us to teach,
Through our actions,
About your love.
Amen.

The day was truly amazing. More that 600 came through the doors of the church. Most ate and left. Many stayed and helped. Many more brought food for donations, dropped the food off with no expectation of reward or praise, and left. Some came by with cash or checks and wanted to know where to donate. Many people came for a short visit and were caught up in the spirit of goodwill and were unable to leave, so they stayed to help serve their fellow women and men. Some laid out their bedrolls and slept, sensing that they were safe in the confines of the church. I was so busy I couldn't think about my talk, now only a few hours away.

I witnessed, with the others, a real miracle in the making. Where I'd been worried about running out of food, people were bringing food for donations in huge lots and dropping them off for the church's food bank. Checks were dropped off. Families came, clean-cut wealthy families, and sat shoulder to shoulder with the homeless men and women. They shared in conversations and in acceptance of each other just as they were.

You could feel the love in the room. It was as if there was a barrier at the front door, a spiritual gateway of sorts, that when you passed through, you left all preconceived ideas behind and only expressed love. Watching the day proceed, I realized that the church was receiving far more that it gave. I also knew that Pastor Tony knew all along this was how the day would unfold. It was truly humbling to experience redemptive goodwill toward others, bringing about a spiritual awakening in the church. In giving, the church received, more than it could ever have imagined. All in the room awakened to new possibilities in their own lives and in the world. I saw clearly that only love could help us and that only love could help me.

Leftovers were abundant, and we began packing up gifts of food for the most needy, the elderly, and those with children to take home. I missed Olivia and the children, but knew I was where I was supposed to be. We began setting up the chapel and announced for those who wished, to join us for good music and fellowship. I was so nervous my mind put me in a dream state. I was going through the motions, but was a bit out of touch. I think this was God's way of keeping me from cracking under the nervous pressure.

Gary was in the front row of the chapel as well as the Maliks. A large crowd had gathered to join us. Pastor Tony began the service with the instructions to spend a few minutes in quiet consideration of all that we were grateful for. So much came rushing to me that I was overwhelmed. I could feel my body shaking and cried as I held my head in my hands. I silently prayed.

God as I understand you.
Fill me with your love,
And allow that love,
To overflow from me,
Into the people gathered here.
Amen.

I came out of prayer with a real sense of peace. My insides and outsides quit shaking. I knew what I would say, at least where I would begin.

Chapter Thirty

Thanksgiving

I was aware of my name being used as Pastor Anthony spoke at the podium. She was wearing a long, bronze-colored, wool skirt that hung nearly to the floor, only exposing her high-heeled brown boots. A warm, brown, knitted scarf hung loosely from her neck and over a shiny, silky blouse, buttoned close to the top of her neck.

The prayers, meditation, and song were over, and it was close to time for my talk. I sat in the front row, petrified and waiting for Pastor Anthony's last words to finish.

"Thank you for coming tonight, we all appreciate your participation in our Thanksgiving celebration. In speaking about gratitude and Thanksgiving, it is my belief that the newest experience, the person closest to receiving the blessings for which they are grateful has the best, most honest, and humble message of all. In that light, I have asked one of our church's newest members to give our closing Thanksgiving talk here tonight. Stanley Pearson has become an honorable member of our church family here. His hard work and dedication to the church over the last four or five weeks have made him a member of our family, in good standing. His experience has also made me strongly believe that he will go onto great things in the world of the Spirit.

"Please help me in welcoming one of our newest church members and a truly amazing individual, Stanley Pearson."

I stood and approached the pulpit. I gave Pastor Tony a strong embrace, pulled back, and shook her hand, and told her I loved her. She, took a seat alongside Gary in the front row. I took a drink from a glass of water that had been left for me. My mouth was already completely dry from nerves, and I hadn't even begun to talk. I bowed my head for just a moment and asked God to speak through me. I looked at the crowd, and they all looked back. I could see the encouragement in everyone's eyes and could feel the love pouring from everyone's spirit as I began my talk.

"I cannot begin to express the level of gratitude I'm feeling to be here today. To be free of drugs, free of alcohol, and to have been brought to such a beautiful family; such a loving fellowship, such a radiant church. To know you has been to know the presence of God in my life. It's all so very overwhelming to me; I've been humbled at depth. From where I came from to now being asked to speak during a Thanksgiving prayer service… in a church!" A few sensed the irony of what I was talking about and laughed with me. A sweet laughter born of gratitude, I continued.

"Just over six short months ago, I wanted to die and was in the throes of addiction. I was resigned to a miserable, lonely and useless existence. I happily awaited the bitter end. I, today, am grateful for that time in my life, for each day today is sweeter than the day before. I have gratitude for the simpler things in life. I know firsthand the dark despair. I now know the brighter, new life, when we come to know a God of our own understanding

"I'm grateful today for this church—for it is a true home to me. Well it actually is my home!" They laughed again many knowing that I lived in a room at the church. I welled up again with emotion, so grateful at the simple idea of having a roof over my head. I'm grateful for the spiritual lessons that seem to show up each day, each week, and each month just as I am ready to accept them. I'm grateful for my children, and for their mother, even though I'm not with them and miss them very much. I'm grateful for the knowledge that without allowing God's love in my life, I'm a failure, and that by being open to God's love in my life, I am successful. God's love was always there, I was just wasn't open to it. I am so grateful to have found this new way of life—the spiritual life.

"I am especially grateful for the willingness I've found to remove those things in my life that block me from God's love, from the Great Spirit, that through this experience I've come to know the truth about myself. I know I'm a liar, an addict, a neglectful husband and father, an ungrateful child. I am grateful to know these things because knowledge of the truth is what sets us free and there is nothing more poignant in that statement of fact than knowing the truth about ourselves. That is the greatest truth there is to know, the greatest discovery of all times. To know that it wasn't them to blame, but my own selfishness and that my only hope is in living the spiritual life. I'm grateful to have those people in my life that are teaching me to apply the spiritual principles that will solve all of my problems. For every problem there is a solution, the solution is always a spiritual solution. Gains outside the spiritual world are always unsatisfactory and do nothing to heal the true soul and solve the real problem. The real problem is me, my ego, my childish demands that others live their life to meet my unreal expectations of how they should live and make me look good. For this knowledge, I am truly grateful.

"What is gratitude? I can only tell you my experience, and that is the feeling you get when a shiver runs up your spine as you realize how good it is to be alive. Gratitude comes from the knowledge of the presence of God, its essence is in the awareness of the presence of God. If you want to know what God's presence feels like, it is the feeling of gratitude. There is no awareness of the presence of God without the presence of gratitude.

"There is no gratitude switch that I can turn on. It's a gift from God, and I arrived at this gift after putting some simple spiritual practices to work. I used a few prayers that the members of this church gave me. I showed up when and where I was told. I wrote when told to write and waited while I was told to wait. I stayed quiet in the presence of another human being, no words were spoken but the language of the heart was heard loud and clear.

"I questioned who was to blame for my bitterness, ill will and dissatisfaction against others. These things, along with willingness, bring me here today in your presence—a very, very grateful human being, knowing the truth about myself and knowing today the presence of God as I understand God today.

"Gratitude is the awareness of God, and in that love, I cannot know fear or hatred or be conceited. Every day should be Thanksgiving, every moment grateful. This is the goal of the spiritual life, to seek real humility and to become right-sized among our brothers and sisters.

"Gratitude is love, and love and hate cannot be expressed in the same moment. Gratitude is love, so love and fear cannot be expressed in the same moment. Gratitude is love, so we see all things clearly and illusion is exposed. Gratitude is the presence of God, and in the presence of God, all problems can be solved. There is no problem that cannot be overcome by the realization of truth. The truth of all that we have, of all that God has provided. Sometimes when we seemingly have nothing, we need to look deeply, but God's presence is always there. Sometimes, it is only the hope for a better day, and we can be grateful for that. This is the intended purpose of gratitude, the awareness of the presence of God.

"I can remember a Thanksgiving, not so long ago, when I spent most of the evening at my family's home in the bathroom. I was deep into my addiction and needed to use every twenty or thirty minutes. I had brought my supply to get me through the evening. I continued all through the night to head to the bathroom and would emerge glassy-eyed and lost.

"I barely touched my dinner. My family was worried, but no one knew what to say, so there was an uncomfortable silence that fell like a dark cloud on the evening. I'm grateful that this Thanksgiving I can come out and be with you. I am grateful that I don't have to spend this Thanksgiving hiding in the bathroom alone with a family that loved me in the next room in disbelief

"Today is Thanksgiving, one day a year we can really think about all that we are grateful for and ask God in our prayers to help us become aware that no matter what our present circumstances—we have much to be thankful for. I live in a church, have no real job, and I'm separated from my family and from my children. I have much harm from the past to clean up, and if the future is anything like the now, I can't wait.

"I love you all so much for helping me from a place of being lost to a place of being found, here with you. I cannot put into words how much help this has been and cannot wait until I can return the love when I find and help one who is as lost as I once was. This is such an honor to be allowed to express my gratitude and to give my Thanksgiving to God in your presence here tonight. I hope you will all stay, and if anyone wants to talk about how I got out from under my problems and rose above that level of thinking, I would love to talk to you in person this evening."

I ended and looked directly at Gary in the first row. He had been there all through my recent journey. He had shown up today, minus his beret, with his long grey hair pulled back neatly and tightly into a short ponytail. He had removed his coat as well, but other than that, he was still wearing the pants, shirt and tie, and black shoes of the Metro uniform.

I stood looking at him as he rose to his feet and began to applaud, a very slow, but powerful and loud clap as his giant hands came together. Pastor Tony was next to stand, then the Maliks and others. Within seconds, all were on their feet, clapping and crying, smiling and happy, full of gratitude and joy. There were also many a lost soul such as I was a short time before who were I suppose clapping because I was finished and they were full of good food and could return shortly against their own will to the suffering with the lost hope that their addiction would once again give them some relief.

For the rest, I knew they weren't applauding me; they were applauding the Spirit of God that moves and performs miracles in all of our lives. They were standing and applauding their own sense of gratitude and well-being. I'd only moved something inside of them. I'd been the vehicle for God to speak about what we all knew and felt deep down within us. I had reminded us all, about the things we know, but so easily forget.

I'd been on the verge of tears all the while, but now wept openly. Pastor Tony, looking as lovely as ever, approached the pulpit, embraced me, and I her. She whispered into my ear, "You told the truth." Pulling back and looking at me with a wide-eyed surprise, and then a smile, a warm lovely smile. She gave me a gentle kiss on the cheek. I took the seat she had vacated in the front row alongside Gary. Gary placed his arm around my chair back and gently pulled me to him. We bowed our head as Pastor Anthony led us in the closing prayer:

Lord of the happy, joyous, and free.
We thank you for your presence with us tonight.
We ask for the awareness of your presence,
In our hearts and in our minds.
We recognize you as the source of all things good.

And so it is.
Amen.

Gary, the Maliks, and many of the others shared in my tears of gratitude and joy. I was so very blessed. I always had been, but now I realized it. I felt fully alive and awake.

Chapter Thirty-One

Blessed Are the Poor, Theirs Is the Kingdom of Heaven

Things had changed so much for me since Thanksgiving; winter was in full swing and had brought a light snow to the area. Christmas was only a few days away. My life was so different, so far better in every way. Most of all, my thinking had changed, my outlook on life had changed, and I seemed to be able to see things as they really were. I had a place to live and a life. I was living, but God was now living my life.

Each day, when I awoke, I would turn my thinking from myself to what I could add to this day, what I could bring to the party, and what I could do to help someone in need.

I still had one thing that, more than any other, still depressed me. I'd not yet made things right with my children. My son, Alex, now nine, and my daughter, Andrea, now seven, were coming to stay a few days for the Christmas break. A miracle in itself as I had long since lost any right to see my children. I had re-established some communication with Olivia, the children's mother, and told her my entire story. I'd promised to make the best living amends to her and the children that I could.

I'd listened as she told me how my former way of life had affected her and the children. We'd both agreed that the best way I could make it right was to be the best father possible and to participate fully in raising our children. To be a loving and supportive father and ex-husband. To help support them financially. I'd begun to live the amends. Olivia had given me something I absolutely did not deserve. A second chance at something I had destroyed. I knew God had touched her heart as well, for her to want me to participate in the family at all was a miracle as sure as any I'd ever heard of.

I had no money for Christmas presents, or a tree, or decorations. I had managed to save a few dollars each week, after paying my support to Olivia, and had just less than $100 in a bank account I'd just opened. I knew I would need the money in the bank for bus fare, food, and personal items to get me through the month. I decided to pray and asked God in my morning prayer what the right thing to do would be:

God,
As I make the amends,
To my family,
Please bring me an answer.
Show me how to be a father,
Show me how to be a loving ex-husband.
Show me how to be an example,
To my children,
Of your love,
Of your way of life.
Amen

I felt tremendous guilt over my past treatment of the children and their mother. Gary constantly reminded me that the damage was done over years and that it would take years to completely make right, and my job was to seek to know and do God's will in my life, and then all things, including my children, would be taken care of.

I came out of prayer that morning somehow knowing I needed to go and see Gary. I left the church and went to the nearest stop on his route and waited. The depression was thickening, and the cloud over my head was becoming darker. Olivia would be dropping off my children in a few hours, and I had no idea at all what I would do for our Christmas together. I had set up a room at the church, and there were toys from the child care center, but there was only so much we could do in the church and I was broke.

It was the first Christmas in five years I could remember having shelter and being with my children. More than one time I had called to say I would be at the family home while they were there. I would say that I'd be bringing presents and to tell the children Daddy's coming. In each case, I would really mean it. I planned on how I would get money, get cleaned up, and get home for Christmas. And in each case, I spent Christmas in a drug-induced stupor, pouring alcohol and drugs into my system as fast as I could, trying to kill the pain.

The memory of what a poor father I'd been weighed on me, along with the self-pity of not having enough money to give my kids the Christmas I felt they deserved.

I pulled myself out of my self-loathing just in time to see Gary's bus pulling up to my stop. I could always tell the exact moment when Gary would see me at one of his stops. He looked at me and always laughed, he could always tell just by looking at me that I had something quite important on my mind. It always turned out to be not nearly as important as I thought. This time though, I was sure it would be different. This was important, and there really was nothing I could do to help the situation. The kids were coming, and I had nothing to offer them.

I boarded the bus and took my normal seat across from Gary. I didn't smile or ask him how his day was. I just blurted out to Gary and anyone sitting in earshot. "My life sucks, Gary. All this hard work, and my kids get another letdown at Christmas. Is that how God would have it, Gary?"

"No," Gary replied, with the same indifference I was giving him. He didn't smile or try to calm me down. He continued driving without even looking my way as he continued. "This has to do with you, Stanley, not with God. That's your first area of wrong thinking on this matter."

"Wrong thinking?" I said, as if the concept was completely crazy, "No Gary, this isn't wrong thinking, I have one-hundred dollars to my name, two kids to be at the church for a Christmas weekend, and no presents. If I use the money, I won't have food. I need to save for a phone. I won't even have bus fare, and I have to put my kids up in cots at a church! I'll probably end up back on the streets. Is that the way this works, Gary? What the heck am I supposed to do here?"

I began to cry, not a hard cry, but a silent cry. Tears ran down my cheek. I felt so low, I didn't even attempt to wipe them away. An angry feeling welled up inside, I was breathing shallow, and my heart was beating fast.

Neither of us said a word. There was a minute or two of silence as Gary made a few stops, picked up a few people, and dropped a few off. As always, these days the bus was packed and if you were talking to Gary, people were listening. All were quiet in the moment. I sat seemingly alone. Gary's voice broke the silence.

"I see that we really have only one reasonable option here, Stanley. You say you have a bank account?"

"Yes," I answered. "I just opened it a week ago. First American on Jackson Street, right by the church."

"The bank closes at 5:00 PM I'd guess," Gary replied. "Go back to the church, meet your kids and then meet me outside the bank at 4:45 PM and bring your kids. I'd like to meet them."

The children showed as planned. They really loved the church, and there was so much to do and so much to explore. There wasn't a lot going on, they were running wildly up and down the stairs and going completely nuts, just being kids. No one seemed to mind, least of all me. It was so great to have them with me and to see them laugh. There had been so many times I'd yelled at them for making this kind of a racket, for being kids. The days of my children walking on eggshells were over.

I 'd seen Olivia as well. It had been difficult, but I could see in her that she sensed a real change had taken place in me. I assured her that the children were in good hands and introduced her to Pastor Tony. Any fears she had were eased, and she was finally able to leave the children and be on her way. I thanked her deeply for trusting me with our children.

I arrived at the First American bank on Jackson street just before 5:00 PM, my children were by my side. Gary had already arrived and was waiting outside the bank. I introduced the children. They immediately liked Gary, and he sparkled in their presence. I had no idea why we were here. I had, however, come to trust Gary and had come to believe that I, most times, had no idea what was best for me.

"Leave the kids here with me, Stanley, and go in and close your account," Gary said with a smile.

I was utterly surprised. I looked at Gary with wide-eyed shock, but didn't want to argue with Gary in front of my kids. He knew I had just opened this account, and he knew that I had less than $100.00

"Get it all in one-dollar bills. We'll wait here in my car," he added.

I noticed the old green Ford parked in front of the bank; a twenty-minute meter was running. Looking at the kids I instantly knew they trusted Gary. He had that quality, the ability to cut through all barriers and gain instant trust and cooperation from anyone. In that moment, I watched first Alex and then Andrea take a step away from me and towards Gary. They knew I was to follow this man's instructions. I knew it as well, I told the kids to wait with Gary and that I loved them and turned and headed into the bank to close and account I had, only a few days before, been so proud of opening.

I did as was told and came out of the bank, having closed my account with ninety-six, one-dollar bills. All ninety-six dollars were in an envelope that I clutched tightly in my hands.

Gary was in his car, Alex was in the front seat with him, and I climbed in the back with Andrea. Both Andrea, and Alex, were laughing hysterically at something Gary had said. It was so beautiful to see the kids loving Gary and having such a good time.

We drove downtown and parked. We bundled up, as it had started to snow. It was an especially cold evening. Gary instructed me to pull the money out and split it up! I wondered to myself how I would eat, this money was all I had! How would I feed the kids! My look at Gary said it all, I took a few deep breaths that could be felt through the entire car and gave each of the kid's thirty, one-dollar bills and split the remaining bills with Gary, as I had been instructed to do. I wished each of them a Merry Christmas and kissed each of my children softly on the cheek. I felt better already giving the kids some money, something for Christmas. The worry about being broke and not having money to live began to leave me, and I was just happy to have given the children something.

We walked a few blocks to a park where I had spent many nights as a homeless drunk. It brought back waves of gratitude to be here with the kids and with Gary. Gary gave away the first dollar and wished a homeless woman a Merry Christmas. Without any further instructions, we all followed the lead. I followed next and gave two dollars and wished him a Merry Christmas. "God bless you," he replied. A wave of gratitude swept over me as I saw myself in the man's eyes. I recognized the hopelessness as I had seen it on my own face so many times.

Gary again handed out a dollar as we walked, and again wished a homeless man a Merry Christmas. Gary looked every bit the part of Santa, and the man called him by name, "Merry Christmas, Santa." With this, the children shrilled with excitement, feeling they were in the presence of greatness. And they were.

Little Alex was next and gave away three dollars to a man drinking wine from a brown, paper bag. He was so brave I thought. His younger sister, Andrea, was a little shyer and not so forward, but soon followed her brother's lead, and the two of them began going from homeless person to homeless person, as was I, handing out a dollar here and two dollars there and wishing each person a very Merry Christmas.

A smile had taken my children's faces captive. I was so proud of my children and tears of joy fell from my face many times in the next hour. It was an especially cold night and now the snow was coming down in flurries. Alex and Andrea were throwing snowballs at Gary, and we were throwing back. I was happy, the children were thrilled, and Gary, looking like Santa Claus, was happy to be with my family. The children, fancying themselves as Santa's little helpers, had handed out all of their dollar bills and looked like the happiest children on earth.

As we headed back to the car we played and joked with each other. We laughed and hugged, threw snowballs. Wished everyone in earshot a Merry Christmas and in general lived in those moments like nothing else in the world mattered but being present in the moment. I wanted it never to end. It was almost 10:00 pm when we were finally settled back into the car and headed back to the New Thought Church.

Gary dropped us off, and he wished us all a Merry Christmas, and turned to me as I got out of the car. "Wealth should always be judged by how much we give, and tonight, you are the richest man I know because you have given everything."

I knew how incredibly lucky we were, and I'd never imagined such joy at being so broke. It was already the best Christmas my children or

I had ever had. When we arrived back at the church we were hungry and headed downstairs to the kitchen. Pastor Anthony had left a note.

To a rich man and a rich man's children, I love you all.
There is stew on the stove.
See you tomorrow,
Love as always,
Tony

The table was set for three.

The next day, friends of Gary's and friends of the church began to come by, one or two each hour and continued over the weekend, they brought food and small gifts for the children. One brought a tree, and one an envelope with enough cash to purchase groceries for a week. These people were now my true family, the family of folks I had met or recognized from rides on the bus and services at church. Many I had come to know just since my talk on Thanksgiving.

I knew it was grace and that I had done nothing to deserve such wonderful friends. I was coming to know a love unlike anything I'd ever known. I was also coming to know a new trust in God and a new appreciation for the spiritual law of giving in order to receive.

Chapter Thirty-Two

Your Heart's Desire

The holiday season had passed, and my beautiful children had gone home to Olivia. My only prayer for the New Year was that I would come to know what God's will was for me. I loved my life in the church. My restored relationship with my children was sweeter than any I'd ever known. There were a few answers to questions about the spiritual life that eluded me though. I knew where to go when I needed answers to the most difficult spiritual questions. I went to Gary and began riding the bus as often as I could. As soon as my chores were done for the day at the church, I would head for the nearest stop and wait.

It was nearly impossible now to even get a seat on the bus. Many times, these days Gary would be completely full of riders, of students. When we pulled up to a stop, if four were waiting, four who had been aboard the longest would have to depart. Some days I would get off and wait the hour until Gary had done one complete round and came back to the stop again. I was not alone. I found it necessary to come very early or show at the very end of the day when Gary would finish his route and head back to the bus depot for the night. I would ride along for those wonderful, special, priceless moments alone with Gary.

At the end of one particularly long ride, I was the last one aboard the bus and had moved forward to the seat across from the driver. As the last person departed, I asked, "Why do you do this, Gary? Why are you helping so many people?"

We sat at the last bus stop of the day. Gary hit a few buttons to move the sign to "Out of service" and flipped a few more switches to shut off the lights in the cabin, darkening the bus interior. Gary turned to me and replied, "I can't, not do this. It's within me, it's my heart's desire."

These moments with Gary, alone, I wouldn't have traded for anything on earth. To be alone in the morning or alone on the bus at the end of the day, alone with Gary was the best. It was, each day, more and more difficult to find time with Gary, as so many were now riding the bus, trying to hear or overhear the words of the master. So many, like I, rode the bus not for the destination, but for the journey. Word had spread through the city that a very special, spiritual man was driving the route number forty -three, University District to Downtown.

I knew how precious this time with Gary was and leaned forward, full of questions I wanted to get out. "How do you know what your heart's desire is?"

His eyes were so bright, even in the dimly lit cab of the bus. It was as if there was an internal light burning. He looked at me, penetrating and softening my spirit with each moment. He stroked his beard, rubbed his eyes, and thought briefly, before answering.

"Your heart's desire is that very thing that you have inside you, but are afraid to talk about. That very thing that you have always wanted. What's your heart's desire, Stanley?"

He had answered my question with one of his own. I always thought the answers were inside Gary. Gary knew the truth: the answers for me, were inside me. He was pressing me to answer my own question. I closed my eyes and thought, but nothing really came to me. I had a few things I wanted, but none seemed real enough to vocalize. "I guess, I don't have one... not really sure... umm... don't know."

Gary laughed out loud and shook in his seat. When the laughing slowed, he said, "Take just a moment here and think about the question. We all have a deeply ingrained desire for something... what's yours, Stanley?"

I closed my eyes again and leaned back firmly in my seat. I let my head rest gently on the window behind me. I looked into my own heart and felt such an attraction to what Gary was doing and wanted also to help others. *I had thought a lot lately about wanting to be a minister. Shoot, what a terrible idea, I wasn't even a good Christian and had been a drug-addicted criminal and general hoodlum most of my life. A minister! Get real:* My mind was racing. Gary's voice startled me and brought me back to the here and now. I sat forward and opened my eyes.

"Well, what's your heart's desire, Stanley?"

I only had to wait a moment for the answer, "I've been thinking about being a teacher, a teacher that pulls from all the great traditions of the world, teaches that we are all the same, and that all paths lead to the one great place, to one God. I want to share this good news with all different people in the world, to bring people together under one roof so that they may hear the good news that one God loves each and every one of us as we are. I want people to know that a heaven of sorts is available here on earth to all religions and those with no particular religion as well—the only requirement is that we live a life of self-sacrifice and service to others, to live the spiritual life." I stopped, somewhat shocked but in the same moment relieved at what had just came out of my mouth. I smiled at Gary, strangely a bit embarrassed by what I'd just said. What if Gary thought I was getting way ahead of myself here?

"You've been brought up to another level here, Stanley. Can you feel a

change?"

"Yes."

Gary took a deep breath and then letting it out, turned in his seat a bit to face me more directly. "What you hold inside will destroy you and what you bring forth will give life abundantly. We all know what our heart's desire is— it's no secret. Mine is helping others to find this way of life."

"Then why are you driving a bus for a living?"

"Because my heart's desire is to help people and ask for nothing in return, no money, no favors, no demand. We've no right to expect everyone to share in our desire and our spiritual experience. I have to pay for my food, and my landlord would appreciate a check once a month. The Tall and Big Shop clothes aren't cheap either, so I need money." He smiled and winked and then looked back to the road ahead and continued.

"I'm so very grateful and thank God every morning that he made me a bus driver so I can earn a living and carry out my heart's desire each and every time I come to work." His voice quivered, and I saw his eyes well up with gratitude, and a single tear ran down his face. He was truly the happiest bus driver in existence, because he wasn't driving the bus to exist. He was so much more than a bus driver.

We pulled into the bus depot and parked in his spot. He would return, like every day after a meal and a few hours' sleep in his chair. I knew the pressure on him these days was tremendous. Everyone wanted a few minutes of his time. I had seen first-hand the huge crowds these days at every stop. I wondered how he could continue. How the city bus authority could allow it to continue. God had hijacked a city bus and word was out.

As we sat parked, Gary shut the engine down and pulled himself from his seat and began collecting his paperwork for the end of the day and his belongings. I wanted our time to never end. I had only time for one more question so I fired away.

"Gary, how do you let all these people feel you really care for each and every one? You have so many coming to you for help."

Gary standing now and looking down at me replied.

"I'm not sure what you are talking about"

He usually understood most questions even before I asked so I was a bit puzzled and rephrased the question.

"You know, how do you give each person such a small amount of time and yet still seem to give them the feeling you care about them so much?"

Gary again looking a bit perturbed by the question answered once more.

"Stanley, I honestly have no idea what you're talking about!"

I pressed once more before coming to the realization I was not going to get a different answer.

"Gary, you have so many people looking up to you, how do you handle it? You just seem to have this ability to give a small amount of time to many and yet they leave feeling like you really love and care for them. I'm just wondering how you handle that?"

I stood to leave with Gary and we walked together off the bus and into the parking lot. Gary smiled very widely and put one of his large arms behind me and around my shoulder. Smiling wide he said one more time.

"I really do not know what you are talking about."

This time I got it. I realized deep down within myself that Gary was truly a humble man. He was absolutely refusing to accept any kind of guru status. Absolutely demanding that I accept him as he accepted himself, a child of God who had been given the gift of driving the bus.

As Gary drove me back to the New Thought Church I one more time had had a spiritual experience that changed my life. I knew that I wanted to be a spiritual teacher. I knew I was solely responsible for the footwork needed to accomplish this, and most of all I knew I was free to use my will in this direction all I wanted. I knew that this was my will and God's will in alignment, and I knew that all true heart's desires were like that—God's will and human willpower in line with each other.

I had stopped on that day, wondering what I was going to do with my life—I knew. It was God's will, God's will for me. I had a vision and an idea of how to accomplish the vision. I knew, without a doubt, that I had the power of God working for me. There's nothing on this earth so powerful as an idea whose time has come. It was time. I had the power. God's power, through me.

Chapter Thirty-Three

Exiting the Silence

Another day, another bus ride with Gary, I thought as I awoke. I sat drinking my morning coffee and trying to practice the morning meditation Gary had taught me. I was on this morning, practicing silence. I'd been given instructions, that for this week, I'd sit in silence twice a day, for twenty minutes each time, minimum. I was to sit with no thought of anything. I did think however, about how I needed to get going to see Gary, how I needed to get my work done and get going. I had to quiet the urge to dash out the door to hurry my day.

I was to allow myself to slip into what Gary and Pastor Anthony called "the Great Unknown." As I practiced the presence of God in this way, I was to watch for what thoughts would pull me out of the silence. At first, I could only sit for the shortest of moments with no real thought, and just observe the silence. At times, I would notice that I was thinking about the silence. I was aware of a thought saying, "Listen to the silence." This wasn't the silence I was seeking, but a thought about the silence. Gary said this was ok as I was aware of the thought and could gently remind myself to relax and observe only the quiet.

I noticed time and again that work around the church was what would come to mind, some phone call I needed to make, or an unfinished letter. I was performing more and more tasks at the church. I was in charge of collecting the money, balance bank account sheets, working with vendors on repairs, and making many of the repairs myself. Always, there was something I needed to do, something I needed to get done, that would somehow make me look better to everyone else.

These were the things Gary said blocked me from God and separated me from a spiritual experience, keeping my spirit asleep. The things that separated you, from me.

There was always something to finish. Some project to be completed. I had a vision of whom I wanted to be and how I needed to get there. I'd indeed been brought to a place I could've never imagined even existed, especially for a person like me. My vision was becoming clear in these times of silence and meditation. I felt the strong urge to carry a message and be of service to others, in the way Gary, the Maliks and Pastor Anthony had carried a message and been of service to me.

I came out of my meditation and noticed I'd been in meditation for twenty minutes without experiencing any real tranquility. I finished my coffee, had a quick bowl of instant oatmeal, and left. It was 9:15, and Gary's bus would be pulling up to my stop in fifteen minutes. As I walked the half-mile to the stop and thought about this vision, I'd felt frustration over not being able to complete this task of helping people and carrying a message about the *sleeping spirit* to all.

I wanted to shout from the mountaintop for all to hear that real happiness came through a spiritual experience as a result of working simple spiritual principles into one's life. I wanted everyone to know it doesn't come through medication taken for the chemical imbalance of depression, from getting the right job, from finding the right partner, or even from repairing my God-given flaws. It came through an honest to goodness spiritual experience. I felt I had something to say, but no platform to stand on. The truth was I wasn't ready, yet. I was far too evangelical about what I had experienced. Honestly, it would be hard for anyone to take. I needed to learn to calm down first.

I came upon my stop and waited. Soon I could see that the bus was stopped one stop away and heading toward me. I was always filled with anticipation for when I knew I would see Gary.

As I boarded the bus, I wished Gary a good morning, the door closed behind me, and as Gary signaled and began pulling the bus back into morning traffic, an elderly woman I'd never seen before stood up and headed to the back of the bus, vacating the seat directly across from Gary. This was a part of the unwritten etiquette of riding the bus. If someone was boarding that needed to talk to Gary and you'd had your time you would give up "The Seat." I knew I had only a few minutes and I would be expected to give up the seat to the next person who came to visit.

"Thank you." I graciously acknowledged, I took the empty seat that faced me directly to Gary.

Gary asked me the first question of the morning. "What one thing brings you out of the silence the most consistently?"

I thought a moment, then answered. "Things I need to get done, you know, work and things around the church, phone calls I need to return."

Men in business suits and women on their way to work, briefcases in their laps, all were leaning in to hear our conversation. Gary was asking me questions and giving me answers, but was not talking to me alone. Gary had told me once. "I talk to you, Stanley... because if I talked to them, they wouldn't listen." They were listening now as Gary asked his next question.

"What would happen if none of those things that bring you out of the silence got done?"

I thought long on this one and found what I thought was the truth. "I'd be a mess, things would fall apart."

"No, think more deeply, not on the surface, but what would happen to you, to the I-am?"

"I'd really feel bad, would feel embarrassed that I couldn't handle things."

"You're really worried about how you look to others, this is what brings you out of the silence and back into the ego. Your sense of self is so large that you won't allow yourself a few minutes of silence without thought of what you need to do to look good to others. You work so you can maintain an image that's not either who you are or what you want to be." He laughed, a deep belly laugh that convinced anyone that Gary saw humor in everything, divine God-given joy. "You're working for them instead of working for God."

The bus slowed, and Gary maneuvered out of traffic and up to the next stop. The other riders and myself were all laughing with Gary as three women and one man boarded. They were used to this in the morning, and all took a seat as close to the front of the bus as they could. No one read their paper this morning, or most mornings.

Gary was right, and by the look on all the faces on the bus, they knew he was right as well. We all could relate to the tireless effort we all exert in trying to live up to other people's expectations. He was right, and I told him so. I went on, as the bus pulled back into traffic and headed downtown.

"I want to carry a loving message to others like you've done."

"My task is unfinishable, Stanley."

I pondered the meaning of this statement, looked around at the others seated with me, and we waited for the clarification.

"When carrying a message to others becomes more important to you than how you look to others, then and only then, can you begin to fulfill your vision. Go into the silence each day, into *the great mystery, the great unknown* until the thought that brings you out is a thought of helping others, a thought that isn't about how you will look to others.

A thought that isn't about how busy you are or should be. When this thought brings you out of the silent meditation on a continual basis, then you are ready to carry a message of love and service; the spiritual awakening!"

Gary pulled over at the next stop and a young man, maybe still in his early twenties was waiting at the stop. I intuitively knew my conversation with Gary was over and that I had received my next instructions. I had sat in the seat for ten minutes or less. It was not all the time I wanted with Gary but it was all I needed. The bus was nearly full now as it was. Nearly all day every day, the bus was packed. I'd come later in the morning and received instructions. I got up, thanked Gary and walked off the bus.

I had a nearly four-mile walk back to the New Thought Church. I never minded the walk after riding. It gave me time to really go over the instructions I'd been given. It was my time with God after my time with his messenger.

Chapter Thirty-Four

Life Is Unfinishable

A few days went by, and I was tempted to go see Gary, but was working more hours, as time passed, at the church. I was now full time, and the church was growing. I'd been given more responsibilities in the church community and in the well-being of all church members and the building itself. I'd recovered and actually had a life beginning to blossom outside of riding the bus.

I was practicing the quiet meditation every morning and again at night. I noticed the trivial thoughts that occupied my mind... prestige, wealth, sex, and importance: I remembered the many times Gary had told me that the deadliest thing to the spiritual life was a feeling of importance. Any time I felt more important than any other human being, I now knew I was in delusion.

I was living an inspired life, and many times had inspirational thoughts about where I wanted to go in life and how my life could best benefit all. I found that when I felt inspired, I could feel the flow of God into me. That when I was thinking of thoughts that were spiritually bigger than myself, I could transmit this inspiration to others with kind gestures and loving and powerful words.

Certain activities brought this about. I had a vision that one day I would be a minister and teacher. I wouldn't preach the traditional gospel, but would preach to whoever God brought to me about the spiritual awakening that's possible by the surrender of self and application of spiritual principles into one's life. The simple spiritual principles that Gary had been teaching me in our sessions aboard the city bus. This vision was larger than I, as it was such a short time ago I'd been a drunken, drug-addicted, broken man, bankrupt in every way, spiritually bankrupt, morally bankrupt, physically bankrupt and of course flat broke. Now I was being filled with the spirit of God to carry the message of hope, oneness, love and recovery through self-sacrifice and service to others.

I knew then what Gary had meant when he'd said, "My task is unfinishable, Stanley." I had a vision of teaching others. I knew that I would be one to carry a real answer to many. I knew now, also, that this was so much larger than I, that it would never be finished. Long after my spirit would leave my physical body, my message should continue in others. The same way that Gary's message would continue in me long after he'd leave the body of the fat, funny and loving old bus driver.

I knew his spirit was now in me and that it would never leave. We were interconnected. As time began to pass, I noticed that when I had a question for Gary, I only needed to be quiet. The answers would come now in prayer and meditation as often as from the conversations with Gary. It came to me then that there was no finish line in life. I could relax and take it easy, as my job was unfinishable, and bigger than I, so there was now no hurry, no urgency.

"My job here is unfinishable." Gary had told me. Now I was participating in life, not just living but a part of life. Something that existed for an eternity before I was I, and something that would continue forever after I was gone. I could relax, I was involved with all of the human race, with the eternal light that flows between us all and will never be extinguished. I knew what it meant to be a part of life at last.

I sat in the church late at nights and wrote sermons on all matter of subjects. Subjects I had struggled with and was finding answers for. I would sit and write and had the certain feeling and knowledge that I was being used as a vehicle for the message that was coming through me. I'd be next in a long line of spiritual teachers. I was willing to go to the mountaintop, if God would have me. The human race has still not received the full gospel—all of the good news. God delivers more of the gospel to us each and every day. My job was to bring whatever God gave me to his children. Daily, I was given inspiration to write, given by a power greater than myself. My writings always amazed me. I had no idea these ideas were in me, and when I went back, some days later, and read, I knew I was being guided by something much greater than myself. My vision, of God's will for me, in my life, was bigger now than anything I would ever accomplish. And much bigger than anything I would've ever imagined for myself. Rather than frustrate me, I was humbled by the overwhelming trust God had in me to entrust such a large vision to one of his children who had turned his back for so long to the love of God. God knew how much it took to get my attention, and now that he had it, he wasn't about to let it go. I now lived the life uncommon, a life of daily intuitive thought. An inspired life. The life we are all meant to live.

Chapter Thirty-Five

Seek To Know Nothing

I t had been almost a week since I'd last rode the bus. February was approaching, and once again a light snow was falling. The temperature had dipped into the twenties. I took the whole day off from work at the church and went to see Gary. I awoke early to get aboard before his route started. As always, he was there. I'd come to count on him. He was there when I needed him, and I always knew how to find him.

I approached, and it seemed that he looked as happy to see me, as I was to see him. He had that effect on everyone, I'd noticed. He had the ability to make you feel he was genuinely happy to see you. You could relax in his presence. I wanted that—and that I did get. I had much on my mind, but Gary was the first to speak.

"Make yourself comfortable. City transit aims to please." He said in a loud voice as if welcoming a crowd. His laughter at this little quip was all I needed to feel at home. He was sipping coffee from his thermos cup, his hands covered in wool gloves with the fingers cut off. A green, knitted scarf hung around his neck. A cold breeze blew in every time he opened the door on these cold wintry days. He was dressed to stay warm, and the extra layers made him appear even larger than he was.

I settled into my seat. "I missed you, Gary."

"Yeah, it's been awhile, are the answers starting to come to you, Stanley?"

I was a bit taken aback, but had come to count on Gary knowing why I'd come. "Yes, I've noticed, Gary, and the more I've noticed, the more I'm inspired to teach the *mystical life* to others. To teach about a spiritual awakening and recovery through self-sacrifice and service to others. I've seen myself helping others the way you do, but I doubt I can have all the answers the way you seem to."

He laughed again, only this time I wasn't so comforted. "I don't have any answers, Stanley, never will, and you'll never have any answers either. You're in luck though, because there's one who has all the answers and that *one* is God. There are many paths to God and many variations on this path, and many ways people view God, but there is only *one* message. The message I carried to you. It is the Father within that doeth the works; it is he who makes the crocked way straight. The same presence exists within you Stanley, and in no fewer amounts. We are the same, you and me. Not a little bit alike but exactly the same!"

He took another large drink from his coffee and continued.

"The message can be found in many books and in many different formats, in many different traditions and in many different languages. There is, however, only one writer working through us all and that one writer is God. There are many different art forms and many different artistic ideas, but there is only *one* artist and that *one* artist is God.

"God works though us, will do nothing for us, or to us, but will work through us. God has worked through me, Stanley... worked through me to awaken the spirit within you. As you go from here, keep your spiritual house in order, and continue to seek to know, and have willingness to have removed, those things that block you from God. Then God will flow through you freely and into the lives of others. You can be a waker-upper any time you decide. There is only *one* who has all the answers and that *one* is God. And the greatest news of all is God is in you!"

He pointed his finger directly at me and he smiled wide, his eyes twinkled like the brightest star in the night sky.

I knew he was speaking the truth. I knew God was within me. At least I wanted with all my being to believe the way Gary believed.

Gary continued.

"With this knowledge, you have your next assignment. Tell yourself, many times each day, 'I know nothing. I've been wrong about most everything in my life. Especially those things I thought I was mostly right about.' Tell everyone who will listen how little you know. And listen to others, really listen.

"The thing that blocks most of us from this knowledge, from the *one* author of all the spiritual traditions of the world is self-knowledge, I don't want to know—I want to experience."

Gary was in his element and was on a roll this morning. He was intense with every word and every word flowed as if he was channeling God himself. His eyes were staring right into mine. He had set down his coffee and was speaking with motions of his hands as well. I was mesmerized, hanging on every word. He took another deep breath, paused for a short moment and continued.

"When I experience something that's good and I can be comforted in the fact that this is my experience, I can share what my current experience is with others.

"When, however, I think I know something, it shuts me down and blocks me from all other experiences concerning the subject. Blocks me from the *one* God! I can carry a message to you because I know nothing!" Gary paused, grinning widely now, almost laughing.

Several people had approached, and Gary opened the door each time until ten or twelve, mainly businesspeople had boarded. All sat as close as possible to hear even a few words from this bus driver, who knew nothing. Gary looked at his watch; it was time to begin the route. He switched on the sign indicating the bus was now in service, checked his mirrors, put the large bus into gear, released the airbrake with a "whisssshhhhh" sound and pulled the bus into traffic. Approaching the next stop, he began speaking again as he slowed the bus once more and opened the door. Another dozen or so boarded the bus, everyone sat as near to the front as they could, some even stood even though there were empty seats in the back, the crowd was already in position. We were there for the experience of the ride, not the destination.

Gary went on. "Stanley, I know nothing, so I become an open vessel for the spirit of God to flow through. His message comes through me and is not of me. I'm just a bus driver, Stanley. It's the God you see in me that carries the message. It's the God in the authors that does the writing—*one* God! It's the God in the artist that does the painting—*one* God! Be free of what you think you know, and God will flow through you and into the lives of many." He had our full attention as he continued to talk and watch traffic maneuvering the large bus through traffic.

"God is all-knowing—that means that he has all knowledge. If God has all knowledge, then how much do you have, Stanley?" He turned and glanced my way, raising his eyebrows in a way that let me know this was not a direct question but something for us all to ponder.

I thought… I knew the answer. I have no knowledge and thinking that I do blocks me from the flow of the *one* who does have all knowledge. Gary knew nothing so he was an empty, open vessel for God to work through.

Gary pulled over, making another stop. The bus was filling quickly, and all were keeping as quiet as possible, to hear what the master had to offer. Gary took a sip from his cup, set it down, and drove the bus gently into traffic. He smiled at me and winked. I knew, that he knew, that he had an audience. He began again. "Once in a while, a man is born that seems to be able to help many thousands, sometimes millions of people, but for most of us, we can take care of our families and try to help a few others along the way. Are you one who will help a few like most of us, Stanley, or are you one of the few who will help the many?"

I was slightly self-conscience of all those listening, but spoke as loudly and as clearly as I could without appearing that I was talking to anyone other than Gary. "I've been trying to figure this out myself."

"Just checking to see if you thought you might know something." He laughed once again and so did several of the passengers.

He added, "The next stop is yours." The door opened, and I wasn't anywhere close to where I wanted to be. I stood up. A middle-aged woman in a smartly dressed suit slid over immediately into my spot. I knew better than to argue, so I got off. I knew that my lesson for the day was over, and the woman in the suit's lesson was beginning. I thought about telling Gary that this wasn't my stop, but knew this would be thinking I knew something. This time I laughed.

I waved good-bye in the early morning cold as the bus full of Gary's students pulled away. I had come to the bus stop full of questions, none of them had been answered directly as I hadn't even been given the chance to ask. They were no longer important anymore. I knew I had been called to help the many. I knew it was their questions that were important. I would seek answers from God now to share with others. I knew nothing, God had all the answers. I only needed to seek God.

I'd come to the bus stop, having taken an entire day off from work to ride the bus. I'd been aboard fifteen to twenty minutes. This was the way it was with Gary now. He had so many coming; I knew that I had been so fortunate to have so much of his time and attention earlier on. I was grateful for every moment I had with him and knew I would take even a few seconds in his presence today. I wondered what I would do with the rest of my day. I prayed for direction:

God,
I am an open vessel.
Take me to my next assignment.
Fill me with your love.
Amen.

Chapter Thirty-Six

The Golden Rule

As I walked toward the church, my mind raced, trying to absorb what Gary had just told me. Was I to help many or help some? What did I think I knew that would block me from God, from *the one*? I'd felt the flow of his presence through me many times. I knew the basic truths of what he'd told me. I knew I was a recovering know-it-all. I knew that when I had all the answers, I was suffering the deepest. Conversely, when I gave up and admitted that I was nothing, my suffering began to subside. I knew that most of my anger was caused by "knowing" I was right about something.

I walked on, the cold weather forced me into stopping. I entered into a small coffee shop and bought a large coffee, and sat down at table in the back. I sat quietly, sipped my coffee, and thought. *One author of all the spiritual literature of the ages? One painter of all the art and sculptor of all time?* It made sense to me, and I began to get out of the way. I bowed my head and went into prayer:

God,
Father, mother, and child.
Lord of the happy, joyous, and free.

I am small and unknowing.
Free me of the shackles that bind me to my own intellect.
I know not how to act without acting.
I know not how to talk with clarity and truth.
I know not how to walk with purpose.
I know not how to help without hurting.
I know not how to be happy, really happy.
I stand ready to move from selfishness to helpfulness.
I stand ready to move from where I am to where you are.
Take me now. I am yours.
Amen.

As I opened my eyes, I could see the patrons of the coffee shop, the baristas and through the window in the cold winter's day, I saw a man. Hopelessness was written on his face in the sad and hollowed eyes and the down-turned mouth. He looked in, and our eyes met through the window. I knew I had to talk to him, and the power of the prayer that had just flowed through me had given me a sense of real purpose. I left my coffee and the patrons of the shop behind and exited onto the sidewalk.

The cold hit me as soon as I opened the door. I pulled the hood of my jacket over my head and looked to my right and then to my left. My new friend had taken a seat on the sidewalk, leaning his back against the brick exterior of the Baxter Street apartments. This was a place I'd been many times. The old building was infamous for the drug dealers and addicts that frequently used these apartments as flophouses, shooting galleries, and places of business for drug deals. I'd been here many times, desperate and hoping that someone would show up and feel pity on me and take me inside to get well. I saw on this man's face the same desperation. I knew if he had money, he would go inside, and temporarily there, find relief.

He was sitting, in the snow and cold, against his will. He was wearing a black knit cap, pulled tightly over his head. The "Raiders" emblem flipped up in the front, exposing his face. He was my age, maybe a little older. His face was sunken-in, exposing the cheekbones and making his eyes appear sunken further into his head than they really were. He was unshaven and unclean. His oversized, extra-large jacket with an Oakland Raiders logo fell over his knees and he had tucked his legs up inside the jacket for warmth. Here sat a man, as hopeless as I'd been, in the same place I would've been sitting less than one year ago.

As I approached, once again our eyes met. I stopped, standing over him, and introduced myself. "You look like you might need a little help. My name's Stanley." I reached out my hand, and he only stared ahead with the blank stare that let me know he saw me and heard me, but didn't care.

"Can you spare some change, Stanley?" He said, without looking up.

Remembering the lessons I'd been taught, I pulled a twenty-dollar bill from my wallet and handed it to my new friend.

"What's your name?" I asked calmly as I handed over the money. I could see I'd sparked some interest in the man, and for a moment, I could see a glimmer of what looked like hope, as the money set off the obsession over the drugs he knew would soon be entering his system. His only hope was really a delusion that there would be any real relief. I knew it, he didn't.

It was an illusion, but I knew to him, at this moment, it was all too real. "My friends call me, Lobo." He finally answered, staring in disbelief at the bill I'd just handed over.

"Well Lobo, I used to sit right here in this exact spot and hoped that someone would come by and feel pity on me and take me inside to get high. I know most all of the dealers in this building." I was nervous but spoke as slowly and calmly as I could.

He looked up at me for the first time. "You don't look the part," he answered with serious skepticism. "Could be the cops," he added.

"Well, Mr. Lobo, when was the last time you heard of the cops handing out twenty-dollar bills to the drug addicts?" I smiled at him, rubbed my hands together, and blew warm air on my now freezing hands.

He stared back at me. I could tell he was listening, but knew I would soon lose him in the obsession for the drug he would soon be buying with his twenty dollars.

Again I slowed my speech and spoke calmly but intensely "You see, my only job is to be helpful, my life depends on it. Depends on you! I was once where you are and have found my way out. Was lost and now am found." I never thought I would hear those words coming from my mouth. I took a deep and intentional breath, looked around and then back at Lobo. "I have a real answer for our type, for any type that is, who is as asleep, as I once was, and as asleep as you are now."

"… Asleep?" he interjected. He smiled and shook his head from side to side as to dismiss me as a religious nut. When he smiled at me, I could see his darkly-stained smile and several missing teeth. Personal hygiene had not been his strong suit.

"Yeah, sure man, asleep," I replied. Speaking quickly now and in a slightly raised voice I went on. I knew I had a minute or two at the outside. "I'm awake, so I can tell you that you're walking around asleep and only dreaming that you are awake. You're so asleep that you are easy prey for drug dealers. They take advantage of your lethargy each time you inject drugs into your body, trying to get the feeling of being well, the feeling of being whole, the feeling of having a purpose, to lose the fear that someone, someday is going to throw you away. Does any of this sound familiar, Lobo? Wake up, dude! I tell you to wake up now and come with me, and I can show you a new way of life. A way to know your creator and to have a sense of purpose. A way to learn to live each day in the sunlight of the Spirit." I inhaled a deep large breath of the bitterly cold air and then exhaled deliberately with a gasp.

I saw the first of many tears running down his face. He was trying to hide them, but now they came. His long shaggy brown hair hung in front of his face, and as he lowered his head, it partially hid what was taking place. One after the other, the tears came, it turned into a stream running out of each eye and no single tears.

"I know the desperation of a spirit asleep. I know because I've been there, and I now believe that there is no more painful condition than for a spiritual being like yourself to be spiritually dead and yet be physically alive. When the internal flame is completely extinguished and there is no hope, none at all, the loneliness is so strong as to take our health and our mind. Once this has happened, there is no pill, no medication, no drug, no partner, and no therapist, that can help. Our only answer is with those who know how to treat the spiritual condition, the spiritual emptiness."

I could tell he was still with me, but not for long. One conversation wouldn't bring this one to God any more than my first conversation with Gary had brought me to live a spiritual life. "Would it be OK with you for me to return to this spot tomorrow at the same time and talk some more?" I asked.

"Sure, do whatever you want, it's a free world, isn't it?"

I looked into his eyes I could see the tears dry, and the darkness once again begin to fill his spirit. His flesh whitened, and his eyes darkened, and within a few moments, he was back asleep and thinking only about the relief he would feel as he pushed the plunger down on the syringe.

I left him and saw him hit the door buzzer to enter the building. I knew that he would use the money for drugs, but also knew that I had a real answer and that he would be waiting for me the following day, anticipating the next twenty I would offer, but also very curious about what I'd said. I've never met an addict like Lobo that was happy. I've never met an addict like Lobo who did not yearn for the end—one way or another. We needed each other.

Chapter Thirty-Seven

Sunlight of the Spirit

The following morning I showed up a little earlier than I'd anticipated, but Lobo was there, waiting as I had expected. I hadn't slept much. I thought many times about Lobo, about how Gary had told me over and over again that this wasn't about me. This was about those I could help. I remembered vividly and fondly, how we'd had long conversations about the bigger picture; the key to happiness would always be in participating in a larger vision.

Lobo now was a player in this new life that had been freely given to me. God had placed him there in front of that coffee shop at the entrance to the Baxter Street apartments. God had placed him there and placed within me the desire and the ability to help.

I approached Lobo and could again see the look of hopelessness in Lobo's eyes as he locked onto me approaching. Lobo was sitting in precisely the same spot as the morning before. Panhandling, waiting, always waiting, and praying that he would find money to buy drugs—before his body was wracked with the sickness of withdrawals. This was his existence, as it had been mine. Hopeless. I knew it, and he knew it. I knew that God had given me the gift to heal Lobo, and deep down somewhere, he knew this as well. He knew I was there to help, and that something greater than he was responsible for us both being there together.

"Lobo, my new friend, you look marvelous this morning," We both knew I was joking. He looked terrible. A skeleton wrapped in black NFL clothing. We both laughed. I'd been shown firsthand by Gary that we could open the spirit using two things: hopelessness and laughter. When someone has a full realization about their condition and realizes that there is no way out short of a miracle, this is hopelessness and it will open the spirit. When someone laughs at themselves, this too opens the spirit and leaves the ego vulnerable for attack. My friend, Lobo, had both. A hopeless man laughing is the most spiritual sight you will ever see. I knew I was in.

I removed a new crisp twenty-dollar bill from my pocket and put it into my left hand. I held open the other hand closest to Lobo, palm up. "I'm offering you two things this morning. Take the twenty, and it's yours, I won't return. Take what's in my right hand, and I will never leave you, will always be with you, and you will awaken from this miserable dream."

He turned his head, spit on the sidewalk, rubbed his forehead, and adjusted his cap. Then, exposing his darkened smile, he answered. "I'm taking the twenty, but want to know. I don't see anything in your right hand."

"Look closer," I said as I brought the empty hand within a foot of his face. "Keep looking," I could see a faint glow in the palm of my hand and felt a warm sensation that started in my heart from deep within and spread throughout my body. I touched Lobo's face and closed my eyes for a moment. I clutched the bill in my one hand, and even with my eyes closed, I knew Lobo was reaching for the bill. I began praying:

God, my one and only teacher.
Show me how to proceed.

I am yours.
I recognize you as the one and only guide in my spiritual journey.
Without you I am nothing.
Guide me here and now.
My life is yours.

I opened my eyes to see that a soft warm light was now surrounding us. A small break in the clouds was allowing us both to be warmed in the sun's loving touch. This wasn't all, as there was also an unmistakable light and warmth emanating from me and into my dear friend. I was still touching his face slightly and removed my hand. I showed it to him, showed him the warm glow of light surrounding us both.

Lobo began to cry, and I watched as the hand that was reaching for the twenty dollars began to drop as if more weight was being added to it, a little more each moment. His arm dropped slowly into his lap, and he continued to cry, tears of relief and joy. I, too, had cried like this. The Creator has given us two kinds of tears, salty tears of sorrow and pain and the sweet tears of gratitude and relief. Lobo was crying his first sweet tears in many years. I was able to put the twenty dollars away. We prayed together now as I kneeled with him, and we both held hands.

Father, Mother, God.
Lord of the happy, joyous, and free.
We are together now.
Show us how to proceed,
Guide our thoughts and our words, but especially our actions.
Show us each step of the way what our next step is to be.
Amen.

I came out of the prayer and raised my head to look directly into Lobo's deep brown eyes. I felt empowered; there wasn't the slight bit of nervousness over what to do next. God was working through me. I'd gotten out of the way. I knew nothing, but at the same time knew exactly what to do and what to say. "Your first lesson is the next prayer."

"The next prayer? Ok, I'm ready" Lobo answered.

We stood in silence, and looking into Lobo's eyes, I held out my hand, and he took it in his. Holding hands, I muttered a one-word prayer.

"Next? Amen."

"OK, that was the lesson, our only job for now is to ask the question, *"Next?"* Then we remain quiet and wait for the answer." We sat for another moment in silence, and it came to me. "Follow me, my friend, and you will live a new and wonderful life."

I smiled at Lobo; he didn't smile back but didn't fight what we were doing either. He was truly done, had been done for a long time. He only needed someone to recognize the hopeless aura that surrounded him and reach a hand out to him. The person to reach out to him had to be someone with a real answer. That someone was I.

We headed for the bus stop on Gary's route to introduce my two best friends to each other.

Chapter Thirty-Eight

A Conversation with God

It was late morning when we arrived at the bus stop. Gary had begun his rounds, and in checking the posted schedule, I could see we had some time before Gary would arrive. As we sat on the bench of a covered stop, we huddled close together. We were both bundled in layers of clothing to stay warm. The sheltered bus stop provided some protection from the wind. Lobo was wrapped in his black Oakland Raiders jacket and had his hood pulled up loosely over his head. My jacket, boots, and gloves provided the protection I needed. We had almost forty minutes until the bus would arrive.

We sat, and I told my story to Lobo—all of it. He was interested, he had to be. I could see he wanted what I'd found and that he was willing to do anything to get it. He listened and shook his head up and down, relating to my misery as I spoke of my years in delusion. He agreed each step of the way, that he'd be willing to do what I'd done as I recalled each step of my awakening. I knew he was willing. What I didn't know, was how it would turn out.

Even the most powerful desire to change, the deepest despair, the most honestly expressed gratitude, sometimes are not enough. I knew he, like I, was a desperate case. I knew I'd lead him to the right place at the right time. I brought him here, in his moment of willingness, to Gary.

We agreed he would go to the hospital when we were done seeing Gary and stay with the Maliks for a few days. Lobo would be the first of many that I would have this conversation with, and the first of many that would begin at Mountain View Hospital.

I told Lobo how I'd first met Gary. I recalled with much gratitude all he'd done for me. The feeling came strongly that this was what Gary had been preparing me for all along. To reach my hand out and give of myself that another may find life. Real life.

The bus pulled up as scheduled, and together we boarded the bus. As always the bus was packed. A man with a young boy got off at our stop. The seat in front was open once again, as it always seemed to be when I needed it. Lobo sat across from Gary, next to the door, and I took the seat on the bench directly next to him. I made the introduction to Gary immediately, "Gary, this is my new friend, Lobo. Lobo this is my old friend, Gary Goldpeople."

There was a slight pause, as Gary drove the bus through traffic, checking his mirrors. The bus was full and I tried to remember that Gary was doing a job as well. I listened for Gary's reply and wondered with amazement at how our willingness was all that was needed to begin. The seats next to Gary were the only ones open when we had boarded, and they were always the seats in the highest demand. Someone had given these seats up, so we could be there. Realizing the responsibility that came with sitting in this seat, I leaned into Lobo. "Pay attention, this'll be important."

Gary, looking at us and showing an ever-widening grin, spoke, "Lobo if you're hanging out with my friend, Stanley, you must be absolutely hopeless," Gary chuckled and shook his head from side to side.

Lobo and I both laughed as well. I laughed, as it was humorous to see that Gary was right. It had been eight short months since I'd met

Gary, and I'd proved to be a very sick man. To have Lobo looking to me for help now, he had to be desperate. Lobo was laughing as he could feel his own desperation and the realization that he was looking to a man who lived in a church and a bus driver for help. He knew also that he had tried everything else. God comes to us in all forms; he came to Lobo that day in a form he could accept, as he had come to me eight months earlier.

Gary spoke again as the snickering subsided from others and ourselves. "To go to Stanley for help." He said as he shook his head from side to side. He really was getting more a kick out of this than I was comfortable with. I had to assume he knew what he was doing. He finally pulled himself together long enough to talk to Lobo.

It always amazed me how Gary could make you feel you had his entire attention. Like so many times before, as we talked, he continued to drive and make his scheduled stops. Folks got on and off the bus. He would sometimes lower the handicap ramp and pick up a wheelchair. Always keeping some eye contact with you and always keeping you holding your breath for his next words. He grew more and more amazing to me as I awoke to what was really happening. The tremendous power of God at work in the lives of normal people. We need not be saints to perform miracles. We only need to be willing. We help as many people as we make up our minds to.

Gary pulled the bus back into traffic after making another stop. He was wearing his glasses, and his cheeks were a rosy-red color. His friendly looks and openly happy demeanor had put Lobo at ease. "Lobo, our answers here are spiritual in nature, and they require willingness on your part to set aside many things you believe you think you know. Are you willing to do that?"

Lobo first looked at me, and realizing I wasn't going to answer for him, spoke to Gary for the first time. "Yes, I think I am. I really just want to get well. I had a good life at one time."

Gary looked at me and smiled, then shot back at Lobo. "A good life is what you will receive here... that and much more... sound good?"

Lobo squirmed in his seat, trying to get comfortable having this conversation with Gary aboard a bus full of strangers. He looked at me again, and I nodded, gently assuring Lobo it was OK to answer and that this was a safe place for him to be. "To tell you the truth, the thought of a good life ever again seems impossible. If I could just find a way out of the constant pain and this feeling of worthlessness. I mean, you all seem so happy, but coming from where I'm at, things seem pretty bad."

Gary had Lobo's attention, lowering his head and looking over the top of his glasses directly at Lobo, he let him know he was getting serious, "Your ideas about hopelessness and what you thought were a good life are of no concern to anyone here."

"OK, well, what is it that you are concerned with?" Lobo answered sarcastically.

"I'm not concerned with anything outside of helping you and asking nothing in return. Your best ideas are of no help to us. As a matter of fact, they may even be a hindrance if your thinking is anything like Stanley's here," He nodded toward me, and the smile once again engulfed his face.

The bus came to another stop, three got off and four boarded. Gary closed the door. I loved this—watching the master go to work. I think the bus, and all its distractions added to the experience. It gave us all a chance to think for a moment about the last thing Gary had said. He had timing down to an absolute art form. The stopping and the starting, the door opening and closing. He was the conductor leading the orchestra. The bus speeds up and Gary hits you with another truth, the bus slows and stops. The door opens and a few disembark, a few board. We look at the faces and then another hit from Gary in the form of the truth.

Gary was again in traffic and headed for his next stop as he continued his symphony. "Lobo my friend, I know you only a little, but if you are anything like me you know loneliness, hopelessness, worthlessness, and despair at depth. Are you drinking? Doing drugs?"

Lobo looked at me, and again I nodded that it was OK for him to answer. "Both." He replied.

"How much?" Gary asked.

"Too much," Lobo responded as his discomfort mounted.

The question and answers went back and forth like a tennis match. Gary firing and Lobo answering back.

"Get sick when you try to stop?"

"Deathly."

"Want to stop?"

"Yes."

Gary looked at me and smiled. He made another stop and several got off. Gary pulled back into traffic, looked at me with a grin... I smiled back. With that gentle smile to each other we could read each other like a book. We knew Lobo was willing, he wouldn't still be with us if he wasn't. And more, we knew God had given us the power to help.

Lobo relaxed a bit and was breathing slowly and waited patiently for Gary's next comment. I watched and listened as the master and prospective student volleyed through another set of questions and answers.

"We can help, we have a way out, are you willing to do whatever it takes?"

"I am, I'll do anything!"

"Are you in need of anything, food, shelter, money?"

Lobo laughed, "All of the above, I've lost my pad and have been living at the shelter."

"Good, Stanley here will take care of all of that for you, just do exactly as he says."

I swallowed hard. I didn't have anything! How was I supposed to help anyone else? I thought hard about saying something, but knew better. I trusted in Gary, that he knew what he was doing. I trusted more in God, that he knew what he was doing.

"I can do that. I can follow instructions and do whatever Stanley says." Lobo replied with a shaky conviction in his voice.

Gary fired away. "No, you can't! That's just it, isn't it? On your own, you will fail at this venture."

"How can you say that?" Lobo answered with his mouth hanging open in response. He looked at me, so I signaled to him to pay attention and listen by pointing to my ear and then to Gary.

"What is your experience, Lobo? Think! You've failed at everything in your life or you wouldn't be here. Right? You've lost everything worthwhile in life, isn't that right?

Lobo dropped his head and hesitated before answering. "Right."

"You'll fail at what we are offering as well if you try to do this on your own."

"OK?" he answered with his head still lowered, looking at the floor.

"Stanley will ask you to do some things, to help to remove all those things in your life that block you from God's power. It may take some time. Are you ready?"

Lobo raised his head, looked again first at me, then directly at Gary. "I am."

We'd stopped and started many times during the conversation. Now, we stopped and Gary surprised Lobo. I knew it was coming. The master at work. Hit 'em hard, and then let them sit and contemplate.

"This is your stop." Gary said, he opened the door. "I'll see you soon my new friend." I stood up and motioned Lobo to follow. He did.

We both got off and looked at each other. I could see that Lobo was going into withdrawals; his nose was running, his breathing starting to labor. We began our walk to Mountain View Hospital. Lobo would be making the same humble beginnings I had.

I pitied him for the sickening torture of withdrawals he would have to endure. I also felt great joy to be taking his first few steps to enlightenment with him.

Chapter Thirty-Nine

We Are Healed But We Are Not Healed Alone

We arrived at the emergency room at Mountain View Hospital. When we entered, I saw in Lobo the same frightened look I'd had when I had walked into the same room at the end of July. I'd come in the sweltering heat of summer. Now, I was here in the chill of a winter evening. This time I was here to give, rather than receive. I saw the sign overhead, "ADMITTING," in bold letters and sitting underneath was a friendly face. Shelly Malik was manning her station. She lit up as she saw me approach.

"Stanley, how nice to have you visit. We had word you were coming."

I felt relief at seeing her and could feel Lobo's relief in the realization that he wouldn't be alone in this adventure.

He could see that there was a friendliness among us that he could be a part of. I knew, and he knew, the next few days wouldn't be easy. When one knows that they've been defeated, and all fighting has been removed, even the most hideous torture can be endured in the knowledge that it may not have to be repeated. It's when we know all our efforts will be for nothing that even the slightest suffering is unbearable.

I'd been standing in his shoes just the past July. Now, I was here with him. I was free. I knew it, and he knew it. It gave us both strength and humility at the same time.

I was now leading Lobo on the same trail I'd been shown only months before. Shelly, with her incredibly warm nature, won his confidence quickly. He was directed, as I'd been, to the trip upstairs to see the social worker and I went with him. Lobo was shaking uncontrollably by this time. His nerves, with the withdrawals, combined to give him the look of what he was: a desperate man. God was using me to help him and using him to help me. In him, I saw what I might be without the awareness of the presence of God.

The next stop was the same room I'd been in, the same bed had been prepared. I could recall the smell, the roommates I'd suffered with. The stale cigarette smoke on the patients and the smell of vomit. The smell of the disinfectants. It was a full room, three other patients and one empty bed. After changing into the robe he'd been given and brushing his teeth for the first time in weeks, Lobo gladly retired to the newly made bed.

I pulled the curtains around him and took a seat in the only chair in the room, pulling it close to the bed so that the curtain would close behind. I pulled a pad of paper and a pen from the bedside table and asked Lobo to write his prayer for grace. I'd done the same thing on Gary's instructions less than a year earlier. The sequence of events that had taken place since I'd written that prayer rolled through my mind now and gave me an intense feeling of gratitude and a sense of amazement that now I was on the other side, giving Lobo the instructions to write.

As he wrote, I told him, as I'd been told, to read the prayer ten times per day for his entire stay in the hospital. I know the power of early prayer. For the most desperate cases, it gives them something... a sense of hope in those moments of deepest despair. It had been so with me. Before I'd seen the prayer, he'd written, I knew what it would say. It said the same thing all the desperation prayers say. No matter how eloquent the writer, they all say the same thing. They say the same thing, that is, when one finally has a realization of the truth about themselves.

I sat as Lobo wrote his prayer:

God,
Of myself I am nothing.
It is you, God, who does the work.
I have blocked myself from you.
Now I need you.
Pleasehelp me now.
Amen.

I talked to Lobo a few more minutes after he'd written his prayer. I shared with him how my life had changed. I told him of the visit he would have on day three from Nurse Shelly and Dr. Malik. I gave him instructions on how to reach me at the New Thought Church. We talked about his plans to stay with his mother when he was well. He could stay, if she knew he was trying. Like all mothers of the walking dead, she wanted her son back, back in mind, back in body and back in spirit.

Lobo, now in bed, was falling asleep. It had been a long day, from our meeting in the morning, off to see Gary, our walk to the hospital, and enduring the admitting process at Mountain View. I was grateful for the rest he would get now, as I knew the torture his body and mind would need to endure in the next few days as he went through withdrawals. He would need his energy. I held his hand as he slipped into sleep. I prayed aloud:

Mother, Father, God.
Lord of the happy, joyous, and free.

Thank you for your presence here,
Thank you especially for the awareness
of that presence in this moment.
Bless our efforts to be healed and serve you God.
That in our healing, we will not be healed alone.
Shine brightly before us a light,
That each step of the way,
We may see what our next step is to be.
In your strength, empower us,
In your mercy, heal us,
In your love, soften us,
In your spirit, guide us,
In your wisdom, teach us,
In your grace, humble us,
That we may know the truth about ourselves.
Amen.

I left Lobo fast asleep. I felt like I never wanted to leave him. In that moment, I knew I never would. I was now a part of Lobo as Gary was a part of me. I knew then the truth about my healing. We are healed, but we are never healed alone.

Chapter Forty

Spiritually Anonymous

February brought with it little change in the winter weather. My own change however was dramatic. My thinking was different, my attitude and demeanor had changed. I looked at everything now through a new pair of glasses.

I had thoughts every day during this process about how much Gary had done for me and how much time he'd given me. He truly was a great man. I'd learned about giving from an expert. This much I knew. I'd told him on one of my recent rides with him how deeply I felt his love for me and how much I appreciated everything he'd done for me.

I knew now that my place was to be of service to others and give back some of what had been given to me. I saw Lobo every day. He was a changed man in just a few weeks. He'd left the hospital on day five just as I'd done. He was now shaved, had received some new clothes and had a small light now shining in his eyes. He was still very much underweight but already showed signs of health. His color and complexion were clear rather than grey. He was clean. Gone was the large coat and the hood pulled over his head. Now he wore a button up shirt and a loose sweater pulled over. His hair was combed and clean.

I had him showing up at the church each and every morning and we talked while I cooked breakfast. This morning I had him come extra early and gave him a few chores while I headed to the bus stop to see Gary.

I showed up at the stop forty minutes early before his route began, trying to catch Gary alone. He was there as he always was, sitting in the darkened bus. He smiled and waved as he opened the door.

"Stanley, how very excellent to see you." He smiled and tipped his head as if paying me a respect.

As I boarded the bus, I was going over all of the things in my mind I'd wanted to tell Gary.

Gary, I knew could see I had a lot on my mind, before I could speak or even sit down, he jumped in, "The love you speak of, how you feel this love I have for you, this is God's love, Stanley. God's love for you. Everything that I do is God working through me. God has no physical way to love you, so God has chosen me to show his love for you."

Once again, the Master had given the answer before the question had been asked. His intuition was amazing. I moved quickly as I realized this was a rare opportunity, almost and impossible opportunity these days. To have a few minutes alone with my mentor was a gift no amount of money could buy.

I took my seat across from Gary. Gary handed me a Styrofoam cup of coffee. I had so much on my mind, and Gary wanted to talk about something I thought I knew all about. "Gary, I understand that, but I still know in my heart what a wonderful person you are and the huge difference you've made in my life."

Gary bit into a small donut, taking half in one bite and washing it down with his coffee. He wiped his mouth with the back of his hand and smiled, realizing that he was a bit disheveled as a few crumbs from the donut fell to the floor. He swallowed, took another drink of coffee and continued, "Not one ounce, not one iota of that is true, wish it were," he laughed with a wider-than-life smile, in that way I had come to absolutely adore.

Gary always saw the truth before I did, and this really amused him. When he laughed like that, I knew that I was about to receive a piece of the truth that I hadn't seen before. He always beamed like that when he saw how confused I was about things.

"Stanley, you see, God loves you through me because God is Spirit and he cannot physically love you directly. God loves us through other people. Everything I've given you has been a gift from God. I would love to take credit for this, and sometimes I try, but the truth is that everything is from God. God doesn't do anything for me, God only does things THROUGH ME!"

He paused, closed his eyes, and breathed a bit heavy. I could see that this man I loved so deeply was slowing down a bit, and somehow, I was clear that I was catching him at the tail-end of his time with us on earth. I'd often wished he would lose some weight, not eat so many donuts each morning, and lay off the drive-thru burger joints at night. So, God had truly worked through this fat, eccentric, old bus driver and reached out and touched me. I was awed by the absolute truth in that fact. I knew God had done the work through me that had touched Lobo and I also knew he was working through me to help many others. In Gary, I now saw myself and realized possibly for the first time that we were *one*.

Gary finished his donut, downing it with another large swill of coffee, and looked up to see me awaiting his next statement, "You see, as much as you would like to attach some very nice attributes to me, and as much as my ego would love to accept those attributes as true, it simply doesn't ring true in the spiritual world. Damn little room for false pride in the spiritual world, it serves only to separate me and you from God. Stop persisting in projecting attributes to others they don't deserve, and never accept those things from others that we don't deserve.

"I'm anonymous in this process; the process of helping others must always be God working through me and can never be about me. As much as I would like to accept all these good things you're saying about me, I can't accept them. I can only be grateful that God is working through me. Any time someone thanks me, I thank God. I want you to go home and thank God for the love and the spiritual truths you have received and kindly leave me out of it. I have enough problems without folks puffing my ego up." He laughed so hard this time his coffee cup shook. He held it away from himself and just let it splash onto the floor. He gathered himself and added "If you allow Lobo to puff your ego up and fail to realize that all the good comes through you from God to him, well then I would expect God wouldn't care for you taking the credit, would he?" He laughed again and managed to avoid another spill.

"Well, I need to take a few passengers, and my route starts in ten minutes. I'm going to spend a few minutes in quiet time myself, thanking God for loving me through you, Stanley. Remember that we are anonymous in this process, it's not about us, it comes though us. If you stand out of the way, many good things will come."

I got off the bus and headed home to pray and thank God for my teacher, thank God for the love, and thank God for the lessons.

The bus hadn't moved. I knew in a few minutes many would be showing up to the stop. I knew that I'd received what I needed. Not what I wanted. Time with Gary was limited more and more as time went on. Pastor Anthony was extremely busy with the daily running of the church and counseling many members of the congregation. I was being prepared for a life of humble service to others. I had to go to God in prayer and meditation to find my answers now. There comes a point in the living of the spiritual life that there are no teachers left, all true teachers want this for their students. I was not there yet but was close enough to see it coming. A few minutes, at the most, every few mornings were all I would get with Gary now. The rest of my time was to be spent helping others and being of service to the church.

I headed back to where God would have me be—in service to Lobo and the church congregation in general.

Chapter Forty-One

Be Still and Know That I Am God

February was here, and winter was in full swing. I was now waking at 4:30 AM in order to get through my morning chores, have a quick tea and oatmeal and arrive at the bus stop before Gary. These early mornings now were not even a sure bet to get one-on-one time with him. Once his route had started, passengers and friends, students and loved ones would fill the seats and ride the bus, to be close to, and learn from "*the Master.*"

I arrived bundled for protection from the cold, I watched as Gary pulled the bus into the stop. I boarded with four others who had been waiting even before I'd arrived. I felt myself instantly relax in Gary's presence and the warmth of the bus's interior. I took a seat across from Gary and we all greeted each other with a warm, "Good morning." The others had given me this seat. It was a privilege and honor to sit across from Gary and we all knew it. I nodded my appreciation. Gary would be pulling out and starting his route in just a few minutes.

I pulled my hat and gloves off. Settling in to my seat, I asked my first question. "Gary, I've been given so many insights into the spiritual life, I can see the huge change in my own life as a result. How do I know for sure how I'm supposed to be living my life?"

Gary paused a moment before answering, he let out a large breath and took another in. I could see he was thinking well before answering. We all awaited the answer.

"I live, Stanley, but God lives my life. Don't worry about living your life, relax and let God live your live for you." He smiled, leaned back in his seat, and let his head fall back in relaxation. He closed his eyes and awaited my response.

I'd heard him say this many times, but I couldn't comprehend what this really meant. I knew that I lived, but wasn't sure about the "God lives my life" part. I showed an obviously puzzled look on my face.

In the silence, Gary picked up on my confusion, leaning forward and opening his eyes, he looked at me, and smiling, he continued, "Yes, God lives your life when you're relaxed and aware of the presence of the Spirit, God will live your life." He again leaned back and closed his eyes, letting out another large breath as his large chest fell.

I was still a bit puzzled, as I knew I'd awoken from a long sleep and was in fact living some moments in the awareness of the presence of God. I knew the manifestation of this presence in my life was evident by the complete personality change I'd experienced. *Why hadn't God always lived my life?* I asked this question of myself, and before I'd said a word, Gary, had started to give me an answer to a question, even before I'd asked.

We were interrupted briefly, as a few more passengers arrived and Gary opened the door. An elderly couple, and a few businessmen boarded and took their seats close to the front. Gary knew this meant his people would begin to show, and I knew my few minutes with Gary were coming to a close. The four who had boarded with me were likely waiting to ask a few questions as well.

He continued now in a slightly louder voice so everyone could hear. "The *ego* is a very strong force, Stanley, strong enough to block out the sunlight of the Spirit in your life. I can look at some people, and without talking to them, I see the living dead, those people walking around dreaming they are awake." He paused for a moment before adding, "They're suffering from high self-esteem mostly."

I'd always assumed my ills, and the ills of many like me, were caused by low self-esteem. He had my attention on this day as he did in every moment now. I hung on his words and realized how precious each answer had become. Several more had now boarded the bus in just the few minutes since I'd shown and had begun listening in as well. Today I wanted an answer, a real answer, and a real answer I got.

Gary took on a few remaining passengers and going through his routine to get the lights on and the sign ready he started his workday by pulling the bus into traffic. As soon as the passengers were seated, he continued. Everyone, myself included, leaned in so that we wouldn't miss a word.

"Many of us live on the *ego* alone. This is the *I*! *I* want a new house, *I* want a new car, *I* want everyone to look at me, and *I* want more attention, more sex, more money, and more recognition. This attitude removes and separates us from our real place. It separates us in our realization of the truth about ourselves. It separates us from God, and it separates us from our fellow man.

"This is the 360-degree mirror: No matter what is in front of me, all I can see is myself and a reflection of how everything affects me." The bus stopped and a few got on, but no one got off from the front of the bus. We were all glued to Gary, this loving wonderful man, preaching to his people and doing his service to society as well.

Once again, as the passengers were seated, he continued, "This is the over-concentration on ourselves. The real spiritual malady that shuts most of us off from the realization that the spirit of God is a part of you, and is not separate from you. This is why therapy is so successful in America. Where else can you go and pay someone to listen to you talk endlessly about yourself?" Gary let out his laugh that let everyone know that he had even amused himself. We all laughed with him.

"We all need a vision, a vision that is larger than ourselves. This is why a spiritual life, the life of self-sacrifice and service to others, is the only real answer for most of us. It is the only way of life with the power to bring us out of our sleep and into a life of purpose. We lose this over-concentration on ourselves and slowly begin to awaken to the fact that this world's hopes lay in one thing and one thing only—*love*. Our current spiritual malady cannot be overcome with a pill, or the right therapist, or a dunk in the tank. These things may very well help, but they will never amount to a real answer. The real answer is to remove those things in our lives that block us from God and allow us to stand as free men and women in the sunlight of the Spirit." He smiled back at us all and concentrating on his driving for a moment took a few breaths.

Gary truly amazed us all. He was our spiritual guru though he would never accept that title. We watched as he moved the large bus in and out of traffic. I noticed how he didn't struggle. Even in the worst traffic situations he remained as calm as when we were parked and eating donuts. Somehow the drivers around the bus recognized the patience and he always had folks slowing down and letting him into traffic as he waved his respects into the large mirrors and out the window. This oversized, out of shape, Santa Claus looking man with a button-covered beret was our spiritual leader. Being in his presence alone gave us all a feeling of being in the presence of God.

Once back into the flow of traffic Gary went on adding: "This process begins with prayer at first, and then this opens the door to the spirit and allows hope to enter. Only in the world of the spirit will hope truly enter the hopeless. Once prayer opens the door and hope enters, our application of spiritual principles in our lives is natural. Making amends to all whom we have ever harmed is the application of the spiritual principle of restitution.

"When we pay the money back that we owe, we open the flow of abundance into our lives. So long as we don't pay or say we cannot afford to pay, we'll remain with a logjam at the dam of giving and surely prevent the flood of all that is good.

"We have all found an answer here, in that thoroughly cleaning our own house and committing to helping others, even at the expense of our selfish wants, we enter the kingdom of heaven on earth. We'll know our creator, the almighty *I AM*."

The bus again slowed, pulled over, and stopped. A few passengers boarded, greeted Gary, and headed to the remaining seats in the back of the bus. Gary lifted his glasses off his nose and held them above his eyes as if to make a point, and looking directly at me, said, "Your next lesson, Stanley Pearson, is to practice the presence of God through prayer and meditation and to make daily contact with your creator. You may only find that place within for a few seconds, but find it, get quiet, as I have shown you, and listen. *'Be still and know that I am God,'* is the mantra to use. Repeat slowly until you become aware of the presence of God within. Then go and do God's work. It's really so simple. He smiled at us all.

Gary returned his attention to the task at hand and eased the large bus back into traffic. Once up to speed, he continued while watching traffic and looking straight ahead.

"Once you have made that contact, take it to the next step. Recognize in you a living God, and become aware that if God is in you, then all that God has is yours! The entire kingdom of heaven is yours, Stanley. Go and help others now. You'll find you don't need me as you think you do.

"You'll find the truth that a student who works hard should surpass the teacher. This is as it should be. I love you, Stanley, as I love all those who come and ride the bus to hear an overweight, quirky, old man ramble about the spiritual truths of our times. I love you so much I want for you to outgrow me. Can you see that when we love one like our own child, we want better for them than we attained?"

I noticed several passengers looking at me and waiting for my answer. I knew the answer, but didn't want to say it. I looked at Gary, and then back at a few of the passengers, and then answered nervously, "Yes, I know you want the best for me." I was elated and saddened at the same time. I never wanted to leave Gary and wanted to spend every minute I could in his presence. As did we all.

The bus came to a stop, and I knew the routine. Gary gave me the nod that let me know this was my stop. I got up, zipped up my jacket, and put on my gloves. "Good-bye, I love you, Gary." Gary smiled and waved good-bye, "I love you too, Stanley."

I left to walk the streets in meditation and contemplation and find my way home. As I walked, I knew what Gary had been saying. I had a vision of becoming a minister. It was more important to my fellow travelers than it was to me. I may carry a message that would reach generations after I've gone on. This experience I'd been having with Gary wasn't really about me at all. I knew then that God didn't do anything to me, that God didn't do anything for me, but that God was working through me. I knew that the presence of a loving God resided within me, in spirit and in soul, and that all that was God's was also mine. I knew then the kingdom of God was mine—It was my inheritance; I knew that I had nothing to fear.

I understood then that there is one hope for all mankind: the awareness of the presence of God. It is our only hope, and I knew it. I also knew that it was my calling. I knew that God gave to each and every one of us on this earth and that there wasn't a single person to spare. I knew that each and every one of us has come with a special gift to offer and that this was my gift. My lesson was already complete. I knew I could go back and see Gary anytime. I also knew I would return as a peer, as a friend. I no longer needed him. I loved him, I wanted to be with him, but I didn't need him. The thought made me cry and jump for joy at the same time. I had to let go in order to be free.

I slowly walked home to the New Thought Church. I entered the sanctuary alone and cried the sweet tears of gratitude and a few bitter tears of sorrow as I felt the beginning of the end of my relationship with the greatest teacher, the most loving man I had ever known.

Chapter Forty-Two

The Lamp Holder

I sometimes went to the bus stop to just think. I wasn't there to ride or to see Gary although I worshiped those moments, I was here now to meditate and contemplate that power that is God. As I sat, I reflected on the miracle that was now my life. My work… God's work with Lobo had gone well, very well. Lobo was now a seeker, a person dedicated to living the spiritual life. He'd taken my job at the church doing the cleanup and the general maintenance. I worked now each day in the church office and took calls, planned the services and counseled anyone who came for help. I was experiencing the transition from spiritual seeker to spiritual teacher. My job as a spiritual teacher to Lobo, and others, was to allow God's love to overflow from me to them. It was also my job to assure those seeking a spiritual way of life that what they seek is real. It was through seeing Gary's spirit shine that I'd come to believe. Lobo was now looking to me for the assurance that his experience was valid. He and others now looked to me for hope.

Lobo was making his amends with his family, was now living with his mother, and paying rent to her, something I'd required. His transition in these four short weeks had been swift and dramatic, mirroring my own recovery. He was only the first in the line of hundreds we would help together. He was a new man, living a new life, with a new perception of the world. He'd made a start into the spiritual life, and I was on my way to living my dream. I would take Lobo with me for as long as he needed, and then set him free.

It was the end of February as I worked with Pastor Anthony in the daily operations of the church—tending to the financial issues, planning the services on Sunday, and spending much of my spare time counseling for no charge to anyone who came to the church with spiritual needs. That included anyone who walked through the door of the New Thought Church. I made myself available to the world of the Spirit. I prayed each morning that God would allow me to be a lamp holder, a light at the top of the hill shining brightly for all to see. I prayed that God would shine through me and allow me to be a man with a real answer, that others would be attracted to me to help them on their own spiritual path.

I found that by setting aside my own needs, or what I thought I needed, I was able to concentrate on how I could be helpful to others. Strange as it may seem, all my needs were met, with little thought or effort on my part. Every possible need was cared for, so long as my thoughts were on others. In all the years, I'd pounded my head in a futile effort to get what I wanted and what I thought I needed, I'd ended up with nothing. Now, with a dedication to setting those thoughts and needs aside, I had everything a man could ever wish for. I had a great relationship with my ex-wife and children. I even had thoughts of one day remarrying, in the New Thought Church, as there was once again a real love in our relationship. My family had come to believe in me and even more in the God that was obviously working in my life.

I had the love of my children, not the broken-hearted love that they had suffered through, but the love of admiration. My children now looked up to me and wanted to be with me any chance they could get. I could see in their eyes that they were proud of me. Hold the hand of a child that looks up to you, and in the eyes of that child, you will see God.

I had the job I really wanted when I looked at my heart's desire. I was headed into a ministry with Gary and Pastor Tony as my mentors. I was so overwhelmed by the life I'd been freely given that at times I'd be moved to tears, sometimes at the most inopportune times. On the bus, walking down the street, looking at my children, and even now, each time I looked at my former wife. A woman I'd at one time blamed for my failure in life. The feeling that life was good, was so overwhelming that I cried the sweet tears of gratitude almost daily. I'd been to the jumping-off place. I'd known the loneliness of the deepest despair. Those days were over now, never to return. It was a dark cold morning, the last day of February, and yet I stood basking in the sunlight of the Spirit.

I knew that we were all children of God. I was now able to disagree with people and ideas, and yet love the person. I knew that real religion would include all people of all faiths worshipping one God, a God of their own understanding. I knew that this was a coming-together time. I knew that it wasn't anyone else's job to wake me up—it was my job. I knew it wasn't anyone else's job to teach the truth, it was my job. I knew it wasn't anyone else's job to love the unlovable among us, it was my job. I knew it was not anyone else's job to carry on the message Gary, the Maliks, and Pastor Anthony had carried to me. It was my job!

With this great gift of life came great responsibility. As I think one positive thought, the world changes—an almost immeasurable shift takes place. When we all think one positive thought, one loving thought, any problem on earth can be solved. The day will come when we will all evolve into what God will have us be. It was my job to be what God would have me be, so that others can see in me what he would have them be.

These were the thoughts that went with me in those days. It was as if a new power was doing my thinking for me. Indeed, it was. These were the thoughts that were with me on that day and every day. So very different from the destructive thoughts I'd had running through my mind the previous summer. I now had clarity of thought, the ability to make a decision, I was inspired, and I was calm.

Chapter Forty-Three

The End of the Beginning

I could see the bus approaching, and Gary at the wheel, his beret atop his head and the smile upon his face as he saw me at the stop. I felt humbled in his presence. Even the sight of his happy face before the bus would come to a complete stop was enough to bring about calm. Some days, I came and just rode, not saying a word to Gary. I knew I had come just to meditate with my teacher and friend, and witness first-hand *"the Master"* at work helping others. Other days, I had come with questions, lots of questions. Always, I left without direct answers, but directions to dig deep inside myself where the only true answers are found. This day, I had come for both, I had questions, and I'd come to pray and meditate with my mentor.

As the bus came to a stop and the door opened, I noticed something was different to me about the way Gary looked. I sensed peace within him and could see the gentle white aura that always illuminated his Spirit. I took the empty seat across from him, just passing the man that had vacated the seat, another of Gary's students and a man who was familiar to me from his weekly visits on Sunday to the New Thought Church. I'd noticed that the man was wiping tears from his face as he exited the bus.

The talk started on the lighter side. The seemingly important questions I'd come with faded into nothing, and what really was important began to surface within me. And that was, spending time in the presence of the man who'd saved my life. It was very important today to just be in his presence. I found that too, when working with people at the church, my students would come to the church with so much on their mind, and as I allowed them to talk, they would come to the realization that they'd really come to meditate with me, to be with me.

So, it was with Gary and me. I enjoyed his presence, and he enjoyed mine. We talked about my family, and I asked him about his. He'd mentioned his daughter many times in the past and told me of his love for her. I sensed that they were estranged, but couldn't imagine how such a lovely man could be rejected by anyone. I only had to look at my own experience, however, to realize that he once was, most likely, a very different man.

Such is the power of God to change the human condition. His past, like my own, was now unrecognizable. A change so complete that nothing could be done to convince anyone that Gary had ever been anything but a totally wonderful, loving human being. I knew the truth about Gary, and more importantly, I knew the truth about myself.

I sat in silence as the talk subsided, complete in whatever it was that I'd come for. The bus driver before me making the stops and starts, the maneuvers in and out of the heavy city traffic. All the while never letting me think for a second that he wasn't aware of my presence with him.

Gary pulled out of traffic, stopped, and opened the door for a large group, then broke the silence as he turned to me. Our eyes met, and he smiled wide, "Our time together is limited."

"Today you mean?" I replied, a bit confused by the suddenness of his statement.

"Today also, but I was referring to our time together in this life, that's limited." He paused, slowly took in a breath, and then continued, "Some people we meet, and we know for a lifetime… this is the rarest of relationships, and we can count these on one hand at the end of our life. Most people we meet, we have some experience with them, and then they will fade, people come and people go from our lives. This is how it should be. Our family is what's important, they are with us the longest, and are therefore designed by God to be our most heartfelt relationships."

I scooted nervously, in my seat, closer to Gary, feeling some fear about what he was saying. I felt like Gary was family and that I should always be with him. *Was he telling me that we wouldn't be seeing each other as much or that I should move on?*

"I want to always be with you Gary. I can't imagine life any other way."

Gary made a stop and looked as deeply into my eyes as I'd ever felt. "I'll always be with you, just not here, in this plane, in this body. I'll never leave you, to be with me just close your eyes, and I'll always be there. It's just that I'm feeling a little tired, and God has other plans for me than to be driving this bus." He smiled wide and chuckled, it wasn't the large laugh of Gary Goldpeople I had come to know and love—this laugh was to quell my obvious fear. This laugh, as most things he did, was to bring comfort to another human being.

I stared at Gary, as he turned away to concentrate on his driving. My mind struggled to grasp what he was telling me. Several others were listening in, and I looked at them with confusion. *What the heck was he saying, other plans? Was he out of his darn mind?* My mind bounced from one thought to the next. *I couldn't get by without our visits, and this was where I'd been receiving all the things that had made my life so worthwhile.* "Gary, enough with the metaphysical stuff, I know you're always with me, I've felt that many times, and I understand that it's God working through you that has touched my life, but do you really need to teach me this lesson now?"

Gary, drove and maintained silence as I awaited his response. It came a few nervous moments later, "I've been to see Dr. Malik, and my heart is giving way. The medicine isn't doing like what they'd hoped, and I'm being relieved of my driving responsibility. I'm taking retirement effective today. I've completed my journey here. I have a lot of people to see today. I love you, Stanley." I could see a lone tear drop from Gary's eye as he checked his mirrors and signaled to stop.

I couldn't bear to look directly at any of the other passengers, for fear of what would happen to me emotionally if I did. I looked down and thought of what I should say. I suppose I'd always had the idea that Gary wasn't the healthiest person I knew. I saw him, so many times, devour two Big Mac's, wash them down with a chocolate shake, and then stop an hour later for coffee and cookies. Cookies by the bagful. I imagined that somehow his close connection to God would protect him from the heavy burden his heart was under to pump blood to a massive body. I had wondered many times about his health. I'd thought about his heart and its enormous job. I suppose I knew all along the day would come when Gary would be in trouble. In trouble with his health.

I knew from the moment I'd stepped onto the bus that day and saw Gary, that this day would be different. I thought about what to say and tears began to form. I wiped the wetness from my eyes and gathered my thoughts. I didn't want to make a scene, "Gary how bad is it, this news from the doctor?"

Gary, obviously moved himself, searched for a response while maintaining his composure enough to keep driving, performing two duties at once. One, keeping his commitment to safety and delivering the bus on time to each stop—serving Metro Transit. The other, serving all his passengers, his students—continuing to teach the spiritual life, even in his time of need.

"Whatever will be, will be," he smiled as he spoke, our eyes met for a long moment, and we deeply connected. He turned away, concentrating on maneuvering the large bus into and out of morning traffic. "The fine doctor's opinion is that the heart would need to be replaced, a transplant. I don't qualify, too old and too fat." He laughed at himself in spite of the seriousness of the topic in discussion.

"How long?" I asked. I now looked around and noticed the other passengers. Businessmen and women in power suits, likely killers in the boardroom, wept openly now. The housewives who came each day to just ride the bus and be with their spiritual teacher, cried with me, and with us. A construction worker, lunch box and hardhat beside him on the seat, sobbed. His face was hidden behind his large worn and weathered hands as he rested his head in his arms. We all awaited his answer together. For a moment, no one could take more than a shallow breath.

"How long is the wrong question, Stanley. What's important here is the time that we've had, the lessons that you've learned. It was never I, never my help, never me who helped you. I'm just a fat, tired, old bus driver with a bad ticker," he laughed a genuine full laugh this time and that brought a smile and momentary relief to us all. Gary had the ability to laugh at himself in even in the most serious times. These moments with Gary showed us all that even in times of our deepest distress there is beauty.

I tried my best to laugh with him. There is rarely something as beautiful as crying and laughing at the same time, and we were both overcome with the two emotions. He paused, stopped the bus, and boarded a few passengers. The bus lurched ahead, and Gary continued. "God is all you need, you will never lose me because you are me. I cannot leave you because I am you. Whatever will be, will be. I may stay and I may go." He paused thoughtfully, and then added, "Most likely go, I presume. I turned in the paperwork from my physical today down at the station and a good friend agreed to hold it until morning so I could drive my route one last time and talk to my passengers and say good-bye."

I kept my eyes on Gary but could hear a slow and subtle weep from several of the passengers. I myself could no longer hold back the flood of tears—Gary cried also. "I love you, Gary," was all I could get out and that barely made it as my voiced cracked.

"I have many people to see today, Stanley, the next stop is yours." The bus slowed and the door opened. "Good-bye my beloved friend, come by the house and see me in a few days" Gary said with a most soft and sincere voice, a calm loving voice, the voice I now use when dealing with frightened children and when showing love to the most emotionally wounded among us. A voice I learned from Gary.

"What am I going to do without you?" I managed to add as I stood outside the bus door waiting for it to close.

"I'll tell you when you get there," Gary said with a wink as he gave me one last nod to let me know that it would be OK.

"Promise?" I responded.

"I promise," he said with a tip of his head and a last smile. The door closed and the bus pulled away.

I stood in silence on the sidewalk, impervious to the cold. I still held my coat and hat in my arms. It had been the journey of a lifetime, I'd boarded the bus eight months earlier, as hopeless, helpless, egotistical, and selfish a person as ever existed. I stood now on this quiet sidewalk thinking of Gary, but also thinking of whom I could help. What I could do to help Gary and what I could do to help mankind. How I could be of service to my fellow travelers.

Whenever I face indecision, I ask Gary, and his promise to me always comes true, he is there. He is I and I am he. Gary's journey in the human experience was winding down. My journey in the spiritual experience was just beginning. Together there was no beginning and no end. We were a part of never-ending life, one with the infinite flow of Spirit's love. For us there would never be an end.

Chapter Forty-Four

Sow and So Shall Ye Reap

Gary lived now, mostly at home. He grew weaker each time I visited, which was nearly every day, many days more than once. Even on my first visit, only one day after his last day driving the bus I could see he was slowing considerably. Each day the crowd grew as well. As word got out that Gary had been medically retired, the large crowds that had once rode the bus began to show, more each day, at his small one-bedroom home.

Each morning when I showed, there was already a houseful of his students from years past, cooking, cleaning, and doing laundry. I recognized many from the bus and knew many from the church as well. Several of his brother drivers from Metro-Transit stopped by each day to see what they could do. We all helped Gary to move around the house as needed and cared for his every need. The scene was awe-inspiring. The law of Karma in effect; Gary receiving payment in kind for the good work he had done through the years. Gary was now making withdraws from the spiritual bank he'd been making regular deposits into for years. He was a giant, spiritually in the eyes of so many. We all felt a deep debt of gratitude to the man who had reached out to the most hopeless among us.

Gary could be found almost full time in his living room, reclining in his old green chair. The old chair sagged under his weight as he laid fully reclined, feet up. Pillows lodged in beside and behind him in an effort to make him comfortable. The house, even with the large crowd had the feeling of calm, much like I'd felt there on my first visit. It was as clean, I imagined, as it had ever been—at least since Gary had lived there. Now with all the help, everyone wanting to do something, anything to help, the place glistened. The cupboards overflowed with food.

Several others as well as myself asked Gary if he wanted some privacy and in each and every instance he declined. He wanted to see his people, the people that had made his life so worthwhile, so satisfying. He now sat and taught in the old green recliner rather than the driver's seat. There were thirty or forty visitors at a time, packed into a small house designed for a couple to barely live comfortably. The few seats on the old vinyl couch were at a premium just like the front seat on the bus had been. Now we gathered around his chair and his couch to listen to him talk. His voice growing weaker by the day but his bright eyes and warm, loving smile never changed, they remained beaming outward indications of the brightly lit spirit within.

Groups gathered in the front yard, in the driveway they huddled, and in the kitchen, was a constant meeting of like-minded folks sharing stories and metaphors from their own experiences with Gary. In the realization that we could no longer lean so heavily on Gary to lead us, we now shared spiritual truths with each other and we all helped to meet the needs of anyone who showed up at the house.

The phone rang constantly starting each morning at 6 or 7 AM and wouldn't stop until midnight, the people on the other end of the line wanting to know what they could bring, what they could do. They all wanted to talk to Gary, and in almost all cases, he simply didn't have the energy for a real conversation, someone would hold the phone up and he would listen and let everyone know he was going to be OK and not to worry, he always made each and every one of them know that he loved them, and he considered them family. Even in his time of need he comforted others.

He took a few calls from his daughter Shelby, telling her to come and how much he loved and adored her; she was on her way she responded. They'd been separated for many years and now she was on her way to join the crowd.

On the evening of the third day after Gary had left the bus for good, his daughter had shown up. Dr. Malik and Shelly had gone to the airport to pick her up. She'd not seen her father in many years. I'd heard Gary talk about Shelby many, many times. I had a picture of her in my mind and knew how happy Gary was going to be to see her. I'd talked on the phone to her, as had many others. Dr. Malik had given her the diagnosis that his heart was failing and nothing medically could be done. We'd all urged her to come quickly. A hat was passed to purchase her airfare and in another example of the law of Karma, now we would all have the chance to see Gary light up when he saw his daughter.

When Shelby along with Dr. Malik and Shelly walked through the front door, Gary began to cry immediately as did Shelby. Shelby approached slowly as the crowd parted to let her through.

"Hello Daddy" were the only words necessary for them both to openly weep with joy at the site of each other. She leaned over to hug her father and he tilted the recliner forward to meet her. The room fell silent during the long overdue embrace.

It was so refreshing to have her there with us all: to have her see first-hand the love we all had for her father; to see her begin to discover that her father was so much more than she'd thought. She had the piercing eyes of her father and the same upturned, likable smile. She was short and round like her father with long shoulder length brown hair. She was very simply dressed and wore no makeup as near as I could tell. It struck me that she was so much like her father even though they had been estranged for so many years. She wore sandals and sweats most days, just like her father; she was very unpretentious in her dress and general appearance.

I asked so many questions, as did we all. Shelby was now the family contact and the main decision maker surrounding the care of her father. We loved having her with us. Everyone treated her like the royalty we felt she was. The only daughter and next of kin to our personal redeemer.

She'd left his life years before and never truly returned. She shared each night with us all the past, as she had believed it to be. We shared with her the truth of who her father really was. She shared about Gary the father and Gary the younger man, Gary the MBA and business prodigy. We shared about Gary the bus driver, the *waker-upper,* the teacher and *guru.* We loved to hear the stories and each night as he slept we sat awake with Shelby and made deeper and deeper discoveries into what this *Spiritual Giant's* past had been. Through Shelby and the conversations that took place between them we all felt so privileged to learn so much more about the man who'd saved so many.

Most of his family had wrote him off years before, many thought or acted as if he had been dead for many years. Sadly, and unimaginable to us all, to them he had been an embarrassment, a failure.

Shelby sat long hours with her father, even sometimes just watching him sleep. She cried with us and laughed with us. She hugged her father whenever she could and sat and fed him soup and milkshakes, whatever he would take. They were unmistakably making up for lost time.

As days past and his condition deteriorated, the oxygen in his blood dropped, and any energy he still had, was zapped away by midday. As days and hours progressed the phone rang every few minutes, the callers would have to be asked to try later and would respond with disappointment and an encouraging word to be passed along to Gary, the messages were simple. "Tell Gary, he saved my life, and I'll always love him."

Another caller saying, "Tell Gary, John, from New Mexico called, and I love him." An older woman with a high pitched grandmotherly voice called and said, "Tell Gary, Betty Wilson, from Quebec called, and I am doing well and have ten students of my own now!" Yet another, "Tell Gary, Marsha, and Paul from Lafayette called, give him a hug for us, and tell him we're all praying for him. The most common comment of all was "He saved my life!"

Calls came from all over the world for the *waker-upper*. I loved answering the phone to hear the same story over and over. One caller saying, "I got on the bus one day and...," another with the same story, only different. "I was visiting from out of town and I got on the bus and Gary was talking and..." And all in one way or another said, "It was during life's most difficult moment that I met Gary, and..."

Visitors came from all over the state and many from out of state. They came to see the man who at one time in their life had done something remarkable for them. Gary had reached out and touched their lives in such a remarkable way that it had become a turning point. Coming back now was a journey home, to one more time see the man who had changed their lives forever.

They stayed in motels close into town. Many who planned a short visit and after seeing Gary in his weakened state stayed for a week or more. The story repeated itself over and over again. "I got on the bus..." "My friend told me about Gary the bus driver and I came to see him and ended up riding for months..." "Gary got me into the New Thought Church and I have taken up teaching myself..." We were now all spiritually related. The family patriarch was none other than Gary Goldpeople.

Chapter Forty-Five

Beauty Even in Death

The call came into the New Thought Church at 6 PM; Gary's breathing was weakening and he was no longer conscious. It had happened so quickly. It was the evening of April 1st, April Fool's Day. Gary wanted the last laugh. He had said to me on more than one occasion, "Don't take things so seriously, Stanley. It's only a matter of life and death." He loved to laugh, at even the most serious of things. He'd left his mark.

I left immediately after making a few calls and arrived at Gary's within the hour. Gary was sitting propped up in his favorite spot made as comfortable as possible by Shelby and others. Shelby was seated in a kitchen chair at the side of her father and was wiping his head with a cold damp cloth. The Maliks and Pastor Anthony had also pulled chairs up close to Gary. Shelly Malik was rubbing his feet. Dr. Malik pulled up closely and laid his head on Gary's chest for a listen. "Won't be long now," he said in his soft accent, looking reassuringly at his wife and then glancing around the room at each of us with a sad and serious look that left no room for interpretation.

I went close and leaned in and gave Gary a goodbye kiss on his cheek. "I will always love you Gary. Thank you for my life." I was barely able to get the words out. I wanted to cry aloud but instead a peace came over me and only a lone tear fell silently.

Gary had been struggling mightily to take each breath. He now rested comfortably, his breathing very quick and shallow but seemingly without struggle. His eyes were closed and his mouth open in a round "O" shape.

The house was over full and Shelby asked us to keep things under control so she could concentrate on the moments left with her father. Lobo volunteered to man the door and several dozen at a time now waited in the front yard. A candlelight vigil was started and prayers were now constant inside and outside the house. Lobo allowed in a few at a time to come and say goodbye to the *Spiritual Giant*.

Inside, two or three took turns answering the phone and passing on the news to come quickly as time was now very short. Within two hours Gary's breathing was non-existent for thirty of forty seconds at a time. He would pause and rest in such a peace that we all fell silent each time. As he would finally take a breath Dr. Malik would reassure us all "not long now." We all gathered close next to, or in and around the old couch and huddled next to the old green chair. One or two at a time they came and said their goodbyes.

Shelby cried slowly but never stopped stroking his head and handing off the towel to whoever was next to her to have it wrung out and brought back fresh. With each fresh towel, she'd continue to wipe his forehead. I held his hand and squeezed, almost imperceptible there was a squeeze back.

Within another hour I squeezed one last time, this time nothing and I knew. One last breath, one last exhale, and we waited. Nothing... quiet...silence...calmness then a voice from Dr. Malik. "He's gone." We were all devastated by the quickness and at the same time comforted in the fact that he had not suffered even a moment.

He'd died just like he'd wanted to, in his big green chair, with his friends and spiritual family near and his daughter with him. He was at peace and died having left behind a way of life that would continue forever. Gary knew he could go, his mission had been accomplished and he'd most definitely made a respectable contribution to life.

His body let his spirit go. His spirit finally shedding the body that had given out. His daughter, his students, and friends were all with him during his final days. I felt strangely at peace. I laughed initially, rather than cried when I realized Gary had left this earth on April Fool's Day.

Dr. Malik closed his mouth for him and Shelby combed his hair. Pastor Anthony took his green beret from the back of the chair and placed it on Gary's head. His mouth was turned upward in an unmistakable smile. He was wearing his uniform shirt and covered from the waist down with a knit blanket. He was at peace and strangely so was anyone who was near him. I found next to the chair on a small table his wire rimmed, round spectacles and intuitively picked them up and placed them on his face and over his closed eyes, tucking them behind each ear. Here sat the likeness of the man who had saved my life.

That night I cried myself to sleep back at my room at the New Thought Church. I missed him already, but reassured myself that he'd given me something of himself that I would never lose. As I reflected I knew the spirit of Gary was now firmly implanted within me was all that was left of what I had known of Gary Goldpeople.

Preparations began at his home, with his family and at the New Thought Church. The celebration of his life would be held at the church in one week's time. The entire Saturday was set aside for a memorial service, music, and food. A time for all to share in the celebration of one of God's most enlightened children: The *Awakened Buddha,* the *Enlightened One,* the *Spiritual Giant,* the teacher, the mentor, the father, the family member, the friend—Gary Goldpeople.

Chapter Forty-Six

Reflection and Awakening

Saturday, April 8th at 9:30 AM, there was the largest crowd gathering in the New Thought Church I'd seen up to that day. The service wasn't scheduled to start until 10:00 AM, and yet here we were, a full thirty minutes before the service was to start, and nearly every seat was filled. The crowd shocked the few family and old friends that had come.

I'd been asked to deliver a eulogy by Pastor Tony. Certainly, I thought she should eulogize our friend. She agreed to say a few words but demanded I talk saying that I was closer to the spiritual experience than she was being newer to the spiritual life. I was humbled at her request and awed by the responsibility. I'd spent much of the last two days in seclusion within the church, spending most of my waking hours in meditation and contemplation of the service to come. Doing my level best to somehow put into perspective all that had happened in my life and trying to piece together the life that had been Gary's existence on this planet as well. I knew I'd undergone a profound transformation that could never be explained in anything less than purely spiritual terms. I knew I would now be going forward on a new journey; the days of going to the bus stop were over now. They were not only over for me they were over for many others as well. They were over for Gary most of all. I knew he'd found peace and a way of living that allowed him to have the only happy life he'd ever really known.

I'd talked only with a select few the days before my seclusion. I talked long in the evenings with Pastor Tony and had a few conversations with Shelly and Dr. Malik. We were all in a state of shock and just quietly shared with each other the amazing stories about how we all had come to know Gary and how he'd changed our lives. Lobo was by my side during the entire ordeal. I saw him look at me the way I'd looked at Gary, with admiration and honor and respect. I saw clearly in this most difficult time that he was giving me more than I could ever give back to him. I knew then that it is by giving that one receives. As I gave to Lobo the right answers would come to my own life's struggles.

I'd also been meeting and talking to Gary's daughter, Shelby, several times each day. She'd shared her story with me the way her father had shared himself with me. She was staying now in the back bedroom of Gary's home. She'd missed so much of her father's life but had come in time to get to know him and she'd been there with Gary as he'd taken his final breath. She opened up to me about her memories of her father and the estranged relationship they'd endured.

Her birth name was Shelby Goldman. She shared in length about how Gary had come up with and began using the name "Goldpeople" to represent the Dr. Jekyll Mr. Hyde bipolar disorder he'd been diagnosed with while he was attempting to unscramble his life after his divorce. During the time after Gary had become sober and stabilized he spent time trying to solve the larger "hole-in-the-soul" spiritual problem with therapists using nonspiritual answers, Goldpeople was Gary's way of allowing humor into a very dark existence. I laughed inwardly as she'd told me the story—and we laughed and cried together. Shelby recalled his name change as something she despised, a symptom of his craziness, a symbol of why her mother was forced to ask Gary to leave the family. She now saw it for what it was, Gary's way of hanging on while he was tortured by his own mind. His way of letting a beam of light into the darkness. Divine humor shining through him. She now loved the name the way she loved the man.

It wasn't hard to see the resemblance, more than a few times in our conversation, when I'd told her of some of our more humorous times together, I noticed her eyes wrinkle and her upturned grin. Her eyes were the bright blue of her father's, her mouth wide, showing the smile I'd come to worship. Her mother and Gary had divorced twenty-five years earlier. She'd had contact and frequent visits from Gary through high school.

After high school, she'd maintained contact with Gary for only a short time, then her own life's difficulties including addictions and eating disorders, along with the selfish lifestyle of her youth, had separated her from her father. Her own resentments about her childhood and the divorce had caused an almost constant separation from Gary. Gary had kept track of her the best he could and she told me he had always attempted to reach her on holidays and birthdays, but she'd kept the conversations short and had always discouraged a closer relationship.

She was now a woman in regret. Regretful that she'd missed the relationship she had always craved. Regretful that she'd wasted time trying to fill the insatiable urge to create a satisfying life on completely material grounds. Time, she could have spent with her father. I held her and comforted her, as did all of Gary's students. We let her know she was now in our family. She opened up to us all and we were so grateful for God sending her to us and she was grateful for our presence in her life as well.

She thought her father was a bus driver, a failure in life. This was especially tough being that he had shown such huge potential in the business world. In her mind to end up as a bus driver was beneath him and beneath his family. She now saw the truth. Even after finding recovery from her own demons, having battled and won with her own addictions—like so many, she'd never found recovery from hatred and resentment toward her own father.

God brought her to me. I intuitively knew it was my job to bring her to the knowledge of whom her father had really been, knowing that that realization would lead her to only one place. A spiritual journey of her own.

We all spent hours with her in those days leading up to the funeral and let her know what kind of a man Gary, her father, really was. I told her my own story and the story of how so many others had experienced his love and compassion. She was moved, and on the day of the service, I could see in her eyes that she was feeling the love of her father and attempting to make peace with the years of lost time with him. I invited her to join us at the church every week for study groups, meditation, Sunday service, and general fellowship. We needed her there. She was another who would help many. She was now, family.

All of Gary's closest friends including Lobo and myself met just before the service to finalize details. We gathered around Pastor Tony's desk as she instructed all of us on our proper place in assuring the service went smoothly. She was moved and her voice cracked and I noticed an almost imperceptible quiver in her hands. She sat behind her desk dressed in her very best. Lobo, Dr. Malik and I all wore black suit jackets and white shirts.

We all listened in as Pastor Tony explained to us all the work ahead. As she sat at her desk she leaned in and fell quiet. Placing the tips of her fingers on her forehead I knew she was seeking the intuitive thought that God would show her what the next step would be. She was pausing in that moment of doubt as we had been shown so many times by Gary. I bowed my head as well and prayed for her, awaiting her to break the silence.

After a very comforting moment or two of silence she leaded back in her chair, raised up her head and turned all attention to Shelby. Shelby dressed in a flowing lavender and yellow spring dress and looking much lovelier than I'd ever seen her, looked around and then back at Pastor Anthony realizing the attention had been turned to her. "You know that you are half-Gary, exactly one half your mother and one half your father."

Shelby began to cry and Shelly Malik who had been seated in front of Pastor Tony's desk rose to give up her seat and Shelby took the vacant seat in front of Sabrina.

She continued talking to Shelby, inspired to make a point to her. "If we cut a lock of your hair and looked closely at the DNA, there we would find fifty-percent Gary."

Pastor Tony took the time and prayerfully the words came to her to explain to Shelby how that was exactly who she was spiritually as well. That her father had never been more than a breath away, she just hadn't noticed. Gary was with her always and forever. It was exactly what Shelby needed to hear and to all of us it was another lesson in the spiritual life. To be aware and awake to the intuitive thought. Pastor Anthony knew Shelby needed to hear this and she paused to take the time to consider if this was the right place and time.

In the days prior to her father's death, in the hours we had together, I'd got quiet with her and we practiced listening to her father in the world of the Spirit, we could both hear him as clearly as when he'd been alive. We had to get even quieter now, but he was there. I recalled with fondness the lessons Gary had given me on listening to the still small voice within. I listened as instructed now and I'd heard Gary, "Everything's good, I'm comfortable now, I'd been uncomfortable for years so it was a real relief to leave this body behind." I heard his voice and his laugh and pictured his body. I shared it all with Shelby and I could see she was listening to her father as well.

I could see now when I saw her in Pastor Tony's office, on the day of her father's service, that the two of them had had a long talk. He was in her now, an invited guest.

We tend to want to freeze-frame people in time. We have a resentment that turns to anger and hatred, and then it festers in us for years. The person we are angry with has in fact changed, as we have. We seem to be completely unable to realize that they are no longer the person with whom we were angry. They've changed in many cases for the better and no longer even distantly resemble the person they were. The anger is within us and is against a person or situation that no longer exists. We harm ourselves as the hatred festers, and in doing so, we selfishly harm the world. Shelby had been healed of that. Her own father, and the words of Pastor Anthony and myself had set her free. She had been brought not only to her father but had been led to us as well. We in turn sought from God the guidance she needed.

When we get well, the world around us gets well with us. It is impossible to harm ourselves, without harming the world as a whole. Those closest to us take the brunt of the harm. Shelby Goldman had seen this realization at a time in her life that had brought with it deep regret. Realizing whom her father really had been brought sadness, and at the same time, great pride in who her father was, and hope in whom she might become. She would remain to pray with us in the New Thought Church.

Gary had tried so many times to get her to come out west, to leave the New York scene and come visit. Come ride the bus and meet his friends at the church he'd helped start. She'd just been too busy. She was a bit embarrassed by the crazy father who had left a family and a high-paying job and ended up driving bus for a living and spending his spare time in a small old church with esoteric, new age, weird ideas about God.

Those in whose lives had been dramatically changed by her father's guidance now surrounded her. She saw that his cause had been noble and that she'd been wrong. We helped her to find peace while learning all we could about the man we all loved deeply.

After our meeting in the office I retreated to my room above and behind the chapel. I came out of meditation a few minutes before the service was to begin. I'd been with God. I was prepared for the spiritual mission before me, that of speaking for us all and putting something beyond words into spoken language to place into words something no words can tell, that which would touch the hearts of those in attendance. To transmit spiritually the life of a great man, mentor, and teacher I would have to transmit more than words I would need to speak the language of the heart. by the spoken word. I'd prepared myself with a simple prayer:

God,
Fill me with your love.
That your love,
Would overflow from me,
Into the lives of those in attendance here today.
That hearts may be touched here,
By the story of one of your greatest teachers.
That those in attendance and many others,
Will be encouraged to do with their lives,
What Gary did with his.
That in hearing the full story of Gary Goldpeople,
Self-sacrifice and service to others,
Will become a desirable way of life.
Where my words won't touch them, let my prayers do the work.
Amen

Chapter Forty-Seven

Love

The sanctuary of the New Thought Church was now filled to capacity. The altar was covered with bouquets of flowers that had arrived from all over the country and several from overseas. Two large pictures of Gary Goldman graced each side of the podium. Both pictures of Gary as a younger man, one with his family, smiling and happy and much thinner than I'd known him, his daughter Shelby next to him as a grade-school-age child. The other picture of Gary as a young high school athlete, sporting his letterman's jacket. Almost unrecognizable as the Gary so many of us had known, except the radiant blue eyes shining through and the unforgettable smile.

Behind me, projected onto the white wall was a larger-than-life image of Gary Goldpeople. The only Gary so many of us had ever known. Sitting in the driver's seat of his bus, wearing his blue uniform jacket and black tie. Atop his head was the button-covered beret. He was laughing, the white aura surrounding him was evident even in the photograph. The brilliant light shooting out from his bright blue eyes. His white beard was neatly trimmed, his head tilted back in laughter. He truly was larger than life, and just seeing the image, had brought tears to my eyes. Many had broken down as they entered the sanctuary and saw the projected image, the dozens of bouquets of flowers and the two pictures, one each side of the podium.

The music played, Gary's favorites, old time gospel. Pastor Tony seated in the front took the few steps to the altar and greeted us all. She herself struggled to hold back tears as she delivered an amazing sermon on the twenty-third Psalm. It was one of Gary's favorites. Gary had used several passages from the bible in many of his long talks with me as I was being prepared to work with others. A prayer designed to let me know the nature of God, the nature of myself, and most of all, remind me to relax and take it easy in this moment. God was leading me in "The path of righteousness," in right thinking and right actions. I was ready; I'd been led to the "calm water." It was comforting to hear her describe the "shadow" of the valley of death. Certainly, I had walked what I thought was the valley of death but truly it was only a shadow, created by my own wrong thinking. God was there even in those hardest of times. "Though art with me" I repeated over and over as she spoke.

Pastor Tony looked striking. She wore a bright red dress, so full of life. Her hair was pulled back tightly behind her ears, and then fell onto her shoulders. A beautifully full white carnation adorned her blouse. I'd never heard her give a talk so filled with love and obvious gratitude to the one teacher she called in her talk, "A Spiritual Giant." She prayed, and as she did, I felt a calm come over me. I knew I was ready and that God was present with me. I heard her introduce me to the podium and calmly I approached. I strongly felt the presence of God working through me. All fear and thoughts of failure left me. I knew the loving presence of God in that moment.

I took a long drink of cold water from the glass that had been left for me. I fought back the feeling of crying as I felt the emotions welling up from the depths of my soul. The church fell into such a silence, a hush I imagined had never before been heard where there were hundreds packed into a small sanctuary. A calm and peaceful silence from heaven. The room was overflowing, many were standing against any wall or pillar, shoulder to shoulder to experience these moments together as a family.

"Thank you for coming today." I heard myself say. I knew I was only a vehicle for the message and I cleared my throat, let go and continued. "I know for most of you that nothing on earth would've prevented you from being here. I've been asked to deliver a eulogy for a man, who using God's strength and his own weaknesses, facilitated spiritual awakenings in the most hopeless among us. When he saw hopelessness he smiled, for he knew this to be where God had him do his best work.

"It wasn't Gary's great strength that attracted me to him. It was his calmness, his lovingness, and his humorous nature. It was that he was a defeated human being in the physical world. Gary had lost all false pride and had no tendency or desire to try to impress anyone. He'd lost all notions that he was accountable to anyone other than his own inner conscience. The internal, still, small voice that is God. Gary was not compelled to try to be considered a success in the eyes of others. Where that had once dominated his life, Gary had found true freedom. I like most of us, had wanted what he had and he wanted and needed to give it to us for fun and for free.

"Gary was a man wholly living in the grace of God. Gary accepted everyone as equal; he never looked down his nose at anyone. Having suffered spectacular failures in his own life he showed us all that we have no room to look askance at any human being or any human behavior. The one quality that most stood out in Gary's personality, in fact, was his genuine willingness to see the spiritual potential in all men and women. He saw in me, and many others who are here and those who are here represented in spirit, great spiritual beings when no one else saw us as even human. What a gift he had been given and what a gift it was, he saw in us what we could not see in ourselves.

"Gary was a person who'd lost all, and in the process, had found everything worthwhile in life. The spiritual awakening comes to many in this form, born of our total and complete defeat in the material world our only friendly direction becomes the spiritual. He taught others from his own experience. He taught us that if we have lost all in the material world, and we recover in the spiritual realm, that we find what is truly meaningful in life. Gary had lost all in his life and yet found everything worthwhile. The most amazing thing about Gary and all spiritual masters, and he was without question a spiritual master, was that he absolutely insisted on giving away everything he found.

"I want to tell you some of what I know about his story, about what made him so great and who he was in his former life that makes his life even more amazing to me. Many of these amazing details about his life, I myself only found out about since he quit driving the bus and began his time at home with us all. They made the experience we all had with him all the more incredible, all the more wonderful and all the more memorable. And that's saying something because we already had an incredible, wonderful and memorable experience with Gary that wanted for nothing."

"Some thirty years ago, Gary began to suffer a psychotic break, he felt as though he was losing his mind. His thinking began to be clouded with suspicion of everyone and everything. He was resentful at how easy it had become for others in life to fit into society and live the American dream. For him, it was a daily struggle to pretend he fit in—a nightmare. Many here today can relate. He described feeling all alone in a crowd. Many of us here can relate. He talked of no longer relating to anyone. In his slide into drinking, and depression, he was fired from his job of over ten years, for what was considered by most to be bizarre behavior. Gary was different than his fellows, again many of us can relate. He quit pretending. He'd spent ten years as one of the most successful stock traders Wall Street had seen and yet he fit into the Wall Street mold less and less with every passing day until it was obvious even to him that he didn't belong. He suffered loneliness at his depth and a crushing feeling of worthlessness and uselessness. There is no greater psychic pain than believing you are worthless, useless and all alone. Knowing this in a crowded room of powerful men and women became more than he could bare.

"He'd lost his relationship with his wife, ending in divorce. He lost contact with his daughter Shelby for many years, she has been with him, never leaving his side in his final days and is here with us today. I hope each of you will have the chance to meet her, she is so like him, her smile, sense of humor and especially her deep intuitive sense of saying exactly what someone needs to hear at exactly the right moment."

I looked over at Shelby and she gave me the kind nod to let me know it was OK to continue the revealing account of her father's life. She wiped a tear from the corner of her eye with her shaking hand clutching a tissue.

I continued after another drink from the glass of water and another moment spent in amazement looking over the beautiful and packed-in crowd. I knew they carried me, supported me and felt the language of the heart that flowed through me. I humbly continued to speak on behalf of so many "While he was struggling with what some may have thought was him losing his mind, he was left with nothing and nobody to help him. Gary tried everything to recover, every doctor, every social program, every treatment... It Like many of us it was in his lowest hour that he awakened to the idea that his problem was rooted in a spiritual emptiness. Gary, after moving west and living in shelters, began attending this very church and found here in this library many of the books he hungered for, books that attributed to his recovery: *The Bible; Sermon on the Mount; Awareness; Alcoholics Anonymous; Experiments with Truth; Varieties of Religious Experience; A Course in Miracles* and others. In the pages of these books, and in the people from this church, he found an answer. He applied the simple spiritual principles outlined in those books to his broken life, and through prayer and meditation, he emerged from loneliness and confusion, from hopelessness and suffering, and his thinking began to straighten out. Today we thank God that in prayer, mediation and study, Gary found the Power and in this found his true self. There is no greater gift than that to celebrate today.

"Gary once again became employable and landed a job as a city bus driver. First as a substitute driver, and eventually, for the last twenty years, the route most of us met him on, Route 43: University District to Downtown Seattle. The only MBA to become a city bus driver so far as I know—Gary always said, 'I love this job, you start at the bottom, with no chance of advancement... take's all the pressure off.'"

The large crowd now overflowing into the lobby and listening through the open doors, laughed, so fondly remembering Gary and his wonderfully attractive, disarming sense of humor. So many commented back in just audible whispers, "That's right," "Yes, he did," "Yep" and "Oh yeah."

I saw so many of the people I loved. My wife, Olivia, with my children: Alex in a little blue suit and Andrea in a smaller matching blue dress. Lobo sat toward the back, sunglasses on to hide his emotion, with his shirt and tie, a haircut and a clean shave he showed the deep respect he had for a man he only was just beginning to get to know.

Nurse Shelly and Dr. Malik were in the front row. Like all of us, tears ran down their faces. Pastor Anthony looked on with such attention, encouraging me and strengthening me with her presence. She held in prayer a loving space for us all. Shelby looked on, and I could see she was painfully remembering so much of her father's past as I spoke, and yet I knew she also felt joy as I talked of his transformation and she saw the huge crowds display of emotion, support, kindness and mostly love for her father.

I recognized several hundred others from the church. Some I knew well, and others I'd only briefly met. More I'd recognized from my bus rides. Many I'd never met. Gary's message of hope and recovery through the living of the spiritual life, had truly reached far and wide. I paused, took a deep breath, and a sip of water. Once again, I gathered all I had to contain my emotion and continued:

"Gary was a teacher for many of us here and many that could not be here. He was a motivator in renaming this the 'New Thought Church.' When this church was failing financially and the entire congregation numbered less than twenty, Gary stepped up and suggested we didn't need a new religion, we just needed to have a new way of thinking about the religions that already exist. *A 'New Thought' Church for 'New Thinking' people.*

"He, along with Sabrina Anthony and a few others, started to explore the possibility of freedom in religion, rather than being a slave to our old beliefs. The idea that a church should be inclusive and never exclusive. That we should study the teachings of all religions and look for the similarities instead of the differences. That we should use these similarities to strengthen our own beliefs and draw us closer to the entire human race. We had the unifying theory of relativity why not a unifying theory of religion?

"Gary, using his newly found ideals saved this church, in fact he was the motivator for our beloved Sabrina Anthony to return to school and eventually become our Pastor. He was the motivator and spiritual leader for Dr. Malik and his wife, Shelly, to take in friends from the streets and to offer hospitalization combined with a spiritual solution to the most desperate in our society. To treat all patients mentally, physically, and spiritually. The purest form of the trilogy; body, mind, spirit.

"Through Gary, many thousands have been helped. He is gone but will continue to touch thousands more. A self-described bipolar... manic-depressive... delusional... alcoholic... drug addict... was healed by God, with the simple agreement that his own needs would be set aside so that he could help others. Any given afternoon, Gary's bus would be filled with us, students, *Sleeping Spirits* being awakened by a Spiritually *Awakened Giant*.

"The most important lesson I received from Gary, is that we never know who the next spiritual leader will be. We would've never picked Gary as our spiritual mentor when he was suffering from a psychotic break, and losing not only his right thoughts, but his family, his livelihood, his home, his daughter, his wife, his self-respect, his will to live, and his place in society as a worthwhile human being. We who have suffered know.

"Not surprisingly Wall Street discarded him. Wall Street discards anything that does not serve its insatiable appetite. His family, unable to understand his dis-ease and cope with his 'giving up' as they saw it, asked him to leave, and all of society followed. Gary was left alone. All of these things were only God's way of preparing Gary for the work he was called to do. As tough as it was it was necessary and the one and only path that would finally allow Gary to follow his heart's desire. God's way to force him to finally and forever pursue his intended purpose. Until we all seek God's will for us we remain sick as did I and Gary did for so many years. When we see others in distress, Gary would have us see them as God sees them, as works in progress. I was given this lesson and hold it dear to my heart. I see from where I am today, standing in a sea of hope, a great tide of a flood coming into the New Thought Church. Many people just coming to grips with what has happened in their lives as a result of a relationship with the man we are here to celebrate today. Sadly, some will slowly go back to sleep and living in their dream but I suspect many also will awaken and join us in helping others.

"Gary saw me not as a drug addict, not as a threat to him, not as a nuisance, not as a lazy person, not as a person with weak will power and certainly not something to turn away from. He knew the truth I was a part of him and he was connected to the whole. Gary saw us all for what we truly are. He saw in us the spiritual potential that no one saw and which we hadn't even begun to suspect existed. Gary saw that I'd spiritually fallen asleep and that all I needed was a simple wake-up call. Or in my case a rather large wake up call. The deeper the slumber the louder the wakeup call he would use. Gary woke me up, like he woke us all up. I know today that from this place of the *Awakened Spirit,* we can see the spiritual potential in our own lives and much more than that, we can see the *Sleeping Spirit* in others an we can now issue the wake-up call.

"In closing, I would like to say one more thing that I know Gary would want me to mention here today. That is our limited time on this planet, in this plane, in these bodies. Many times, I've wished that Gary would have had just a few less double Quarter-Pounders with cheese. Selfishly, I wanted more time with Gary, but one thing we talked about, and I've come to know as truth, is this: Gary is here with us today. His death is only an illusion. He has only pretended to die. He lives on in me and all of you. He literally lives on in his daughter, Shelby, who is here with us.

"We are him—so he is always with us. *The Great Truth.* If we could all remember that any sense of separation between us is an illusion, that we are all connected to the *One Source.* If we can remember that to bring harm, in any way, to another human being is to bring harm to ourselves, that to help another human being is the only real way to help ourselves... If we all just could understand and believe in this one thing, that we are all connected, all real problems would cease to exist for humanity. Gary showed us the answer. How to heal not only ourselves, but to heal the world.

"I love you all and bring you love from our mentor and friend, our Father, family member, and loved one—Mr. Gary Goldpeople. Thank you all for this opportunity to be placed in such a position to share with you all some of the life of the *Awakened Giant.*"

I stepped back from the podium in front of me, looked out over the crowd, nodded happily to everyone and scanned all those who had been such important figures in my life these last many months. Still even in that moment was just starting to realize that he was gone in this realm. I turned as Pastor Anthony approached and cried in her gentle embrace. I walked down the few steps tearfully smiling at all those I loved and they are smiling back. I took the seat in the front row that had just been vacated by Pastor Anthony. Once again, I had done something I'd never imagined I would ever do, or have the strength to do. I always imagined someone giving a eulogy for me and saying how pitiful a life I'd lived, I know knew it wasn't going to end like that God had restored me to my right thinking. Now here it was me who'd given a eulogy for a man who'd done something spectacular with his life. He had risen to a level most never reach. He had been in heaven and on earth simultaneously.

Pastor Anthony took to the podium once again, flanked by the photos of Gary on either side. She was absolutely superb in the moment, her red dress with the white carnation adorning made her stand out even more magnificently. She bowed her head for a moment and dabbed her wet eyes before continuing. Her voice cracked as she began. "I'd ask your permission here today to close this service with a prayer. Please pray with me now"

We all bowed our heads, the sound of men and women weeping quietly was the only thing that disturbed the long and deliberate pause Pastor Tony took before she uttered our final prayer.

"God,
Thank you for the life of one so great,
Thank you for allowing Gary to stand,
As a window into the spiritual life.

Allowing us all a glimpse into the infinite possibilities in our own existence.
We realize you've not taken Gary from us, but taken Gary home,
Allow this to serve as a call to us all to come forward.
We come forth, willingly and gladly.
Allow us to now be the windows for others,
To see what they might be.
We are ready to now be like the lighted lamp.
We follow you today Gary, to the mountaintop, to shine brightly
For all to see!
Bless us all on this journey and give us strength.
Bless the New Thought Church.
Thank you, God, for Gary Goldman.
Thank you, God, for Gary Goldpeople.
Thank you, God!
Amen. "

Chapter Forty-Eight

Full Circle

The days and hours at the church following the funeral were dreadfully long without Gary to be able to visit. Even so, I loved everything and everyone in my new life but there was an emptiness about my existence. It had been two months since Gary had made his transition. One year since I'd wandered onto Gary's bus and stumbled onto the solution that would save my life, and I hoped the lives of many others. I still had visions of becoming a minister like Pastor Anthony. I worked day and night at the church, doing what I had done now for a while. administering the paying of bills, the working with vendors on the maintenance, keeping Lobo busy making repairs and counseling anyone in need who came into the church.

I missed going to the bus stop. I'd ridden several times just to meditate on the old bus but found myself stuck with loneliness in each case. I prayed a prayer for direction as I sought out the answer to the question that had been plaguing me since Gary had passed. What should I do with my life? I'd thought I knew so solidly when I was with Gary. I now had constant waves of doubt. I consulted Gary's spirit in mediation each morning asking that he show me what to do. Each time I received the same instruction. "Keep praying and the answer will come." So, prayed, I did.

Mother, Father, God.
Lord of the happy, joyous and free.
I know not where I am going.
I know not what direction to go.
As I seek to do your will in my life.
Gently guide my way.
Amen.

On the twelfth day of reciting the prayer and spending an hour in contemplative meditation I had a vision, then I knew. I felt lead and knew what I had to do. I left the church after morning tea and consultation with Pastor Anthony. She assured me I was on the right path.

I stood an hour later outside the large brick building. It was summer again, I stood in the hot sun looking at the old brick four-story building from the sidewalk. Streets ran uphill on each side of the building and a constant flow of downtown morning rush-hour traffic passed by on both sides and on the street beside me. I stood at the main entrance at sidewalk level. The sounds of the city fully awakened nearly drowned out all thoughts, horns honked, impatient drivers yelled and the hundreds of folks walking the sidewalks talking and running created a low-level drone that existed just under the louder noise of the traffic. A siren wailed in the distance.

A large set of cement steps rose to a large platform and a double wide set of swinging glass doors. I walked up the steps, mixing with the crowd coming and going and counted each step as I rose. At the count of twelve I stood atop the landing and stared at the large golden seal emblems that adorned both of the heavy glass doors that were in constant motion as the workers preparing for the day entered and exited.

'**Metro Transit Authority**' it read in a circular arraignment around the logo showing an airplane, a train, and a city bus all on each side of a triangle. I grabbed the large brass handle and swung the door wide and took a step inside. Everyone around me seemed to know exactly where to go as they passed by me on all sides. I stood motionless in the crowd looking for a sign as to where to proceed. My heart pounded as I saw the sign pointing to the left. '**Employment.**'

Another set of glass doors separated the foyer I stood in and I could see several people through the glass waiting in line at an old wooden counter that ran the length of the room. I walked up, pulled the door open and got in line.

I waited as I heard the women at the counter ask the questions. She was wrinkled from years in the sun and her voice told of years of gin and cigarettes. Her peppered, gray hair was cut short giving her a masculine appearance. Around five feet four inches tall and thin as a rail I watched her command each person one after the other until it was my turn.

"What can I help you with sweetheart?" she asked in the friendliest manner she could muster.

I looked her square in the eye. I had worn my best shirt and tie and was filled with confidence knowing I was doing the right thing. "I'm here to look for work. I'd like to find out about becoming a driver."

"Well honey we aren't hiring drivers right now. Do you have your commercial license?" She said, as she looked beyond me to the next few folks in line.

My confidence waned for a moment and my heart skipped a beat. I swallowed, thinking well before speaking. "No, I don't have the license but I have a serious desire and I'm in no hurry, so I'm willing to put the time in. I really just need some information on how to get started."

"What's your name darling?" She shot back in a slower, gentler tone. Her demeanor changed and her attention was back on me. This time she was looking directly at me.

"Stanley Pearson ma-am." I answered as I smiled and gave her the warmest look I was able.

She smiled wide exposing a pleasant grin. Her eyes locked on me and she eyed me up and down. "Well Stanley Pearson, wait right here, don't go anywhere." She said as she shook a finger at me to emphasize that I was to stay put. She turned and walked away.

I watched as she whispered into the ear of a fellow coworker sitting a desk at the back of the room, he in turn got up and I saw him talk to several others. A quietness settled into the room as several workers behind the counter slowed their progress and looked in my direction. I stood looking around the Metro Transit Authority Employment Office and distinctly felt like everyone was looking back.

The grey-haired, weathered women approached again from the back of the office with an envelope in her hand. Somehow, she looked twenty years younger and several degrees friendlier than she had just a few moments ago. She stretched her hand out to give me the envelope and she smiled widely once again calming me with a warm and friendly smile. I reached out to accept the envelope and she pulled back slightly. "Gary left this for you, said to give it to you if you ever came in." She said as she chocked back a small display of emotion.

She thrust the envelope to me and I took it in my now trembling hand. I couldn't believe what I'd just heard. I struggled to regain my breathing, first realizing I was holding my breath and then releasing and struggling to get anything back in but a shallow short gasp. Trying to regain a moments composure to ask more about the letter in my hand I heard her say in her loud, commanding, gravelly voice "Next, I can help you right here." I looked up and she was waving the next man in line forward and was once again looking beyond me as if I was not in the room.

I backed away slowly, turned and slumped into an old wooden chair against the wall, seating myself next to several others who were waiting and filling out applications. I trembled as I looked at Gary's handwriting on the envelope. STANLEY PEARSON. I carefully opened the envelope and pulled out three documents. I looked over what I held in my hand. An application for commercial driving school, an employment application for Metro Transit and a note from Gary. In awe and utter contentment with my heart's desire, my life, and my place in the world. I read.

Stanley,

Route 43, University to Downtown is yours when you're ready!
I knew from the day I met you.
Thank you for taking over, I needed the relief.
Laughter and Light my friend.
Love as Always,

Gary

About the Author

Kenny Down runs New Thought Life (newthougthtlife.org) an organization dedicated to those seeking a higher consciousness through the practice of spiritual principles. A New Thought Life for New Thinking People.

In addition, Kenny owns Seaquest Ventures, a small maritime contract and investment advisory company in Seattle. His work in corporate America included six years as the President and CEO for one of the largest participants in the Alaska fishery using only hooks (no nets). Kenny spent years lobbying, organizing and, most importantly, leading national policy in support of low-impact fishing efforts. His efforts are obvious as a leader in sustainable fishing practices, what may not be quite so obvious though, is the tremendous sense of power that lies within him, and it's a power that's genuinely derived from Spirit.

But it has not always been this way for him. It is a state of being he's been brought to by the way of a spiritual transformation. He'd spent many years struggling with addiction, both with the tragedies that tend to lead to relying on such a dubious resource and the fallout of reaching for such an empty relief. After a troubled youth that included a broken home, homelessness, group homes and institutions he found solace at age eighteen working on fishing vessels in Alaska and after finding sobriety ten years later eventually leading to a long career in the industry. Truth be told all the trials in his life have turned out to be his greatest blessing.

After thirty years of being deeply involved in the clean and sober lifestyle and helping many others to make their bed and walk again, Kenny shares some of his personal wisdom and experience in Awakened Giant / Sleeping Spirit and through his writings and videos shared on the New Though Life website encompassing all things for a New Thought Life and a path to follow for New Thinking People.

He now expands his efforts on being a fisher of men—by helping to relieve those in spiritual despair, whether through addiction issues or other spiritual maladies. While he has been writing for as long as he can remember, he officially began with small articles and short stories. Today, his main goal as a writer is to help people find solutions to the problems in their lives through the application of the spiritual principles he's put together in this novel, *Awakened Giant, Sleeping Spirit*. Although some of the storyline in *Awakened Giant, Sleeping Spirit* is based on his own trials while learning to "wake up." Many of the spiritual principles highlighted in this book and expanded on through his other writings are concepts intentionally kept basic. These are drawn from universal truths compiled together for a simple message of hope to those suffering—whether they may be "awake" enough to be aware of it or not.

When he's not writing, helping others, working to maintain, encourage and promote sustainable fishing practices, he may be found spending time with his most valued treasure—his family; his wife Shannon of over twenty-years "The Beautiful and Wonderful Shan" and his two adult children son Jake and daughter Jessica.

K.D. lives in Seattle, Washington USA where he has spent most of his life. He is a man that genuinely understands what it means to wake up the Sleeping Spirit and allow the Awakened Giant to appear. His other writings including a book on relationships "The Care and Keeping of a Shan" and can be found at www.newthoughtlife.org along with many more of his writings, lessons, blogs and vlogs.